Philomena Houlihan

Time After Time Before Time

Time After Time Before Time

Copyright © 2020 Philomena Houlihan

Second Printing

All Rights Reserved

The moral rights of the author have been asserted

This book is sold subject to the condition that it shall not, by way of trade or otherwise, be lent, re-sold, or otherwise circulated without the copyright owner's prior consent in any form of binding or cover other than in which it is published and without a similar condition including this condition being imposed on the subsequent purchaser.

No part of this publication may be reproduced in any form by photocopying or by electronic or mechanical means, including information storage or retrieval systems without permission from the copyright owner.

ISBN 979 867 415534 8

philomenahoulihan.com

This book is

Dedicated to The Ancestors

Time After Time Before Time

Chapter One

My son-in-law Daniel found me lying face up in the mud in the far corner of the top field. I must have scared the hell out of him, looking as I did, covered in mud, with bloodied hands and feet. Even before he touched me to see if I was still alive, I felt his rising panic. I wanted to tell him to go away, that all was well. What I could not, must not, tell him, was that I had simply decided to die.

Simple as that. I had no need to carry on living. However, I hadn't counted on being found so soon after leaving the house. I had been relying on the heavy rain and the strong wind to do their job before anyone even noticed I was outside. I also hadn't counted on Daniel's raw strength. He picked me up as easily as one of his hay bales and carried me back to the house. He used my feet as a battering ram to push open the kitchen door and gently laid me down in the armchair next to the cooking range. The kitchen warmth did its work and quickly catapulted me back into the present moment. He placed a mug of steaming hot tea in my hands and told me to drink. I suddenly felt very drained and helpless. I assured Daniel that I wasn't hurt in any way, that all I needed was a hot bath and a warm bed. He knew this wasn't the time to ask me questions. "If you're absolutely sure you're all right, I'll go and run you a bath. Mary will be home any time now."

My family are worried about me. "What on earth were you doing Dad, lying outside in the mud in this weather?" demanded my daughter Mary a little later, in a

Time After Time Before Time

tense angry voice. "If Daniel hadn't found you, God knows what might have happened to you. You're not a young man any longer; you need to be taking it easy now." Her anxiety and worry about me makes her breathe fast and erratically. A shot of remorse hits my stomach because I know that in her condition, she should not be subjected to too much stress. I can feel her fear seeping out through her skin and threatening to catch me in its net. Her love tethers me to this time and this place. I feel trapped. Again. What can she possibly know of my need, my deep, piercing need to walk out of the comforting warmth of her home to seek my true happiness?

    Mary sits beside me on the bed. She places one hand on my forehead and the other on her rounded swelling belly. "You're running a high temperature Dad," she says softly. "If you're no better in the morning we'll phone the doctor." Daniel, her husband of five years, stands in the doorway and asks me how I'm feeling. I know he cannot possibly understand why, when he found me, I was absolutely naked, lying perfectly still in the corpse position with my hands lying relaxed by my sides.

    For their sake I make an enormous effort to speak calmly. "Oh, it's just a touch of cabin fever, should be right as rain in a few days. Don't know what possessed me to go outside in this awful weather." Even as the lie slips out of my mouth, I feel the ancient betrayal wrapping round me like a cold shroud. I am afraid to speak the truth. I am trapped by their love. How can I tell them of my other lifetimes, of hardships and sorrow and love and betrayal, of oppression and of kingship? I have been too long in this lifetime, and I am weary. I am weary of my aching old body and my mind is slowly caving in on itself. I want to walk among the hills again, see the red kites whirling above me and go down to the river to bathe. I feel my life-cord being stretched gently now and the familiar sensation of floating wraps itself around me. There is no struggle. I have done this many times before, so perhaps this time I will remember how to do it with dignity and in full consciousness. I have lived my allotted years and now my time has come to leave. I would like to die outside where I can feel the wind on my skin before my soul takes flight. I have memories of other deaths when the wild open spaces were denied to me at the moment of my passing. This time will be no different unless I can trick Mary and Daniel into leaving me alone. I turn my gaze on my only child, "You're right Mary love, I am feeling very tired so I'll try to sleep for a while. Before I sleep tell me, have you and Daniel decided on a name for the baby yet?"

      She places my hand on her belly, and with shining eyes, she said proudly, "We're calling him Seth, after you Dad." Her love, sweet as honey, washes over me and I feel its grip closing in on me. I close my eyes feigning tiredness to shield me from her love because it is the only thing that will crack my resolve to die. Why does she love me with such fierce intensity? Her love is what has stopped me leaving many times before today. When her mother died five years ago, Mary persuaded me to move into the farm with her and Daniel.

      Lightwood Farm has been in Daniel's family for several generations. It is more of a smallholding now because most of the fields had been sold off long before Daniel was born. The grey stone farmhouse nestles into the western side of the lower fields and from what Daniel tells me it doesn't seem to have changed much since it was built by his great grandfather. Daniel has installed central heating

Time After Time Before Time

and knocked the two small downstairs rooms into one spacious morning room. Apart from these minor alterations nothing has changed much. Daniel loves this land and walks its borders most days. Sometimes he does it twice in the same day when he has something on his mind and he needs to clear his head. The line of ancient oaks in the top field is his favourite place to pause on his daily round. He often sits there for a long while gazing out over the valley below. This I had forgotten when I chose to lie down beside the biggest tree up there. After they've left me to sleep, I resolve to try again as soon as I can. I sleep without dreaming.

  Daniel woke me next morning with tea and toast. Except it wasn't morning, it was two thirty in the afternoon. "I'll be up working in my study if you need anything," he said as he left me to drink my tea. As well as running the smallholding, Daniel is also a successful writer. He has published two books on the ancient farming methods of Ireland. Usually when he's working on a book, we wouldn't see him until supper time. Mary, it appears, had just driven off before I woke, to do the big fortnightly supermarket shop and I knew this meant I had a good clear two-hour slot before she returned. It hadn't been easy for me to get myself up to that spot where Daniel found me yesterday. I am not a young man but neither am I so old that I cannot get myself to the top of that hill again, or so I told myself.

  I pulled on some clothes but in my haste to get out while the coast was clear I forgot to change out of my slippers. I slipped out the back door and the icy wind and near-horizontal rain almost took my breath away. I walked across the yard and before I opened the gate into the bottom field, I turned to check that Daniel was still upstairs. I could see him in the half light, hunched over his desk. He is a good man; he loves my daughter and they have carved out a successful life for themselves in this place. I am sorry for the pain my actions will undoubtedly heap on their ordered life but nothing must stop me now.

    I quietly shut the gate behind me and my slippered feet immediately sank into the muddy field. The recent exceptionally heavy rains had saturated the land. After three or four paces I abandoned the slippers and began to make my way straight up. The mud made it very difficult to keep my balance and I fell face-down several times. I slowly made my way over to the fence on the far side, and gripping on tightly I used it like a banister. I slowly began to inch my way upwards. My hands were bleeding from gripping the fence but I couldn't feel much because they were almost frozen with the cold. I didn't mind the searing pain of the cold on my chest and face either. "This was all to the good," I told myself. "Makes my final task a lot easier." My breath was coming in huge gulps now as the strain on my lungs got heavier. From my bedroom window this field didn't look very steep but trying to get up it now was almost defeating me. "Please God, don't let me fail. Don't let me die before I reach the top." My lungs were screaming now and I could hear my heart pounding in my ears, with a low rushing white noise. The pain in my chest was frightening. I sank to my knees in a desperate attempt to breathe normally. I gulped in huge draughts of air but the pain in my chest continued. "It's OK, it's OK," I repeated over and over in an effort to will my heart to beat normally.

    I've no idea how long I stayed hunched over on my knees, but gradually I began to feel my chest calming. As soon as I felt steady enough, I continued slowly upwards. I willed my feet to keep on moving. Nothing must stop me now. I could see the sun beginning to sink below the top trees. I needed to hurry. The biting January cold cut into me

Time After Time Before Time

but I hardly felt it as I was sweating heavily. I heard a buzzard calling. Its plaintive cry gave me a momentary happiness which I snatched like a starving man. The day was dying and me with it. I reached the top as the last rays of the winter sun were disappearing. The mossy hollow where I lay down is where the veil between the worlds is always thin.

    The ancestors had also come here to die. I could feel their presence all around me. It feels like my mother's arms holding me. I am safe. My soul is breaking free. I asked for death to be quick. I had been born and had died many times before but this time I was choosing how I was going to make the transition from life through death and beyond. I brought to mind all those I loved in this lifetime and who loved me. I asked for their forgiveness in choosing to leave in this way. Their pull on my heart almost unnerved me. I blessed each and every one and released them from my orbit. As my last conscious bodily act, I, Seth O'Neill, 85 years old, placed my awareness in my third eye and looked for the light. I needed a strong image to take me through the door from living to death. Now I need to breathe easily so I can slip away gently.

    The outer dark is now all around me, but I am slowly in my mind's eye making my way towards the white light. Some magnetic force is pulling me onwards towards this beautiful blinding radiance. I have no hesitation in responding. I open my arms in welcome. I freefall into blissfulness.

Chapter Two

It's high noon when I regain consciousness. I am alone by a stony river bed. I'm alive in a different body in a different time. I'm sure about this because I can remember my final act in the other life. I have no other memories apart from that.

I lie still and inhale deeply. My chest hurts, as if a heavy weight is pressing down on me. I try to sit up but a searing pain in my back makes me cry out. My feet and hands are torn and bleeding. I lie back on the grass. My breath is coming fast and hollow in my chest. I can hear voices, sweet singing voices, coming closer and closer. I try to move again but the pain has me in a vice. Through the pain I hear the voices all around me now and I can see shadowy forms looking down at me. I try once again to sit up, but I pass out from the pain. When I next open my eyes, I am lying face down on a straw pallet. There is a pungent smell of herbs. I turn my head and as my eyes adjust to the dim light, I feel something moving on my naked back. I try to move. Gentle hands hold me down.

"Be still, my child, you are safe now." Hands caress my head and I slip back into sleep.

I awaken to morning light and the sound of rain. As soon as I try to move, my painful back makes me cry out. Immediately someone comes to my side. I recognise the voice from the night before, the voice which made me feel safe. An elderly woman is squatting on the floor beside me. She helps me to turn onto my side. "What is wrong with me?" I ask her.

"Your back has been badly lacerated where you fell on the stones, but it will heal in time. Your hands and feet will heal much quicker. You have also had a fever these last three days."

"How long have I been here?" I ask.

"We found you on the day of the full moon, quite a shock you gave the young girls who were on their way down to the river. You were very close to death when we found you. But you are young and your limbs are strong. All you need is to rest. Naduree will come soon to change the dressings on your back and give you a potion to ease your pain."

As she rose to leave, I grabbed her hand and said, "Where am I?"

"You are in the hut of Naduree, the herbalist. He has been treating your wounds for many days. He will be happy to see you are awake at last. I will leave you now."

Despite her age she rises gracefully to her feet. Slowly and painfully I pull myself up on one elbow and look around me. I am in a small round hut. There is straw on the floor overlaid with animal skins. Apart from the pallet I was lying on, the hut is completely bare. I feel a strange disquiet in the pit of my stomach. A shadow blocks the light from the open doorway.

A tall white-headed, slim man enters and squats beside me. He has a dignified and strong presence. Our eyes meet and I have a fleeting sense of recognition which I cannot understand. I see infinite tenderness in his eyes before he closes them. He utters a low rumbling sound like distant thunder on a hot summer's day. It comes from deep in his belly. The sound gathers momentum and bounces from one wall of the hut to the other. When the sound finally stops, deep velvet silence takes its place. A silence so deep it made my own breath sound like a galloping horse. He draws himself up to his full height, spreads his arms wide and once again makes his extraordinary sound. When the last reverberations fade away, he begins to move his hands about six inches above my body. Almost immediately I feel very hot but strangely elated.

Images of flowers and high mountain meadows race across my vision making me laugh out loud. I see myself as a young child rolling down the hill with delight and strong tender hands catching me at the bottom. I see a beautiful young woman scoop me up, throwing her head back in laughter as she sits me on her shoulders. Many more images come thick and fast but I cannot hold onto them. Finally, the old man, for I could see now that he was indeed older than his graceful and lithe body would have me believe, places his hands on my forehead. I feel something move in my head and suddenly I know who I am. "My name is Solasa," I say in a trembling voice as I incline my head towards the man, "and you are my beloved grandfather."

A smile explodes across his face as he leans over and clasps my hands. "I am indeed your grandfather. I have waited for this moment for a very long time. You need to rest now because you have been re-aligned and this takes a toll on the physical body." He places his hands on my head and I immediately feel very tired and close to sleep. In that microsecond before I drift into oblivion, I thought I heard him say, "My beloved granddaughter, she has come back to us."

Solasa is sitting on a flat mound outside the hut, her face upturned to the morning sun. Her back is healing but she can only walk a short distance before she needs to rest. She is a striking-looking young woman. Her long golden hair, lithe limbs, and statuesque height mark her out as different from the other women who live in the settlement. Despite her differences, she feels part of the life around her. There are twenty huts in the settlement which at this time of the day are mostly empty. They are arranged in an inward-facing circle on the top of the hill which she has been told is called *Sliabh Mor*. The view in all directions is unobstructed and movement in any of the four directions below can be immediately spotted. It's a well-chosen spot for a settlement.

    Despite the early hour everyone is outside with the daily activities getting under way. Some of the women are in the woods collecting firewood directly below where she sits. Solasa can hear them talking softly to each other. There are several small children with them. She's noticed that whenever a child cries, all of the women begin to sing together and almost immediately the crying child is soothed. The older women and men sit outside in the sun and, like Solasa, not much is asked of them. They seem to be simply taking life easy. The young boys have already gone off with the goats for the day and the babies are busy crawling around getting in everyone's way. The men and older boys hunt every day from dawn until dusk. Solasa has come to love the daily rhythm and finds a deep happiness welling up in her when someone smiles as they pass by her. She cannot explain it to herself, but she knows she belongs with these people.

    As yet, not one person has asked her who she is or where she's come from, even though she's been here for many days now. It's as if they've been sworn to silence. They show her respect but she's puzzled by their lack of curiosity. Naduree has not been seen since the day she told him her name. She'd tried asking about him but always gets the same answer. "You must be patient. He will be back soon."

Chapter Three

Naduree walked for many days through the far forest propelled by the enormity of his mission. The path he navigated took him deep into the unknown interior but he felt no fear. Although he was no longer a young man he could keep up with the best warriors in his own settlement and his fighting skills were legendary. The key to his survival however and that of those under his care was his extensive knowledge of the plant kingdom. Ever since he was a small boy, he had loved collecting herbs and other edible plants and seeing if they could be ingested without harmful effects. He had used himself as a guinea-pig and on more than one occasion had nearly died from the toxic effects of one or other plant he was working with. Gradually his knowledge grew to include grasses, and fungi found near the summer settlement. Most mornings he could be seen leaving his hut before dawn to gather the medicinal herbs to make into his healing potions. He liked to gather the plants while they still had the dew on their leaves.

He believed that the life-force held within each plant was at its greatest just before the sun rose each morning. He was always careful to handle his plants with care and he never took more than he needed at any one time. Sometimes he could be seen sitting in a meadow without moving for hours at a time. Once, one of the young men asked him what he was doing. "I was listening to what the plants had to tell me today," he replied in a voice of deep reverence and love. He successfully treated the open wounds of the hunters and warriors with a mixture of his herbs, laying hot poultices on top and finally binding the wound with strong grasses. If death drew near, he always offered a special drink to ease pain and hasten departure. He knew precisely which herbs to be used to draw out fever and bring on sleep. The barren women came to him for help. Sometimes he was able to help and there was great joy when some months later a child was born.

His knowledge also included those plants and fungi that were used in ceremonial rituals especially at the summer and winter solstices. In certain places within the landscape at certain times of the year the veil between the earthly worlds and the unseen worlds was very thin. At these times Naduree prepared and drank a potent mixture which deeply altered his state of everyday consciousness. His personal preparations were meticulous and lengthy on these occasions. He fasted for three days and nights, during which time he sat alone in his hut and spoke with no-one. On the fourth day he would stand in the river water for many hours. This was hard on his body, already weakened from fasting but during the winter celebrations the freezing waters gave him immeasurable agonies. The younger warriors watched him from the bank ready to help. Naduree was stubborn and not until he fell face down in the water, did he allow helping hands to support him. The ceremonial conditions were faithfully upheld by the whole clan, sitting round waiting for his visions to unfold. Over many years Naduree had tried in vain to train several of the younger men and women in the ways of the plant kingdom. None expressed a desire to learn. This greatly troubled him.

On the day of the solstice itself the whole clan would fast and do no work. They would sit in a circle without talking from dawn until evening time. As the light faded and darkness rolled in over the hills, soft murmurings could be heard in the circle as talk of the ancestors began. Hushed voices spoke of the magic of the Tuatha and the winsome ways of the *Sidhe* [1]. They listened for the wind in the trees telling them that the Sidhe were riding in the sky towards the new light. If it should rain on the solstice night the people knew that they had to be extra watchful because the Tuatha always came with the rain.

The *Tuatha dé Danann* [2] were the magical people who lived deep in the underworld and they could instantly turn a man into a tree or a rock if they so wished. In that liminal space of the fading of the light Naduree would come out of his hut holding a cup filled with the sacred elixir which he had prepared. He slowly passed from one person to the next, offering the cup and laying his hand on each head in blessing. When all had drunk, everyone turned to face the east to wait for the rising sun. Naduree stood with them, silent and unmoving. The preparation he'd given them did its work quickly.

Some fell down almost immediately into a deep sleep while others gathered in small groups to talk. Only Naduree continued to stand, his back ramrod straight as he saw visions and made bargains with the gods. As the drug took deeper and deeper hold on his conciousness he felt his mind floating free and his deeper visions began. He saw his own, and his people's, past deeds of violence and killing, starvation and death. He saw scenes of such terrible savagery that he begged for blindness but still he had to look and witness what had gone before. He heard the moans of the dying and starving as they crawled around on their hands and knees plucking at the grass. One moment he was

---

[1] Irish fairy folk
[2] A supernatural tribe in Irish mythology

Time After Time Before Time

crawling on his stomach in the mud dying from battle wounds, the next moment he saw hands raised towards the light and the vision changed. He became at one with the natural world. He saw the lovingness of the trees and the streams and the flowers and clouds and birds and worms. He felt the life force of the earth herself pushing up through his feet and into his veins. He upturned his face to the sky and felt his body swell in the vastness.

    As the hours went by, he began to tire and gradually the visions lessened. He walked a short distance out of the camp and sat with his back leaning against a rock. He sat in stillness until the first rays of the sun coloured the sky. He asked for a sign to take back to the people. He waited until the warmth of the sun began to fill the creases in his weathered face. Still no sign. His bones were soft with fatigue as he slowly eased himself onto his feet. Two of the older women had been sitting at a distance from him and as soon as they saw him moving, they came forward to help him. They had done this for him many times in the past as they knew that the strength of the sacred potion he drank was far greater than what he had passed round the circle. They knew he would be weak and unable to look after himself for the rest of the day and perhaps even the following day. They took their places either side of him taking his full weight on their strong arms as they slowly and painfully made their way back to the settlement. After each third or fourth step they had to pause to allow Naduree to catch his breath. The final few paces to his hut were the hardest as his strength finally passed out of his body and the women had to carry him. No man was allowed by custom to touch him while he was still gripped by his visionary powers. He made no protest as the women stripped him of his wet clothing and laid him on his pallet. They covered him with his warmest hide. They took it in turn to sit beside him, keeping vigil as he tossed and turned and called out in his sleep. He called out in words they couldn't understand and they knew it would be a while yet before his body would clear itself of the toxins produced by the plants he had ingested. His weakened and ageing body rode the waves of his rising fever and the women feared for his life. Finally, he settled into a peaceful sleep which lasted for two whole days and nights. When he finally woke, although weak and hungry, his senses were on high alert for what he knew was to come.

Several weeks later at the time of the next full moon he received the sign he had been waiting for. At that time it was the custom for the young girls to go down together to the river to bathe. They believed that magical powers of the light coming from the moon in its fullness would increase their fertility. They sang as they made their way down through the long summer grasses. Half way down they had stumbled upon a young woman lying half hidden in the long grass right next to the river bed. At first glance she appeared to be lifeless but then she moaned and tried to sit up. She immediately fell backwards into the grass. The girls inched forward to examine her more closely. She was not of their clan and they were scared, wondering how she happened to be there. One of them ran back up the hill to the camp calling very loudly for Naduree. He came down immediately and he could see that she was badly injured. He gave orders for her to be carried up to his hut where he could take stock of her injuries.

It was because of this young woman that he was now into his third day of travel towards the east. As he neared his journey's end, his thoughts travelled back in time to when his only daughter Granuil was alive. She had been born at the time of the deep snows when life was always hard for his people. The winter she was born was especially hard because snow had been falling for many moons. Vehuna, the child's mother, already weakened from prolonged wintertime hunger survived only a few days after the birth. Naduree used all his skills and knowledge, but failed to stop her life blood seeping away. When the women came to clean her up and get her ready for burial, Naduree, wild with grief and fury wouldn't let them come near. For three days and nights he stayed alone with her in their hut. On the fourth day he staggered out into the sunlight like a wounded animal. He walked through the camp and on down to the large stone west of the river. His roars of grief were continuous and frightening. It seemed as if even the birds dared not disturb his howling. Sometime in the late afternoon his quietened moans were like the thud of arrows cutting deep into the warm animal flesh of his own body. His sorrow spilled out onto his face like flood waters that might never recede.

    He stayed by the great stone for the whole of that long night and by first light his grief was done. He carved into the face of the stone his love for Vehuna and his hopeless wish that she was still alive. The two long parallel lines he etched with his flint snaked down the smooth rock surface and crossed over each other at the bottom. He finally made his way back up to the camp, his sorrow clinging to him like the scent of a slaughtered animal on his skin. His grey face and sunken vacant eyes were piteous. He brushed aside all offers of food and drink but asked to see the child. She was nothing much to look at, mewling and skinny but she was of his loins, so he would protect her all the days of his life.

Chapter Four

    Granuil grew to be a strong child, long limbed and wild natured. From a very young age she followed Naduree everywhere. When he went off hunting, she would scream in tempestuous rage because she had to stay behind in the camp. All the time he was away she spent her days scanning the horizon hoping for a sign of his return. Naduree poured into her all his knowledge and love for his plants and with tender patience told her repeatedly the names of each edible plant they picked. As she grew older he began to initiate her into the deeper mysteries of the healing properties of specific plants. She knew which plants were poisonous to the human system if taken in leaf form but which would be beneficial if mixed with another plant and eaten as powdered matter. Naduree was a hard task master but Granuil was a willing pupil. When she was younger her interest in the plant kingdom was simply generated by her desire to be with her father. However, as the years went by and her knowledge grew, she became more and more eager to learn.

    Naduree regularly checked her knowledge of what he had already taught her before he introduced her to a new plant and its uses. Time after time she surprised and pleased him with the accuracy of her answers to his probing questions. When she had been learning with him for fifteen summers, Naduree knew it was time to initiate her into the making of the substances for use in the sacred rituals. First, she had to prepare her body and mind because she was well aware of the enormity of what she was about to learn. She was scared of the expanded mind states that Naduree would guide her into but she trusted him absolutely. He had made it clear to her that before she could work safely with his mind-altering substances, she would need to experience the effects for herself. Naduree gave her detailed instructions about how to prepare herself before they began this new level of work together. For one whole day and one whole night she was to stand naked in the river waters without moving or adjusting her position. She intuitively knew that the safety and efficacy of her future work depended greatly on her level of personal discipline. Being patient came naturally to Granuil because she had spent many years sitting by Naduree's side when he was working with his plants.

With the first light and without taking food Naduree led her down to the river in silence. He motioned for her to walk into the centre. He withdrew a small pouch from beneath his clothes and placed a small amount of strong-smelling powder in her hand. He motioned for her to place it in her mouth and swallow. Finally, he laid his hands on her head as he spoke. "You will stand here in the river without moving until I come for you. Remember what I have taught you. The river, the cold and the darkness are your allies. Do not be afraid and you will not fail." She nodded her head in understanding and he turned and left her.

Alone in the river, she stood tall and erect and radiant in her youthful beauty. After some hours however, the cold of the rushing water began to seep into her bones causing bouts of almost continuous shivering. After the third or fourth bout she became aware that she no longer felt cold but pleasantly tingly. And she continued to stand. As the daylight hours passed away however, she felt her strength leaving her and she longed to simply sit down in the river bed. Her legs grew tired and strained. Each time she staggered and looked like she was about to sit down

Time After Time Before Time

Naduree appeared as if by some unseen signal in the water beside her. He laid both his hands on her shoulders and a flood of warmth and energy coursed through her like a spring tide. She knew that he was using his deep healing magic to keep her upright and focused and to learn this from him was the very reason she was enduring the extreme agony of the river water. Three times during the twenty-four hours of her task Naduree appeared before her and each time she absorbed his healing strength. Naduree kept vigil with her through that long and agonising night. Time after time he longed to go and fold her in his arms to give her rest and end her agony. But he knew she must endure alone. His eyes never left her, tracking her every thought and emotion. And they endured the long dark night together, father and daughter.

When the first pink light began to colour the sky, Granuil was still standing, her eyes trained on some unseen object in the far distance, her body resembling an old coat hanging on her bones. She looked like a standing up corpse. Naduree stood before her one more time and began to make a low sound in her left ear, calling her back from the places her mind had travelled to during her river initiation. Slowly and carefully he called her name, being aware of the delicacy of her mindstate and fearful of unhinging her from normal life. She slowly walked towards him. He rubbed her face and hands and wrapped her in his furs. As the warmth began to seek a way back into her flesh she finally let go and collapsed into his arms. He carried her back to their hut and never left her side until the following morning when she awoke. During this time he had his first doubts about what he was asking of her. "Was she too young for such an ordeal?" he asked himself over and over again. "Would she be able to take on the responsibilities of such a deep and profound initiatory step?"

On waking, she was eager to speak of her experience but first Naduree led her outside to sit in the warm sunshine and to make sure she had something to eat. After her meal, he took her by the hand down to the standing stone where he had spent the night in wild grief for Vehuna her mother. They sat with their backs to the warm stone and Granuil began to speak. "What happened to me in the water, father?" she asked. "My mind was stripped of its power to control what was happening to my body. At first, I thought I could not endure the cold and the fatigue but as the hours crawled past, my body ceased to be part of me. I could see my freezing body struggling in the river waters but I, Granuil was not there. I was standing next to my body but I was not of it. All my pain and terror had evaporated. I was standing in a parallel reality where I had ultimate control over what happened to me. Everything around me grew luminous and brightly coloured. I could see through my hands into the bones and sinews beneath the flesh. The trees and rocks began to call to me in a language I could immediately understand. I saw the grass actually growing before my eyes and I heard the river water offering itself to the thirsty birds flying past. Such exquisite joy I never thought possible. My consciousness was vast, streaming with radiance, when without warning everything changed. I was plunged into a world of horror and pain and suffering, and black snarling despair. What was happening to me father?" she asked in a voice still full of fear.

"You were being cleaved in two by your mind," he answered. "It is always this way in the beginning. Each time you take this plant into your body you will be able to stay for longer and longer periods in the blissful states. The power of the dark will begin to lessen its grip on you. For now, you need to learn about the dark powers so they cannot take you by surprise. You need a period of recovery for your body and your soul before you can take this substance again. Spend long hours in the sunshine to energise your mind and heart and we will both know when you are ready for your next experiment."

In the days and weeks following this harrowing experience, Granuil spent long hours wandering in the hills and meadows. Sometimes she gathered plants to take back to Naduree, but mostly she simply walked as she tried to unravel what had happened to her mind on the night of her first initiation. She had recurring images of blackness and terror which at times threatened to overwhelm her. Sometimes these images plunged her into mindless panic where she felt body and soul were being wrenched apart. At the peak of these terrifying moments, Naduree's voice would rise up within her, telling her not to bend to this force. Gradually over the lengthening days of spring and early summer her distress grew less and less. The time finally arrived when she could look at these images with a cool detachment and say, "Be gone. You have no business with me."

As her mind settled and stabilised into equanimity, she was happy taking part in the life of the settlement doing the daily chores with the other women. As high summer approached, she felt she was carrying inside her a secret joy. She knew she was ready for the next step. Naduree had been preparing for the summer solstice when she approached him. "I am ready father. I am no longer afraid of my mind. I now ask for my visionary powers to be expanded."

Her father looked at her long and hard until she began to see pictures in his eyes. "Tell me what you see," he said. A deep stillness came over Granuil. She then accurately described her own mother's death, the mother she had never known. Naduree was deeply affected by the accuracy of her vision and with a great effort to keep his voice steady he laid his hands on her shoulders and said, "You are ready. We will prepare together for the solstice ceremony."

Chapter Five

Not many days later while gathering plants by the river, Granuil heard a soft rustling in the trees high above the river bank. She thought it would be good to cross over and lie down among the trees and rest for a while. The rustling sounded mysterious and other-worldly and Granuil responded now without hesitation. She crossed over the water and climbed up the bank. As she gained the top, she became instantly on her guard because standing under the tallest tree she saw a young man wrapped in a long golden cloak. She was utterly transfixed by his beauty. A dazzling white light surrounded him, and a soft blue light was streaming from his fingers. When he spoke, his voice was the sweetest sound Granuil had ever heard. "I am of the Sidhe. My people are of the fairy blood and you mortals cannot usually see us with your human eyes. The rustling in the trees was me calling you to come to me. I've been watching you for a long while now and when you are by the water I cannot keep away from you. Today I allow myself to be seen by you." He opened his cloak of enchantment and held out his hand to her. She didn't hesitate but stepped forward into his waiting embrace. He enclosed her in his arms and she knew bodily pleasure for the very first time. They lay together with his soft light flowing over her white skin until nothing else mattered except the feel and the weight of him. Afterwards they slept. As the day slipped into the night, they parted with the promise to meet again the following day.

He watched as she crossed over the river again towards her own people. She turned to have a last look at him. He smiled at her one last time, placed his hand on his heart before he dissolved into the trees. She could hear the soothing rustling of the leaves and her heart opened wide. She wandered into the camp and lay down in her hut without speaking to anyone. Next morning she was waiting by the river before sunrise. As the first rays of warmth spread across the land he appeared on the far side of the river. He held out his hand and she crossed over. Once again they spent the whole day together entwined in each other's arms. He wrapped his light around her and she breathed her human love into his veins. He told her of his world, the world of the Sidhe. He spoke of the time long ago when humans could call upon the Sidhe for their support and seership and magical powers. "At one time," he told her, "my people would bestow gifts of protection upon the human kingdom. Until we were driven underground by human greed and lack of respect and gratitude. Now we no longer wish to make ourselves known to your people. But you Granuil are different from your people. Your heart is pure. Its radiance has pulled me into your orbit and so we can see each other and be part of one another."

The summer days continued with the young lovers meeting every day across the river. Naduree guessed what was happening but he decided to say nothing until the time of the summer solstice drew near. He had observed that Granuil was not collecting plants every day as she had been doing since she was a young girl. He had taken to following her in the early mornings to see what she was doing with her day. He observed her walk briskly down to the river, and then he saw something which confirmed his suspicions. He saw a magnificent smile break across her face as she rushed into the water and up the bank on the other side; her arms open wide in greeting. He couldn't see anyone of course, but he knew that she was with the fairy folk. He watched for a short while until she became more and more shadowy, then he knew that she had fully merged with her fairy lover.

He felt a cold spasm shake his body because he knew what the outcome of such a union would hold for all of Granuil's people. He turned his back on the river waters and slowly made his way back to the camp. That evening he asked for Granuil to accompany him to the place where her mother had been buried. They sat by the small cairn watching the sun go down. As he looked at her blossoming figure and shining eyes, he knew that she was with child. He turned to her and with infinite kindness in his voice and said, "They will never let you keep the child you are carrying. They will come for it, perhaps not immediately, but come they will."

The girl child was born some months later and was named Solasa because she came from the light. The birth had been easy for Granuil. The infant fed greedily and grew fair and strong. She took the infant down to the river only once to see her lover. She knew he was there because of the rustling in the trees but he didn't show himself. Granuil knew then that she would never see him again. The child was a constant joy and everyone in the camp was drawn to her. Granuil continued to go out each day looking for herbs and medicinal plants but she always took the child with her. They would run and play together in the long grasses, and one of Solasa's favourite games was to roll down the small hills and be caught at the bottom by her mother's arms. In the evenings while her mother was mixing and making potions, the child would usually be found sitting at her grandfather's feet. She seemed perfectly content to sit quietly waiting until Naduree rose from his place and together they would walk down to the river. One evening as they sat by the river, she began to hum a most beautiful song. It was the song of her soul calling to her unknown people. Naduree felt a shadow pass over his heart. When he tried to prepare Granuil for the imminent separation from her daughter she refused to listen. "She is my child and mine alone. She will not be taken from me," Granuil said in a firm voice. It was not to be.

    One evening, some months later while Naduree, Granuil and Solasa were sitting quietly outside their hut, a shining figure with light streaming from his fingers and head appeared in front of Granuil. She could hardly breathe as she gazed upon the face of her lover. What she saw in his face however, was not love but a steely determination. Although he did not speak to them, they each heard his voice clearly in their heads. "You will go to the Mound of the Hostages at Tara the night before the next full moon. You will place the sleeping child in the cairn and leave her. You must not look back. We will leave you something precious which you must always keep safe. It will safeguard her return someday if she so wishes. The time has come for her to be with the Sidhe where she belongs. I have been allowed to tell you, if when she is grown into a woman, she wishes to be with her human family then we will allow it. If you do not bring her to Tara, she will die very shortly, before your eyes. A death you will not be able to prevent." With a sudden rush of warm air he was gone. Granuil tore at her own face and hair in her anguish. How could she live without her beautiful child of light?

    Naduree prepared her a calming potion and after several more hours of wild weeping she finally slept. Naduree knew he had very little time in which to imprint into the consciousness of the child the story of her birth, images of her mother and grandfather and the taste of human love. So, for the remaining time left to them, he spent every waking moment with her that he could. He pointed out landmarks in the landscape, he named the surrounding hills and valleys and tried to get her to repeat their names back to him. He sat her on his knee and told her the stories of her ancestors. He took her out into the meadows and told her the names of some of the medicinal plants. He taught her the songs of her people but mostly he simply loved her with a fierce intensity.

With everything he sought to teach her in such a short time he tried with all his mental powers to imprint on her mind a picture of a place that he hoped would one day remind her of where she had come from. The days quickly went by until the time nearing the full moon arrived. As the day for their departure for Tara drew near, Naduree made their preparations for the journey. Granuil was no help to him as she was still locked into the grief at the prospect of losing her child. Granuil insisted on going with her child. They set off carrying enough food for three days for each of them. The child was excited because she had been told she was going on a special trip with her mother and grandfather.

They set off just after sunrise. Every member of the camp stood on the hilltop and silently watched as the three figures set off on their journey. All members of the camp had been told by Naduree what was going to happen to the child. Although there were many protests and cries of "We can fight the fairy kingdom like we did in the past," Naduree silenced all voices.

"It has been agreed and I will not break my bond with the fairy folk," he said with an air of finality. They walked slowly because of the child and it wasn't long before

Time After Time Before Time

she was being carried on Naduree's back. Towards noon the heat of the day forced them to stop and seek shade. They stopped at a small stone circle where the shadow of the stones provided some shade. Granuil simply lay down and turning her back on her father, promptly fell into a sound sleep. The child climbed into her grandfather's lap and she too fell asleep. Although he was weary from the walk and the many sleepless nights he had recently endured trying to console Granuil, he sat with his back against one of the larger stones and gently rocked his granddaughter, all the while whispering in her ear the stories of her tribe. A deep sadness washed over him as he contemplated the loss of the child. He listened to the call of the buzzards as they wheeled above him in the blue cloudless sky and once again he questioned his decision to allow the child to be taken from them. He loved her with an intensity that gripped his heart like an iron cage. And because he loved her so much, he would let her be taken from them. To refuse meant her certain death. He must not waver now, because he knew that every move he made was being watched by unseen eyes. He held the sleeping child close and asked for her forgiveness. He finally allowed his own weary body to sink into sleep. He woke as the sun hung low in the western sky and he knew that they had to make haste.

      On waking, Granuil looked at him with such a deep loathing that his blood ran cold. When the child was fully awake, they began to walk forward again. Granuil made no sound until they reached their destination. When she saw the opening into the burial chamber she began to wail in a low pitiful voice. She threw herself at her father's knees and begged him not to take the child inside. Although his own heart was breaking, Naduree pushed her aside and walked the child into the chamber. The child went willingly with him into the dark interior because her grandfather was with her holding her hand. When they reached the place where the offering bowls were laid, he drew from his belt a tiny phial and gave it to the girl to drink. She willingly obeyed as she was thirsty. They sat down together and within two minutes she was sleeping soundly. He placed a long tender kiss on her cheek, blessed her and whispered in her ear, "Please remember us and come back some day." He took one last look at the sleeping child and turned quickly to leave. Granuil was kneeling on the earth, tearing at her hair making a low pitiful wailing sound. He knew that if sleep escaped her now, her mind would break. He pulled her to her feet and pushed her in front of him away from the entrance. When he judged they had covered sufficient distance, he sat her down and offered her a drink from a phial which he used when one of his people was nearing death. She knew immediately what it was and took it willingly. Before she swallowed it, she let out a piercing cry and said, "May my life end now. I cannot live without Solasa!"

"You will not die," he told her, "but you will sleep deeply." When he was satisfied that she was soundly sleeping, he covered her with his cloak and walked back to the tomb entrance. And so began his lonely silent vigil. He stood at the entrance like a sentinel on duty through the long hours of the night. Every fibre of his heart was being shredded as he fought down the urge to race in and scoop up the child. Instead, like the warrior he was, he remained without moving until the first rays of light came over the hills behind him. When he felt the first wave of warmth on his back he knew it was time to go inside. The winter sun illuminated his passage into the cairn until he was at the very centre where the burial bowls were laid out. Sunlight was shining directly on the central earthen bowl in which he had laid the child.

In her place was laid a beautiful white stone. His knees buckled under him as his sorrow burst out of his heart. "*Fan liom mo leanbh, fan liom,*" [3] he uttered over and over again. He picked up the stone and kissed it over and over, muttering her name, until the very walls of the tomb seemed to drip with his pain. Finally, when the sun moved higher in the sky, the chamber was once more plunged into darkness and Naduree knew it was time to leave. He placed the stone in his clothing next to his heart and groped his way out into the daylight. Granuil still lay sleeping where he had left her. He woke her gently and said, "I promise you, she will be returned to us some day." But she stared at him with unseeing eyes and he knew her sorrow was too much for her delicate soul. It took five long days to gently lead her back to their camp. Day after day he watched her letting her life force slip away and he knew there was no help he could give her. None of his potions or herb mixes would give her the will to live without her daughter. One morning she didn't rouse from sleep. She had mixed her own death potion and Naduree knew she would have died instantly. She was placed in the cairn next to her mother and once again Naduree was heard to make the sounds that come from the soul when wild grief takes up residence there. He lived all over again his loss of Vehuna her mother. He cried aloud to the sky and the trees and the river "There is nothing left for me, take me too. Take me too."

---

[3]   Stay with me my child, stay with me

Chapter Six

Now, all these years later, as Naduree spurred his horse quickly eastwards, the white stone safely tucked away on his person, memories of the previous journey he had made to the Mound of the Hostages came flooding back. His grief for Granuil's brokenness, which had never gone away, began to loosen its grip when he thought about the return of his grand-daughter Solasa. She was now a beautiful strong woman and her return made him feel like a young man again with a sense of urgency filling his veins. There would be time enough to explain to Solasa how she had been taken to live with the Sidhe. For now, he needed to replace the white stone in the mound in order to make the exchange complete. For all the long years after that terrible full moon night, when she had been taken from them, Naduree had guarded this stone with his very life. He never lost the hope that one day he would exchange it for the life of his beloved grandchild. That time had finally come. He once again passed the hilly outcrop where he had rested with Granuil and Solasa on that last fateful mission. He rode on by and didn't stop until he came over the rise and the Mound came into view.

As he approached the entrance, he could feel the silent presences in front of him and behind. He knew the Sidhe were watching him closely. He crouched low and groped his way forward deep into the centre of the chamber. He knew he had reached the centre when his searching hands found the large earthen bowl where he had laid his grandchild on that terrible night. He took out the stone, held it aloft and said, "I return you, O living stone, to your right and proper place, among the Sidhe." As soon as he placed the stone in the bowl, a strong wind funnelled into the passage and hurled him against the wall.

He heard the words "Go now, O human one, and tell your people not to mix with our kind ever again. We have released the human child to you because she wished it. She knows of our ways but she can never enter our world again. For this we are sad, because we had grown to love her and she was one with us."

Slowly the atmosphere changed and Naduree knew it was finished. He groped his way out of the tunnel into the light of the dying day. He felt cold to the marrow of his bones and weary in spirit. There would be no rejoicing for him until he was safely back with his own people. He knew the Sidhe were capable of great treachery and he feared for his life because he knew too much about them. He rode through the rest of the day and most of the night until finally he came into the valley and met up with the young warriors who had come to escort him home. He had fulfilled his mission. During his absence Solasa had heard many stories about this giant of a man who was her grandfather and she looked forward with deep longing to getting to know him. She was waiting with the others to welcome him back into the settlement. She was shocked to notice how tired and frail he looked. Stepping forward, Solasa helped him as he dismounted, and led him into his hut. Helping him onto his pallet she watched as he instantly fell asleep. She sat beside him during his long sleep and made soft soothing sounds over him whenever he thrashed around while in the grip of some hellish nightmare.

While the rest of the people went about their daily tasks, they would frequently stop to listen to the beautiful haunting melodies coming from his hut. Solasa's singing was like a soft cool breeze blowing across warm skin, soothing and calming. After two whole days and nights, Naduree finally woke and reached out his hand to Solasa. The look of love in her eyes was so strong he felt he was standing under a cool invigorating waterfall. All of the mental and emotional exhaustion which the meeting with the Sidhe had generated, simply dropped away from him as he bathed in Solasa's love. No words were spoken between them as he laid his hands on her head in blessing.

  As the weeks and months went by, the old man and the beautiful young woman could be seen on most days walking down by the river or sitting quietly together by the big stone. From early on, Solasa expressed a desire to learn about plant medicine because she intuitively understood that this would bring her closer to knowledge of her dead mother. Because she knew how fragile her grandfather's health was, she stopped herself from asking him direct questions about her early childhood and the events that led up to the death of her mother, Granuil. She was content to learn from Naduree everything he could teach her about his medicines and their uses. Like her mother before her, she was quick to learn and it was no surprise to Naduree when the day arrived when he realised that he had nothing more to teach her.

  One day when they were resting their backs against the stone, with their faces raised to the sun, she asked him to tell her about the secrets of water initiations. He knew the time had arrived to break his silence. All through the heat of the day he told her about her mother's first initiation in the cold river waters and the strength of her visions. He spoke of her skill with plant medicine and how she had been a willing pupil of his from a very early age. There was great joy for Naduree in telling this early part of Granuil's story but as the narrative moved forward, he realised how a vice was beginning to tighten round his heart. He knew his grandchild, this beautiful young woman sitting beside him, held a vast longing in her heart to know all there was to know of those who had gone before her. Rising from their resting place and with Solasa's helping hand, they made their way down to the river.

Pointing to the dell on the other side, Naduree said, "This is where it all began for your mother." Great silent sobs escaped from his lips and the pain once more closed in. Solasa already knew from her time in the fairy realms that water, and rivers in particular, are gateways between worlds. There was a very particular way to cross a river and many precautions were necessary to make the journey safe. They each looked across at the beautiful trees and grass of the dell bathed in the summer light and gripping the hand of Solasa's very tightly Naduree began his tale. "Granuil often came here to collect plants and to bathe. One day as she was sitting by the water, dreaming, she heard a beautiful sound which instantly made her forget everything else. The music locked into her heart and despite her fear of crossing the river she simply stepped into the water and crossed over. The glowing beauty of the dell wrapped round her as she fell under its spell. The trees were glowing and murmuring and inviting her to sit awhile amongst them. She saw a beautiful shimmering light appear before her. Gradually the light became a beautiful fairy man. He called her to him and wrapped his cloak of enchantment around her. They remained together in deep ecstasy and her heart was no longer her own. She came to the dell many times over the next few months, always drawn by the music and in expectation of meeting her beautiful lover. I knew a deep change had come over her at this time but I didn't understand until much later that she had merged with the fairy world."

"Some months later I realised that she was carrying life deep in her body. I feared for her when she told me of her encounters in the dell. She said he would not come to her again but she had this very precious gift of his love inside her. As her belly swelled my fears for her began to lessen and I thought that perhaps the Sidhe would leave her alone. And her time to give birth came and you Solasa were born. She named you Solasa because you were like the sun in her life. You were strong-limbed and Granuil carried you everywhere with her. She took you on her back when she gathered the healing plants and she loved to play with you. Your favourite game together was rolling down the slopes of the hills and falling into a tangled heap of arms and legs together at the bottom."

Solasa let out a cry of joy. "I remember that, I remember arms catching me and a laughing face. Not until now have I been able to make sense of this image. It has been with me always, in my waking and my sleeping."

Naduree felt the pain of her lost childhood with them over again when he saw the look of pleasure on her face. He continued the story. "Your early years with us in the camp were filled with many pleasures and adventures. You especially loved the trees and whenever you heard the wind rustling their leaves you would rush to Granuil and say 'the trees are calling me.' At those times your mother would clutch you to her and a look of fear would cross over her face. She loved you so much, perhaps more than one human heart is capable of. She knew you were special and that made her love for you so intense. Although we never spoke of it, we both knew that there would be a price to pay for the gift of your birth. That price would turn out to be that which killed your mother and took you away from us." Naduree fell to his knees sobbing as the dark memories spilled out. Solasa knelt beside him and cradled him in her arms wishing she could sing away the pain and suffering he had stored up for so long. When his grief subsided, Naduree rose and together they slowly made their way up from the river and back to their sitting place by the big stone. As her grandfather regained his breath Solasa waited silently by his side, knowing that the worst of the story was yet to be spoken out loud.

Naduree closed his eyes, leaned into the stone as if for comfort and seemed to have fallen asleep. Solasa rose and was about to leave his side when he clutched her hand tightly and said, "Don't go, child. Stay with me." He immediately recalled how he had said these very words to the sleeping child as he abandoned her in the burial chamber all those years ago. His sorrow flowed out of him and swirled around him like a pale sea mist. He heard the call of the buzzards overhead and he knew that he must not pull away from the truth. "I need to tell you all, dear child, before this day is past because I will not - cannot - speak of it ever again. The sorrow coming from it will destroy me if I do."

And so Solasa learned how the Sidhe had come for her in her fourth year, the long terrible journey to the mound; how her grandfather had led her into the chamber and how her mother's mind was destroyed by this. She wept for her mother's terrible pain and for the guilt her grandfather had carried next to his heart for these past long years. He explained how he tried to heal her mother's mind but he knew she was beyond any help he could give her. Her sorrow at losing her child starved her of all desire to live.

"She was a skilled medicine woman," he told Solasa. "She knew how to let her life force flow out without causing her any pain. She simply lay down, drank the preparation she had secretly made, and went to sleep."

Solasa sat beside her grandfather, hugging her knees to her chest and rocked backwards and forwards. Her grief was silent as vague images of what she now knew to be her mother flashed in and out of her mind in rapid succession. These pictures were delicate like butterfly wings but each time she reached out to hold onto a memory it floated away. She had one burning question which she was afraid to ask Naduree in case she deepened his sorrow. But finally she had to ask, "Do I look like my mother?" Naduree turned his gaze on her and said with a timeless tenderness in his voice

"Oh yes, you do, oh yes, but you are more beautiful, because you have the fairy radiance running in your veins. Your inner beauty shines bright like the stars at night and you bring great joy to all who cast their eyes upon you. Tomorrow, when I am rested, I will ask you to tell me about your life with your father's people in the fairy domain."

They sat quietly side by side until the sun dipped below the far-off hills and the cooking fires in the settlement called them homewards to eat and sleep.

When they had gone, it was as if the big stone gathered up their sorrow and took it inside itself. As if this was its purpose; to hold the pain of these people so that they could continue to live.

Time After Time Before Time

Chapter Seven

    At sunrise the following morning Naduree and Solasa were already making their way back down to the big stone. This was the place where all sorrows could be expressed. Solasa never looked more beautiful than she did that morning as she gently led her grandfather to their chosen spot. Her natural poise and gracefulness, combined with her golden hair and soft elfin-like features gave her an almost ethereal beauty. She slowed her pace to keep step with the faltering stride of Naduree. She noticed how her grandfather seemed to have aged significantly since she first saw him on that momentous day when she recognised him. She knew that death was walking behind him now and would soon catch up with him. Before that happened, Solasa could give him her gift; a gift which she hoped would soothe his heart in the same miraculous way that his potions healed the ills of his people. She guided his steps over the uneven terrain until they once again settled into their familiar places by the stone.

    They sat close together, backs to the warmth of the ancient rock and bathed in the shared silence. Far below them the river sparkled in the early morning light and way over on its far bank Solasa could see the dell where her story began. She fought down the huge swell of longing for her fairy family which now rose up inside her and threatened to undo her. She looked at Naduree and taking his hand she said, "Grandfather, please close your eyes, so that you may picture more clearly what I will tell you of my life after you left me in the chamber." And so she began her extraordinary tale.

"My earliest memory of the Sidhe, my father's people, is of colour and sound. I was in a flower garden surrounded by a ring of beautiful elfin women who sang me into wakefulness. I felt no fear. The women were dressed in clothes of iridescent loveliness. All were barefooted and they danced around me with wild abandon. The light surrounding them made my head hurt because it was so bright. They looked at me with wonder and amazement because no human child had ever come into their realm before. I was a curiosity. At an unseen signal, they broke the circle and became utterly still. A soft perfumed breeze blew across my face and sitting beside me on the grass was a very beautiful man. Remember, Grandfather, I was a small child so I simply accepted whatever I saw happening. I didn't wonder how he had suddenly appeared, or the women for that matter, and I didn't wonder where I was. Everything around me was pure delight to my child's eyes. The man had a strong electric magnetism which made him glow. He stretched out his hand to me and blue light streamed from each of his fingers. I put my hand in his and I felt very warm and very lovely. I curled up in his lap and I guess I must have slept again because the next thing I remember is lying in a soft grassy bed and hearing soft musical voices. I couldn't understand what they were saying but it really didn't matter. I was content to stay where I was."

"The beautiful man sat down beside me again and this time he spoke to me. He told me his name was Mactus and that he was my father. He asked what my name was and said, 'I will call you by your name, but everyone else will know you as human-child.' He asked if I remembered where

I had come from. I said 'no' and this brought a great wave of joy from all the others who had gathered round while he was talking to me. Everyone was smiling at me and touching me and dancing round me and singing. I felt so excited and so happy. He picked me up in his arms and whispered in my ear 'you have much to learn of our ways, my little one. We will begin tomorrow.' Two young girls came to play with me. They were much smaller than me but they could do such amazing tricks. They could make themselves disappear at will and fly like birds in the air. The running game we played was not much fun for me because I couldn't leap into trees like they did. I started to cry from utter frustration. They were frightened by my tears and vanished right in front of my eyes."

"My father appeared and asked if I would like to learn how to fly. I nodded my head and we began. 'First you have to have a very clear thought in your head of what you are trying to do. Flying is a little bit hard to learn first-off, so let's begin with something easier. How about learning to make something move without touching it.'

'Yes, yes' I said, and clapped my hands with delight. A juicy green apple appeared on the grass in front of me.

'Look at the apple', Mactus said 'and tell it to move over here.'

I said out loud 'Apple - come over here.'

My father laughed and said 'No Solasa, you must say what you want to happen without using words. You simply think it in your head.' I tried many times over and over but the apple never moved. When I finally gave up trying, my father made the apple appear in my hand. That was my first lesson, Grandfather, in how energy follows thought. I quickly learned that whatever we focus our full attention on increases in power."

Her grandfather nodded his head because this made perfect sense to him. He had witnessed, while working with his plants how the healing effect was much stronger after he had held the medicine in his closed hands, while thinking thoughts of deep healing for the person he was about to give it to. "Can everyone in the fairy world work with energy?" he asked her. "Oh yes Grandfather, even the tiny children have powers beyond anything we know here in our world." At this point Naduree asked her to describe the landscape of her fairy home. She paused for a while with a faraway look on her face as she struggled to find the most suitable words to describe a world that was impossible to describe in language. "My words, Grandfather, will not do justice to such a beautiful world, but I will try. The fairy kingdom is like a mirror image of our own forest landscapes but with one huge difference. It lacks the solidity of dense matter. It is a world of extraordinary magical mystery and beauty. There is no sickness, no cold, no hunger and no sorrow. Everything is alive and can be seen to be alive. When the wind blew across the trees we could see the air spirits flitting in and out among the branches. The trees loved to play with the sylphs, and the small children would gather round, clapping their hands in unbridled delight as they watched the antics of the air spirits. The birds would join in, darting in and out of the branches playing a game of hide and seek. 'Come and play with us, o human child' they would sing over and over. They would gather round and sing their beautiful songs for me. I understood the language of the birds and trees and flowers and grasses. The trees and the birds became my dear friends. Because of my father's fairy blood running in my veins, I quickly discovered I had the gift of far seeing and deep hearing. So, you see Grandfather, I could speak with the birds and the trees and the rivers and the waterfalls and I could see and feel the vitality of all growing things.

"Each day I discovered some new delight. I can recall very well the first time I really saw and understood the living qualities of water. At the top of our dell was a beautiful powerful waterfall. I could hear the deep low sounds of its voice following me around each day, calling me to it. I especially liked to sit at the foot of the waterfall where it tumbled into the deep velvet pool below. The water in this pool, Grandfather, was truly alive. It sparkled and jumped about with energy. Because I was new to far-seeing, it took a while before I understood that the water was filled with myriads of water spirits which my fairy family called *Undines*. They could change shape quickly and easily. They were the sparkling energetic forms which gave the life quality to the waterfall and the pool. They could change their shape at will and they manifested in a different form depending on who was looking at the water. They could appear as ancient men telling the stories of the people, or they could be tiny flickers of light twirling and tumbling across stones and riverbeds carrying messages and colours and sounds across the valleys and mountains. The waters were the record-keepers of all that passed among the people each day."

"Here in our world, Grandfather, we know that the rivers are sacred containers for our ceremonies. We honour and respect the water but we don't see its deeper hidden life. We know not to cross over the rivers because we fear what is on the other side. My mother crossed over and for a very short while she developed far-seeing. I believe she could actually see and feel the light and luminescence which was how my father appeared to her. For that brief period she must have experienced exquisite happiness like nothing she might ever have experienced before. That same light called me into being. I too was very happy and content living among the fairy folk. I didn't realise I was different in any way until the day my father came to me and said 'Today, Solasa, I have something important to teach you. We are going on a journey. You must at all times do what I say without hesitation.' My instructions were to hold onto the hem of his cloak which he wore at all times, keep my eyes firmly shut, and use the mind technique of simply willing myself to be in another location."

"'Where shall I will myself to be, father?' I asked quickly because I was afraid he would leave without me and I wouldn't be able to find him. 'We will travel to the borderlands of the human kingdom. Stay close to me at all times.' I held onto his cloak, took a life breath deep into my lungs and on the exhale, I asked to be taken to the borderlands."

"I shivered violently when I opened my eyes because a strong biting wind was blowing all about me. My father stood close to me with a very sad look on his noble face. He lifted his arm and pointed to where I was to concentrate my attention. What I saw was so alien to my eyes that I immediately turned my back on it. 'No,' said Mactus, as he turned me round to face this scene once more. 'I am your father, no harm will come to you, but you must see and understand what the humans do and how they live. This knowledge will be your protection for evermore.'"

"The scene before me was very confusing at first because there was a lot of activity and a lot of voices all talking at once. The people were on the top of a hill. They were sitting round a central fire, eating and drinking and shouting across to one another. They wore rough clothing made from animal furs and their bodies seemed large and heavy. They needed the heat of the fire because it was a cold wind blowing around them. There was a great deal of wild shouting and some of the men were fighting. We gazed for a long time, watching without being seen. Once or twice some of the older men stood up and took a few steps in our direction. I made to disappear but my father placed a restraining hand on my arm. 'Don't be afraid, they cannot see us. They can feel something is different in the atmosphere where we are, but they have not the sight. They know we dwell beyond their lands and they are afraid of our magical powers. It was not always so. A long time ago, they respected our hidden places. They left us alone and we never intruded into their daily life. In time, though, they invaded our peaceful glades and dells and their noise and constant activity drove us out of those places. Those spots on the earth are now quite dead and it is up to us to breathe new life into them. Since that time, we no longer wish to live alongside the humans.'"

"We stayed in our silent sentinel positions, watching until darkness fell. The people became very quiet as sleep overcame them. Just as we were about to leave, the leader of the group, shook off his sleep and stood up. He quickly walked in our direction; his hands held above his head. As he neared us, I experienced a very strange sensation. He stood in front of me and I heard a crack. The sound came from deep inside me. He turned away and I heard the crack again. I had no understanding of what was happening to me but suddenly I was no longer afraid of these people. I began to reach out towards this man, but my father quickly grabbed my hand. 'Let us go now. It is finished.' We stood, with eyes closed and once more I was back in the sunny green dell which was my home. Mactus faced me and said 'So you see, my child, the humans are not like us. They would destroy us if they could. You are never to go there again.' But something drew me back day after day."

"It was you Grandfather. Your longing for me, cracked open my heart when I first looked upon you. Your longing kept calling me to return to the same spot day after day until I too could feel a longing. I didn't know who you were but I wanted to be with you. Time passed but the longing didn't. My father could see what was happening and because he too loved me, he released me from the fairy world. Before I left, he said I could tell you where I had been, what my life had been like in the fairy kingdom, but once I had told you the story, all memories would then be erased forever from my mind. I've no idea how I came to be lying in the river bank the day I was found. But as soon as I saw you, I knew I was home. My body was heavy like all humans and all my special gifts were gone apart from my gift of healing. I want to learn with you Grandfather like my mother did before me." Naduree's eyes spilled over with hot burning tears. Solasa knelt before him. He placed both his hands on her head in blessing and thanksgiving.

For the remaining years of his life, Naduree took Solasa with him on his daily search for herbs and plants. Her skill with using the plants never failed because her seership gave her deep knowledge into what was needed to affect a cure. Her grandfather came to rely on her completely and she was never far from his side. In time he grew too frail to accompany her on her daily foraging trips but on returning to the camp each evening she would go to him and show him her day's collection. One morning near the time of the spring equinox, there was no sign of Naduree when she woke from her night's sleep. She found him down by the big stone stretched out on the grass. Stifling the icy fear which immediately gripped her heart she knelt down beside him. She could see he was close to death. "Stay with me," he asked of her, "But promise you will not try to delay my leaving. I know you are capable of healing me but my time to go is now." He looked up at the sky and said, "They are calling me. They will be my companions on my journey."

A pair of beautiful buzzards was circling overhead. Dipping their outstretched wings, they flew down close over and over again. Their beautiful plaintive cry went deep into Naduree's soul calling him onwards. Solasa cradled his head in her lap and together they listened to the buzzard's song of death. As his breathing grew more laboured and Solasa could see he was near the end, her searching eyes never left his face. At the final moment he stretched up his hands to the birds and said in a surprisingly strong voice, "Take me home."

Long after the breath had left his body, Solasa continued to hold him. Sitting with her back to the stone of sorrows, her grandfather's lifeless body across her lap, she knew she would meet him again. She knew because the cord which bound their love still held in her heart. As the day gave way to evening, she propped Naduree against the stone while she returned to the camp to announce his death. When she returned with several of the men, there was no sign of her grandfather's body. At the foot of the stone she found four beautiful buzzard feathers. She touched them gently and whispered, "Goodbye Grandfather, we will meet again in another time."

Time After Time Before Time

Chapter Eight

Shepherd and sheep were huddled together behind the drystone wall trying to find shelter from the blinding snowstorm and howling wind.

It had been a harsh long winter so far, the worst the old shepherd could remember. He had set out at first light that morning to check on his few surviving sheep. Already this winter, half of his small flock had perished in the deep snowdrifts which covered the eastern half of the island. He himself hardly fared any better than his sheep. The relentless cold seeped through his thin clothing day after day and his gaunt face and sunken eyes spoke of the gnawing hunger which was his daily companion.

He pressed himself further into the stones of the wall as if he might find some comfort there. He sat among his sheep waiting for the blizzard to ease, trying to find some warmth from the body-heat of his animals. As he waited out the storm, his thoughts drifted to the events of the past few years when his life had suddenly spiralled into a deep bottomless morass.

He had been born on this island, as had all his people before him. There were stories woven around the arrival of the first people to their island, stories to which he loved to listen on winter nights when the cold stalked humans and animals alike. Their island had been chosen because it had been revealed to one of his ancestors in a dream. An island of fresh clear water, sheltering hills and far from the ills of man. So a small group of people, men and women, following a dream, had set sail into the unknown in search of a new life. And, as his grandfather was fond of saying, "They found it."

Shepherding was what the men in his family had always done and he was no exception. From a very early age he had gone out with his father and grandfather to roam with the sheep across the length and breadth of the island. He was quick to learn and very soon he could handle the sheep as well as a grown man. He loved the rhythm of those early days following the sheep as they cropped the short grass. The flock which was passed from his grandfather to his father numbered more than two hundred. The work was hard but the family wanted for nothing. His mother and grandmother were in charge of the milking ewes, the men saw to the birthing of the lambs, shearing the fleeces and preserving the skins. The daily, monthly, and yearly rhythm was dictated by the needs of the flock and the rhythms of nature. The women of the family always took him with them when they searched out the plants and the roots they would boil down to use to colour their woven cloth. His mother was quick with the spindle, which his father had made for her from the wood of the holly tree. She could spin deftly and quickly, so each season the new fleeces were quickly woven into practical garments for each member of the family.

He had never been off the island and had no curiosity about what lay beyond the horizon. He missed his grandparents when they died, but death was part of his life, so he didn't mourn them for long. Sometimes on a summer's evening when the sheep were resting quietly, he would walk up to the cairn on the hill where they had been laid to rest. He especially liked being there when the sun was setting over the sea, and the glowing pink sky wrapped itself around him. In those moments he was as close to the eternal as any

Time After Time Before Time

man can be on earth, though he would not have named it thus. If you had asked him, he might simply have said, "It's a goodly place, this island of ours."

At one time there had been twelve families sharing the island. Disease, old age and hardships in general had taken their toll on the small population. Although he and his parents were the last remaining family now, he never felt lonely. The whole of the island was his kingdom to explore. This was all he knew and this was all he wanted. He knew the habits of all the animals and he especially loved to listen to the birds singing. He particularly liked the sound the buzzards made when they were calling to each other, as they twirled and dived in effortless aerobatics. His heart always jumped slightly in his chest whenever he spotted them. He didn't understand why he liked to hear them so much but he missed them whenever they weren't around.

From a very young age, so long as he had done his chores, he was free to roam as he wished. His parents understood perfectly their son's need for freedom so they left him to his own devices. He grew into a strong lean young man, with an innate ability to scale the sea cliffs in search of gulls' eggs to supplement his family's diet. He loved his parents and they him. The small family survived alone on the island because they worked as a successful team. If his parents missed the company of the earlier families who had once been close by, they gave no indication of this. His father, like his father before him was a gifted story teller. He told his son tales about those who had gone before him and how their spirits were all around them.

Nothing much changed in the island rhythm until the day many years ago now when the young lad stood up by the cairn and saw a small boat heading towards the island. He came down to tell his parents, and all three of them raced down and took up position on the beach where they knew the craft would surely land. As the boat drew closer, they could see it contained three men, several animals and sacks of provisions. The breaking surf launched the boat into the shallows and all three men leaped out. They pulled on the boat to clear it of the surf and onto the beach. As the young man and his parents looked on in silent amazement, the three men threw themselves on the sand, face down, arms outstretched and began to make strange murmuring sounds. When they finally became upright again they noticed the three islanders for the first time. Without hesitation, the tallest of the three men, bowed his head in greeting. "We have come a long way to this island. We are men of God, and we seek to live in peace and solitude for the remainder of our days. We will find a quiet corner of the island in which to settle and set up our place of worship. We will not intrude on your lives in any way." While his dumbstruck parents continued to stare, the young man came forward to greet the men. "You are welcome to our island. But tell me, what made you leave your homeland."

The three men exchanged glances with one another until finally the man who had first spoken said, "We have been called to serve by silence and prayerful simple living. We have taken vows to serve. There are many men and women like us all over these western isles, seeking out remote places where they can live in prayerful peace. We will not disturb or harm you in any way so rest assured."

The young man and his parents left the beach and went home to their small hut which nestled near the only wooded area of the island. This was a grove of ancient holly trees where his ancestors had come to perform their ceremonies and celebrate the changing seasons. The hut where the young man and his parents lived was sheltered from the worst of the winter gales by these now barely-alive red berried trees. They had been damaged by the remorseless activity of the sheep over many a year past. Still, it was a place where the young man loved to sleep on summer nights when the sea was calm and the moon rode bright in the sky. Sometimes he dreamed that the trees uprooted themselves, and carried him aloft in their arching branches, out of the hollow and up to the top of the highest hill on the island. On waking he would look at the trees, standing silent and solid in their usual places and wonder. But the practicalities of his daily work kept these wonderings from developing. He knew the feeling texture of each tree almost as well as he knew the feel of his own skin. They felt like a part of him, a feeling he would have great difficulty in naming had he been asked. Although he rarely, if ever, felt fear when roaming about the island in search of his sheep, the time spent in the grove gave him a deep sense of protection.

Just before sunset, while finishing the evening meal, he spotted the three strangers labouring up the steep slope on the far side of the holly grove. They looked more like beasts of burden, so great was the load that each man carried on his back. They made slow progress as the slope of the land grew steeper still as the hill summit came into view. Like ants following a trail they slogged one after the other until they had crested the hill and disappeared over the top. They were headed for the clearing at the bottom of the hill where a fresh spring gushed clear waters throughout the seasons. Being in the lee of the hill they would find good shelter from the gale force winds which regularly visited the island in the hard season. "But how did they know that was the very best place for them to settle down?" he asked himself in astonishment. His parents were wary of the newcomers and urged their son to have nothing to do with them. He, however, was very curious about the men and secretly watched them whenever he got the chance. Flattening himself on the top of the hill, he could watch their comings and goings without being seen, or so he thought. What he saw seemed normal enough. Each man had dug out a hollow space where he lay down to rest at night. Each man slept with his feet facing in towards the centre where a low burning fire kept the extremes of the night cold at bay. The rough shelter they had made using the animal skins which they had brought with them, barely kept the rain from flooding their sleeping quarters. They looked a sorry sight as they spent the days dragging large pieces of wood from the forest. Their days began to fall into a pattern of collecting wood for building purposes, with periods for rest and food. Gradually their little camp began to take on a more permanent shape, as they slowly and laboriously built their individual huts.

They kept their two goats tethered not too far away from the camp and several mornings he had observed them milking and drinking the fresh steamy milk. The smallest of the men, and by several years the youngest, fished off the rocks above the pounding surf every few days. The shepherd and the young stranger crossed paths several times in the evenings when they were each homeward bound. The one young man wearing a long rough brown garment, carrying his pole with one or two fish dangling from it: the other smelling of sheep with his small herd following on behind him. They never spoke but always acknowledged each other with a slight nod of the head.

The days and weeks tumbled into each other and the young man didn't go up to the top of the hill very often now. Until the day when the sound of a bell ringing out at regular intervals throughout the day and the hours of darkness, whipped up his curiosity again. Wherever he was on the island he could hear the bell. On the third day after he had first heard the bell, he once again climbed to the top of the hill, made himself small on the grass, and prepared to wait and watch. After some time one of the men stopped his work, struck the bell which was suspended from a tree nearby, knelt down in the clearing and waited. In time the two other men appeared together, carrying a long thick branch between them. They looked hot and tired, but without stopping to quench their thirst, they too fell to their knees. After a moment's silence, the oldest man began to sing some words which the young watching shepherd had never heard before. The two other kneeling men joined in. All three had their eyes closed, their hands crossed over their hearts. The sound of their voices rose up out of the clearing and seemed to mingle with the wind in the trees and the low murmur of the tide receding over the rocks. The young man listened utterly transfixed. The words had no meaning for him but the hypnotic call and answer sounds of the music filled him with a happiness he had rarely felt since childhood. Not since the time when his father had given him his first lamb to look after. When the men had finished with their prayers, they stood together for a moment in silence, before they began preparing their food.

    Just as the young man made to leave his hiding place, the oldest of the men below looked up in his direction and called out. "Please come down and join us." The young man hesitated, but because the sound of their singing voices was still fresh in his ears, he came slowly down the side of the hill. When he finally stood among them, such was the sense of peace and calm in their settlement, that all fear and suspicion he might have had, instantly vanished.

Time After Time Before Time

"My name is Brother Conall, and my companions are Brother Aedan and Brother Fergal. And now tell us your name," said Conall. The young man replied, "I am called Fiachra because I was born at the time when the young eagles are learning to fly and leave the nest."

"Yours is surely a good name," replied Conall as he smiled at the young man. "Why do you ring the little bell and sing your strange sounds?" asked Fiachra. Brother Conall laid his hands on Fiachra's shoulders and said, "This day is drawing to a close. Tomorrow, myself and my brothers will have a day of rest. Come down to us with the first light. We will sit together and we will show you our real work. Go your way now, and may peace be with you this night."

Fiachra began to climb the hill, with a light heart but with many questions whizzing and spinning in his mind. However, he was a young man of infinite patience, garnered from his years of shepherding his flock and waiting for their broken limbs to heal. So he would sleep tonight like any other but with an unfamiliar tiny flicker of expectation budding somewhere inside him.

Next morning saw Fiachra still sleeping when the first light crept across the sky. His parents were already outside seeing to the morning chores. Fiachra slept on, deep in dreaming where he entered a strange world of dangerous rivers, magical objects and rituals involving great hardship. When he finally surfaced into wakefulness, his sense of the world about him felt clouded. The images from the dream tugged at his memory in a way he didn't understand. He went quickly over to the water container, splashed his face with the cold water, over and over, trying to wash away the images that still clung to his mind like cobwebs on the grass on a winter's morning. Without stopping to break his fast, he headed off up the hill. When he crested the top, he stopped for a moment to observe the scene below. The lack of the usual morning work of the brothers gave their camp an air of time suspended. A loose stone rolling away from his footfall gave notice of his coming. The three men looked up and waved to him. Minutes later he stood among them, feeling an unusual sense of pleasure to be among them.

    Fiachra was welcomed with wide beaming smiles by all three men and was invited to sit with them under the tree where the little bell dangled. And so began one of the most extraordinary days in Fiachra's young life. Brother Conall nodded to one of his companions who immediately went to fetch a covered box which was resting in the hollow trunk of a nearby tree. Brother Conall reached in and withdrew an object which was wrapped in a cloth. The three brothers laid their hands upon it and closed their eyes for a few moments. Fiachra's curiosity was aroused even more when each of the brothers now kissed the object in turn. Finally the cloth was removed and there sitting in bother Conall's lap was the most beautiful thing that Fiachra had ever seen. It was a book - with exquisite colours and interlacing patterns adorning the outer cover. Blues, greens, red, yellows, and even gold filled the spiralling, snaking patterns which ran all around the outer edges. Fiachra was transfixed by its beauty.

    "This is the work of a great many of our fellow brothers in our monastery beyond the sea. It tells the story of the beginning of time and the beginning of love. It is very precious to us. It tells the story of the kingdom of heaven and the descent of a mighty loving force into our world. Each of the brothers who worked on this precious book had a different job to do in it. Some spent day upon day searching out berries and roots, oak galls and lichens to

Time After Time Before Time

provide the material for the beautiful colours you see. Others fished for shellfish which were also an important source of colour pigment. Others collected the soot from the burnt animal bones which were good for giving the deep dark black you will see in many of the pages. The more skilful and patient of the brothers were expert in using the quill. They spent their days bent over desks, painstakingly creating each letter as perfectly as was within their means. And because they believed they were doing this work for the glory and honour of their saviour; they performed the same tasks year after year. Those who were asked to do the most intricate and delicate lettering paid a huge price because after years of such close eye and hand coordination, they frequently found their eyesight failing them. When the time came to hand over their work to younger and brighter eyes, they did so without murmur because completing the work was what was important."

    Brother Conall looked down at the book resting in his lap and said, "As you can see it is not a very large book, but it took thirty of the brothers in our monastery seven years to complete it." Then he slowly and reverently turned a page and beckoned Fiachra over to have a look. The vivid serpentine animal shapes and intricate knotwork which lay on the page before him, plunged Fiachra into a deep pool of shifting, swirling entwining colours. He was like a man drowning in beauty, unable to help himself. He stood rooted in his looking, unable to turn his face away from the bedazzlement before his eyes. A strange dizziness and unsteadiness flooded through his body as he sank down onto his knees. Finally Brother Conall closed the book, wrapped it in the cloth and signalled to the youngest brother to take it from him. He put his arms around Fiachra's shoulders until the young man had stopped shaking.

Fiachra's voice finally burst from him with "What is the magic that is in this book, that makes me forget who I am and makes my eyes and skin peel away from me? What is in those shapes and colours that could surely take my life from me?"

"The magic you felt when you looked upon the beauty of the book is not magic as you and your ancestors might have known. This book is impregnated with all the prayers, blessings, dedications and love of the men who made it. What you felt was the very essence of that fierce combination of love and praise. This has the power to make grown men and women fall down and weep with joy. Battle-hardened warriors have turned away from killing and become simple holy men after exposure to this very book. You see Fiachra, this precious book contains the word of God and nothing on this earth is more powerful. We are the guardians of the book for now. We need to make sure it is always safe so that those who come after us can read the words of praise in its pages and come to know the way of love."

From that day onwards Fiachra developed a thirst for knowledge of this God that the brothers spoke of. He began to spend more and more of his days with them. As time unfolded, the brothers, with Fiachra's help, began work on building their chapel. The work was hard, and it continued day after day, month upon month, throughout all the seasons except for the times when the fierce sea storms were blowing. The day finally arrived when the little chapel was complete. All that was left to do was to make a permanent position for the bell. Fiachra was asked to build a small tower on top of the roof to house it. The building's tiny interior was dominated by a very large tree trunk, placed at the front upon which rested the book. The brothers went into the chapel four times a day to chant and worship. Fiachra, however, preferred to sit outside and listen to the rise and fall of their voices. He didn't understand the sounds or the words the brothers sang but he liked to listen all the same. Sometimes he was lulled into a half sleep when the human voices mingled with the call of the buzzards surfing the air. Sometimes Brother Conall would come to search him out over the other side of the island to invite him to come and sit with them while they read from *An Leabhair Mór,* [4] which was the name that Fiachra gave to the book. Fiachra loved those moments when the cloth was removed, the book revealing itself to his hungry eyes, and once again he could feast on that rare and exquisite beauty. He especially loved the way Conall's face seemed to light up from the inside when he was reading from it.

Many years passed in a pattern of harmony, work, prayer-filled days and nights for the brothers and moments of silent contemplation for Fiachra. He never joined the brothers in their little chapel but he loved to listen to the sound of the bell as it was carried on the wind. Sometimes he could hear it clear across the other side of the island. His friendship with the three men, but especially with Conall, increased and flourished. His parents meanwhile never visited the side of the island where the little chapel and monastic huts were located. Although they had listened as their son told them with shining eyes about the magical colours and shapes of the book which the brothers had, they expressed no curiosity about it or desire to see it. Their lives were centred around the coming in and the dying of each

---

[4] The Big Book

day and each season. The power of the natural world was what they worshipped. Their lives were dominated by the wind, the sea and sky. They reverenced the elements and they appeased their gods with animal sacrifice.

    Fiachra too shared the old rituals with them, and felt no conflict with his new knowledge of the Christian God. On Summer solstice mornings when the first light of the day broke through the darkness of the night, the little family would go to the top of the hill above the holly grove to greet the sun. Standing with outstretched arms and turning in all four directions, they murmured their thanks for the warmth on their bodies. During the long hot summer days, they repeatedly gave thanks for the abundance of the berries and edible wild plants growing on their island home. Fiachra had learned from an early age which plants were good to eat immediately after picking and which were best left to dry in the sun and used as medicines when needed. He had many successes with plants which he ground into a paste with clear water. This he used to help seal surface wounds on himself and those of the sheep who frequently lost their footing near the cliff edges. He seemed to have an innate understanding of the healing properties of certain plants. Using some inner thread of knowing he found the smell and colour of a plant told him how to unleash its medicinal qualities. Sometimes when he was perhaps seeing to an elderly ewe that was haemorrhaging after lambing, images unbidden came into his mind of women in childbirth. Images of one particular woman. He tried over and over to bring these images into focus within his mind's eye but it was like wading in the mud flats when the tide was low. As his grip tightened around the blurred images, they simply slipped the noose and floated away. "It's no matter, it's no matter," he would repeat to himself in an effort to shake off the lingering feelings of sadness which sat heavy on his heart after these episodes.

Each year before the worst of the winter gales visited their island, the little family would again pay homage to the elemental world. They would visit the inner sanctum of the holly grove, circling the trees and petitioning the spirits of the forests to protect them and their animals through the coming darkest months. Fiachra felt the benign unseen presence of the trees wrap round the family, so he never experienced the nightly fears which plagued his parents during the dark months. Yet, each year, the family survived the vicissitudes of weather and hunger. The holy brothers too survived as best they could and began to take on the lean look of men who work hard and never have quite enough to eat. Even the island seemed to wrap itself up against the wild storms lashing its shores during the winter months.

In the tenth year after the brothers first landed on the island, Brother Conall seemed to suffer more than usual through the long dark months. His tall frame began to visibly shrink now as the winter illness took hold of him as it did all of them every year. However, with the arrival of Spring Conall showed no signs of getting better. Walking taxed his strength so much so that he was content to spend a great part of every day praying by himself in the tiny chapel. He still clung to the rhythm of spending time with Fiachra, turning the pages of the great book and explaining what the symbols and words meant. Fiachra genuinely liked everything he heard about this new God so beloved of Brother Conall. He listened with rapt attention to the stories of the man called Jesus, about the miracles he performed. This seemed like true magic to Fiachra. When Brother Conall explained how Jesus had died and subsequently became alive again, Fiachra was puzzled. This was very difficult for him to accept because all his life he had seen living creatures die, and be no more. He had watched his parents die some years before and his grandparents before them. Nothing was left of them now inside the cairn except a pile of bones. Every spring he had seen many of the old ewes die while birthing their lambs. Death was final and that was that. How come Conall believed otherwise? Could he too not see that death was the end of life?

Fiachra never voiced these questions because during the long years of their friendship he had grown to love the gentle Brother Conall. He especially loved the way Conall was always willing to stop whatever he was doing and sit and talk. Fiachra observed the myriad little ways that Conall showed kindness to the other brothers and to himself. When food was scarce he would relinquish his portion saying he had no appetite that day. He would point out how one of the brothers had done a good job building the fire that day, or how good it was to be alive and how they should thank God every day. Fiachra still believed in the powers of the natural world and the need to be in communication with the spirits of the rocks, trees, air and water, but for Conall's sake he pretended to believe in the kingdom of heaven as well. He experienced no conflict in this.

Brother Conall died before the first spring flowers appeared on the grassy slopes of the island. In the following days and weeks Fiachra experienced loneliness like never before. He missed the man so much. He wished he had never met this good man because now he had to live without him. Not even when his parents died had he felt such a gaping hole inside him. He moved around the island like a wounded animal, sometimes shouting out in anger at the sky. Other times he sought solace from the silence deep inside the holly grove. Why had this great love he had felt when near

Brother Conall been taken from him? His pain would bellow out from him across the island. Time did not heal his pain. There was nothing else to replace this love. He continued to shepherd his sheep but with no Brother Conall to talk with, he became like one of his own animals wandering aimlessly around the island. At least they wandered in search of food, he wandered in search of the ghost of a dead man.

    The years that followed took their toll on Fiachra. Two summers after Conall's death, the remaining brothers left the island early one morning without saying goodbye to Fiachra. Although he had had very little to do with them in the intervening years, they were his remaining link with Brother Conall. As he sat atop the cairn that particular morning, looking out to sea with a vacant stare, he saw the little boat pushing off from the beach below. The brothers were busy navigating the boat over the surf and out into open water, so they didn't see Fiachra, arms flailing, flinging himself down the hillside and calling out to them. By the time they had cleared the surf and looked back to what had been their island home for so many years, Fiachra was a broken sobbing mass on the sand. The taste and feel of salted water lapping his face tumbled him back into the world he no longer wanted to be in. He left the beach and slowly made his way up the hill again and on down the other side to where the tiny monastic settlement now lay abandoned.

    For two days and nights he lay in what had once been Brother Conall's bed. He neither ate nor drank but dreamed of the love and kindness that had been so freely given to him. On the third day, he woke with a new lightness in his heart. He knew what he had to do. He let himself into the tiny chapel, in a vain search for the book, knowing full well that the brothers would not have left it behind. He placed his hands on the altar space where it had lain and closed his eyes. Once again he allowed himself to drown in the swirling colours and patterns and he thought he heard the soft voice of Brother Conall reading aloud from the living pages. When he at last came back out into the sunshine, he had found a new peace. Just before he set fire to the chapel and sleeping quarters, he removed the bell from the chapel roof and placed it to one side. He watched until the flames began to lick the roof timbers, picked up his crook and bag and turned his face away from what had been. He walked back into the land and spirit of his ancestors. He carried the bell up the hill to the cairn. He placed it with the bones of his family members, his final farewell to the love and friendship of Brother Conall.

    For his remaining years he lived and roamed his island like a spectre. His flock dwindled from his lack of care and attention, until there was only a handful left. He suffered badly each winter and never quite regained his vigour when the warm days returned. He neglected his body in the same way he neglected his sheep. He lived in his memories and his body could do as it pleased. He was an old man now although still only in his early middle years.

    Fiachra stirred and floated up from the velvet blackness of his memories. He pushed his frail body further back against the wall and wrapped his arms around the body of a sheep. The searing cold was arrow like in searching out the few remaining unfrozen areas of his wasted flesh. He closed his eyes, as he pictured the kindly smiling face of Brother Conall bending over him. He heard the buzzards calling to him. His frozen body lay among the carcasses of the sheep throughout the remainder of that winter. When the thaw came, nesting eagles picked his emaciated body clean. There was no living person to gather up his bones and lay them in the cairn beside those of his family members. The bell remained silent in its hilltop resting place.

Chapter Nine

The boat moved silently along the river. The night was dark. Ada sat in the hull, cold and frightened, wrapped in her thickest cloak which was still no barrier against the damp air of the river waters. Standing silent and proud in the prow was her brother Pamu, who had pledged to deliver her safely to the women's quarters. Ada felt the heat rise off the glistening backs of the men who rowed the boat. Although the night was calm, the river currents strained their muscles as they pulled on the oars, trying all the while to make reasonable speed. Their father had been due to accompany her as was the custom, but a lingering bout of illness had prevented him leaving the house. His physician had warned against making such a journey, when the river dampness and nights sleeping under the stars would take their toll on his already fragile health.

Seven days earlier Pamu had been called for and was asked to swear an oath to protect his sister with his life, and to make sure she reached the city without harm. He knelt before his father, and with bowed head received his father's blessing. Pamu was excited to be given such an important task. Although he had just passed his seventeenth birthday, and was only two years older than Ada, the up-coming honour of taking her to the city gates, conferred all the privileges of the older male. This included being obeyed instantly and without question while on the journey. Ada loved her brother and his new status did nothing to stop her continuing to tease him and play daily silly tricks on him. While pretending to be now above such childish and silly games, Pamu allowed Ada to chase him round the garden playing catch, and generally being free and fun loving together. He knew, and possibly she did as well, that all this would change as soon as they set foot on the boat. So for the remaining time before the journey began, they were allowed to frolic like young dogs without a care in the world. Once on the journey, this simple uncomplicated relationship between brother and sister would change forever. They had been forbidden to speak with each other about the upcoming journey.

Not until the last evening before she left her father's house, did young Ada understand the honour that was being conferred on her. "You have been summoned to the palace," her father told her in a soft voice. "The king has sent for twelve young maidens for a special ceremony. You are one of the chosen."

"I would rather stay here with you and Mother," replied Ada.

"Do you not understand the honour, my child," said her father. "You will live in the temple and wear garments of gold and stand next to the king and queen. This brings great favours to our family. Because of you, your brother will have the opportunity to become one of the king's chief personal warriors. Tales of your beauty have reached the king's ears and our household has been singled out for his attention. We are proud of you and we willingly send you to the palace." Ada rushed at her father and flung herself sobbing into his arms. Although Ada knew she had absolutely no choice in this matter, she clung to the tiniest of hopes that her father might not send her away. "Can I not stay here with you and mother?" she asked in a small choking voice. Her father tenderly but firmly disentangled her arms from around his neck, and holding her away from himself said, "It has been decided. We cannot disappoint the king. Go now, my child. Tomorrow you begin your journey."

Ada went out into the garden in search of her mother. She found her sitting by the pond, her sewing abandoned in her lap. As Ada approached, she saw that her mother was silently weeping. Large tears flowed unchecked down her cheeks. When she became aware of Ada's presence, she simply held out her arms to her but continued to weep. Ada laid her head against her mother's breast and muttered soft low soothing sounds. For several minutes, mother and daughter clung together with wave after wave of unarticulated sorrow washing over them. When she felt her mother's weeping subsiding, Ada pulled away and looked questioningly into her mother's eyes and asked, "What is wrong Mama?" Her mother rose and putting her arm through Ada's, led her down through the meadow to the river's edge. Here they sat together, once more hands entwined, silently watching the river rushing by.

Finally, her mother spoke. "I have always known that this day would arrive. At the time you were born, your father was serving in the king's army. He was well liked by all the men who served under him and he had also earned the admiration of the king for his bravery and loyalty. Something happened around the time of your birth which brought deep and lasting changes into our lives."

"What was it Mama?" asked Ada, sensing a stiffening in her mother's body. "Your father had been assigned as personal body guard to the king, a duty which he faithfully carried out. Your father slept next to the king's bedchamber, except for those occasions when he came to my own bedchamber. On that terrible night, two days after you were born, your father was awakened from sleep by a strange strangulated sound coming from the king's chamber.

Time After Time Before Time

Clutching his small dagger, your father rushed in and plunged it into the neck of the man he saw trying to strangle the king, causing instant death. By this time, the king had groped for his own small rapier which he always kept near while he slept and just as he was about to sink it into his attacker the man rolled over and the blade instead went deep into your father's side. The king, mistaking your father for his attacker continued his frenzied attack on your father. By the time he realised what he was doing, your father lay dying sprawled across the king's bed. By now, many guards and servants raced into the room adding to the confusion. The lifeless body of the intruder was dragged from the room. For six days and nights your father hovered between life and death. The king came to visit him daily and engaged all the best physicians and herbalists to attend to his wounds. Against all the odds, he beat death but never fully recovered his previous strength or agility."

"One day, two months after the attack, the king came to visit your father in our quarters. Most of his injuries had healed fairly well in this time, but he still found it difficult to walk unaided. No longer able to perform his official work duties, he sank into a deep lethargic state. On the day when the king came to visit, your father was sitting holding you in his lap. He used to do this quite often which was unusual for a man in any case and more so in your father's case as men of his rank never had any dealings with their children while they were little. He tried to rise when the king entered but the pain in his lower back prevented him. With a sweep of his hand, the king motioned for him to remain seated."

"'I have had a house prepared for you and your family away from the palace where you can spend your days in rest and quiet' said the king without preamble. 'You may leave whenever you feel strong enough to make the journey.

You saved my life and for that I am grateful. I will not forget.' He pulled his cloak across his breast, turned and abruptly left the room. From that moment, our fate as a family was sealed."

Ada's mother looked at her young beautiful daughter and not for the first time stifled the rage and anger she experienced daily since she first heard about her daughter's invitation to the palace. "How can I willingly let her go to such a fate?" she asked of herself over and over without finding a single answer. So she turned her anger on her husband for giving his consent. For several days she had come to him to plead for her daughter. Her husband listened to everything she said. He too loved his daughter and feared a great loneliness without her joyful spirit in his house. He also loved his wife who had patiently looked after him for so many years now as his health and vigour declined. He could deny her nothing except what she was asking of him now. He could not say no to his king even though he would possibly never see Ada again. All the while that his wife was raging against him for letting her go, he was fighting down his own demons.

He had been a young virile man in the king's service so he knew first hand the likely fate of his daughter. She would be a consecrated virgin in the first instance, then after the king had had his fun with her she would be passed down through the ranks of his generals and warriors. She would receive the finest honours and accolades but would always remain a glorified plaything. On the night before her departure, he sat alone in his room and let his mind sift through his memories of his daughter. He recalled the steady gaze she lavished upon him as a tiny infant whenever he held her in his lap during those early days of his recovery. Had fifteen years really gone by since she lay peacefully looking up at him? Sometimes it was as if she were asking him questions with her steady baby eyes. He found great comfort in looking at her. Her eyes seemed to be offering him reassurances. These same pure baby eyes seemed to tell him stories of other places, other lives and other loves. Sometimes he felt slightly unhinged when he looked deep into her green eyes. "I'm imagining all of this," he told himself over and over, "she is a tiny infant, without thought or speech or comprehension, totally helpless and vulnerable."

He loved this child with a love that became all-consuming as the weeks and months went by. He was confined to the house because of his injuries so he and the baby whom they had named Ada, spent a lot of time together. When she smiled, his world became soft and gentle, which was thrilling in its newness for him. He had been a warrior from the age of sixteen and was battle-hardened by the time he came to the attention of the king. His world had been dominated by male camaraderie and the excesses to be found in the unmarried male quarters. He had bedded a great many young women, who came to him willingly. Their erotic skills satisfied his youthful lust but not once did he experience a sense of connection or companionship. This was not something he was looking for either in or outside of his bed. He had his favourites of course but he never spent time with them outside of the bedroom.

Until the night Ada's mother came to him for the first time. She had a fieriness which immediately excited him but it was her refusal to accept his gifts which made him curious. For several successive nights he specifically asked for her to be sent to him. "Why do you refuse the gifts I offer you?" he asked her, when on the fifth night she refused once more to accept the bottle of precious scented water he held out to her. "I come to your bed because I am ordered to. I do not want your gifts. We are master and servant but when I refuse your gifts I am free."

    He looked at her with renewed curiosity. Slowly over many weeks she began to inch herself into a place in his heart. He started to send for her in the early afternoons to walk with him in the gardens. They both enjoyed these walks and so began his appreciation of her keen wit, and tender heart. For her part, she began to see that underneath his hard, commanding exterior, was a likeable, kindly man. Their fondness and indeed love for each other grew steadily over many months. They were married with the king's permission and were granted quarters close to those of the king. When his firstborn child, a son whom he named Pamu was declared healthy in every way, he was pleased. He was less pleased when his second child was female. Her mother named her Ada. It seemed the gods had smiled on the young family until that fateful night when the king was attacked in his bed chamber. As a consequence of his deep injuries and forced rest, his tiny infant daughter became his favoured companion.

    He had loved her with a piercing intensity then, and he loved her still. "How can I let her go from me?" he asked over and over, biting his fists to stifle his cries. All through that long dark night before her departure, he paced the floor, torturing himself with images of the sexual acts his beloved child would have to perform. He felt angry with his king, to whom he had sworn undying loyalty. How can a kingly honour hold the promise of so much pain and degradation for his child? He felt angry with himself for agreeing to hand her over believing that duty to his king outweighed his family loyalty. But mostly, through that long painful night, he was angry with the gods for allowing life to be as it was for human beings. As the pale comfortless morning light crept silently into his chamber, he allowed all the questions to simply fall away. "I have given my word, it cannot be taken back, so my daughter will leave our home today."

When the family assembled for breakfast, her parents appeared haggard and exhausted as was Ada herself. The three of them ate in silence, too exhausted to speak. Pemu was already down by the boat, checking that everything was in readiness. Many of the household servants were busy loading the provisions needed for the three-day journey. When he was satisfied that everything had been stowed on board, Pemu returned to the house. Although he was extremely excited about his new responsibility, he was sensitive to the sorrow wrapping itself around his parents and his sister. He waited in the garden until he got the signal from the boatmen that all was ready and the time for departure was upon them. He bowed respectfully as his father came out leading Ada by the hand. His mother followed behind, leaning on the arm of her personal maid. Father and daughter walked the short distance to the landing place, each of them rigid with the effort of controlling their desperation. In those final few moments before she stepped into the boat, something hardened inside Ada. A thin sliver of ice was laid down in her heart, as she acquiesced to her fate. She faced her father, bowed her head and stepped on board. Her father made an involuntary movement to catch her arm, but she was already out of reach. Her mother dashed forward, attempting to get on the boat, but she was restrained by her husband barring the way. She let out a low howl of pain like that heard from a snared animal.

The barge moved silently away from the landing stage and within minutes was lost to sight as it rounded the first bend in the river. The river quickly settled back into its sleepy tranquillity and only the low voices of the servants returning from the landing stage to their normal chores broke the empty silence of departure.

Ada kept herself apart from her brother during the three days of the river voyage. Pemu was fastidious in his care of her during the days and nights it took the barge to reach the palace. She accepted the food he himself served to her but she rebuked his attempts at conversation. For the whole of the first day, she remained sitting in the same position in the stern of the craft. A lone figure, wrapped in a cloak, seeing nothing and speaking to none. Her eyes stared into the distance noticing nothing. Once or twice her body shook with suppressed emotion and a long low animal whimper took hold for several minutes. Each time this happened Pemu made to come towards her, deep concern in his eyes, but she waved him back. She wrapped her cloak tighter around her girlish body and retreated further into herself. As the first day wore on, and the mist failed to lift from the river, her limbs stiffened from the damp and cold, but still she did not move. Towards dusk, her brother gave the signal to the rowers to make for the shore. Pemu gave her his hand and helped her onto the bank.

Most of the men busied themselves setting up camp, getting a fire going and making preparations for a meal. Ada wandered off by herself. Pemu ordered one of the men to follow her at a safe distance. Unaware that she was being followed, Ada quickened her pace in order to put as much ground between herself and the camp as possible. When she could no longer see or hear the camp sounds, she waded into the river.

The shock of the cold water made her heart beat fast and her breath came in huge gulps. Tendrils of river weed wrapped around her legs causing her to cry out in fear. But still she continued into the deeper part of the river. She tried to stay upright for as long as possible but the current finally knocked her off balance. As she swallowed gulpfuls of the murky waters, she flailed her arms about in an effort to breathe. Her head went under for a second time and this time all fight left her. She allowed her body to be taken by the waters. She lay on her back and for the first time since her father had told her of his decision to send her away, she experienced a sense of peace. She looked up at the night sky and listened to the soft sounds of the river. Images of her parents and scenes from her childhood painted a watery canvas on her mind. She didn't hear the change in the sound of the river as the water gathered speed on its final run towards the falls. The urgency in the water carried her faster and faster tumbling her body round and round in its foam. She no longer saw the sky, as her bruised body went hurtling over the precipice like a rag doll.

  The man who had been ordered to follow her, knew the river intimately. When he caught up with her and saw her in the grip of the current, he didn't hesitate. He knew this section of the river well, so he realised the futility of trying to wade in after her. She was already nearly out of his sight. He raced along the bank, past the falls, and then waded into the centre of the river. The current was strong here too, but he was a river man and had no fear. He was only just in time because the body of Ada came hurtling over the top. He caught her dress as she was sweeping past and held on with all his strength. His years of rowing barges up and down the river had made his arms strong like trees. Yet it took every ounce of his strength to hold on and try to drag her into the shallow waters at the edge. Several times he thought he would have to let her go as they were both pulled under. But he had been assigned to look out for her and he would die if need be in his efforts to save her. As they both went under a third time, he felt hands pulling on his body and shouts of the men.

Willing hands pulled them out of the water. As he lay gasping for air, he looked over at Ada who lay perfectly still beside him. Pemu knelt beside her, shaking her violently and shouting at her not to die. He flipped her over onto her front and began thumping her back. The men were silent as they watched his frantic efforts to revive her. When it seemed to all those watching that there was no hope, she spluttered and spat out quantities of the river water. Pemu gathered her up into his arms and headed back to the camp. He took off her wet garments and was so engrossed in getting her dry and warm that he failed to notice her budding womanhood. He held her close to him and wrapped them both together in his large cloak as she lay compliant in his arms. Waves of tenderness and anger mingled together in his heart as he looked down at her sleeping form. Several times during the long night she moaned and called out and began to flail her arms wildly. He soothed her body and hoped that the terrors in her mind would lessen. As the night passed and he realised how close he had come to losing her, he discovered how much he loved her.

As the kaleidoscope of images from their childhood unfurled across his vision, he held her closer still. As he rocked and soothed her through that long night, a wave of strange and forbidden sensations rolled over him. The weight of his sister's body folded so closely against his own, generated a deep longing to have her as his own. He brushed the river-stained hair away from her face and bent to kiss her mouth. What a sweetness there was in such an innocent pleasure! She moaned in her sleep and entwined her arms about his neck. Even while he luxuriated in her bodily closeness, he knew he could play no further part in her life. She was bound for the king's chamber and his job was to get her safely to the palace gates. For the first time in his young life he experienced an unfamiliar feeling of dread. What could have made his sister want to end her life? To his mind she had everything to look forward to and should be feeling very special to have been called for by the king himself. Why was she not happy? Why did she not want to leave their father's house? What made her throw herself into the raging river waters?

   He battled with these questions throughout the night as he kept his vigil by the side of his now peacefully sleeping sister. When the first streaks of pink began to pierce the sky, he still hadn't found a satisfactory answer. Ada woke with a start from a dream which she had had many times before, a dream of running in wild green hills and listening to the call of the sea birds. Always the same sense of freedom and joy in the dream. She had no living image of such places but somewhere locked inside her rested a memory, so thin, that whenever she tried to hold onto it in her waking state, the ephemeral thread snapped, just like her mother's sewing yarn. On this, the morning after her plunge into the river, she could smell the salt air in her dream. A voice calling her name pulled her up from the depths of the dream into the cold air of the early morning light. Pemu was shaking her awake. She grabbed his hand and with tears spilling out of her eyes she pleaded with him in a tiny childlike voice to help her escape. "You've got to help me," she said while her fingers gripped his hand more tightly. "Please send the boat on without us. I know I will surely die if I go to the palace."

The look in her eye was pitiful and it tore at Pemu's resolve. He loved his sister and more than anything he wanted her to be happy – just like she had always been throughout their childhood days. But Pemu was his father's son and his sense of duty was deeply ingrained in him. Before the look of hope and pleading in her eyes unhinged him from the task given to him by his father, Pemu sprang into action, barking orders at the men to break camp and prepare the boat for the next leg of the journey. Not for a moment did he take his eyes off Ada's movements. He knew where she was and what she was doing at all times while he simultaneously checked and re-checked the loading of the boat. When everything was in place, he led her onto the boat, making sure to seat her close to him.

The early morning mist continued to wrap itself around the figures in the boat. The men were silent as they concentrated their efforts on the work of rowing. Ada sat wrapped in silence, all thoughts of escape evaporating from her mind as the boat negotiated the river currents. She looked an abject and desolate figure, the hood of her cloak hiding her face from view. She rebuffed all attempts at conversation by her brother. "Just leave me alone!" she hissed at him whenever he came over to her side and tried to talk with her. "If you will not help me to escape, then we have nothing to say to one another."

"Please Ada, please, help me to understand what is so awful about being chosen by the king. Is it not an honour?"

She pushed her hood back, showing her face turning ugly with the force of her anger which she spewed in his face, "Why is it an honour to become the plaything of the king? Tell me, tell me!" she repeated over and over as she pounded her fists into his chest. Pemu made no attempt to ward off her feeble blows. He waited until the anger had exhausted her and she slumped against his chest sobbing uncontrollably. He held her in his arms whispering soft soothing words over her head until he felt her go limp. She allowed him to guide her back into her seat. He knelt before her and tilting her chin upwards, he forced her to look at him

"I cannot change your destiny," he said softly, so only she could hear, "But I will always be your defender."

His eyes never left her until the boat prepared to pull once again alongside the river bank to make camp for the second night. Ada went straight into her tent and didn't emerge again until first light. She ate a small amount of food but spoke with no-one. The boatmen were familiar with the daily rhythm now, so very little time was lost eating breakfast, dismantling the sleeping quarters and readying the boat for the final day of the journey. The pre-dawn mist cleared rapidly and it wasn't long before the first rays of the sun began again to warm the naked backs of the rowers. As the morning gathered momentum, the warmth of the day lifted everyone's spirits except for Ada's. She continued to huddle in her place but the mid-morning heat forced her to discard her cloak.

Without it she looked pitifully thin and her almost boyish figure revealed how young she actually was. She maintained her silence until late in the afternoon when the outer walls of the palace came into view as the boat rounded the final bend in the river. A deep guttural sound escaped from Ada's lips as the boat made for the jetty. However, once she was handed ashore, she stood tall and dignified, her head high. Pemu caught a final glimpse of her as she was led by a group of older women towards the open palace gates. Just before she entered through the gates, she turned and raced back towards her brother. She hugged him tightly then turned back toward the gates. Although he didn't know it then, this would be the last time he would see his sister alive.

    The women guided Ada into the women's quarters. She was shown into a room where several young girls were seated around a low table, eating. A place was made for Ada. As she sat down, the fatigue and stress of the past three days overcame her. She put her face into her hands as tears spilled out between her fingers. She cried for herself, for her lost home and for the friendship and love of her family. She felt as if she was drowning in lonesomeness. When she finally composed herself, she felt a visceral recoiling as the silence in the room hit her. There were fourteen young girls and several older women in the room yet there was an eerie silence. Her eyes widened in incomprehension as she looked around at the beautiful young faces. She began to introduce herself but was stopped by one of the women who shook her head and put her finger to her lips indicating that speech was not allowed.

    A bowl of food was placed in front of her. The smell of the food hit her stomach. She ate hungrily and greedily not once lifting her eyes from the food. When the meal was over, the girls were led to a large bathing area. Each girl was assigned her own woman attendant. When her clothes had been removed, Ada was led into the warm scented waters where she was sponged down quite gently and ceremoniously by her attendant. After each girl had been washed, they were taken to the sleeping quarters.

    Before they were allowed to rest they were addressed by the oldest of the women. She spoke with a quiet air of absolute authority. "You girls have been specially chosen. In the morning you will be dressed in the finest of pure white robes. Each of you will be presented to the king, then you will be initiated into the inner houses of pleasure and everlasting happiness." Her cold eyes swept the room, and with a swish of her purple gown she was gone.

Despite her anxiety and fear, Ada slept almost immediately as exhaustion took hold of her. In the morning she was surprised to find that she was one of the last to wake up. Her attendant from the night before once again escorted her to the bathing pool. Her young nubile body was massaged with oils of elemi and myrrh. Standing in her gleaming vestal robes, with her hair braided and coiled around her head, she was the epitome of womanly beauty. What made her appearance all the more startling was that Ada was an innocent and had no idea how her beauty could arouse strong emotions, particularly in men.

The girls were led into the inner sanctum where the king sat on a resplendent dais surrounded by the high priests, chancellors of the court and courtiers both male and female. Each girl was taken in turn up to the king where she was encouraged to bow low. With each girl the king lifted their face and asked of them, "Do you swear to do whatever is asked of you from this day forward?" When it came to Ada's turn, the king held her face for a long time before asking for her loyalty. She held his gaze and said in a low trembling voice, "I do not swear, my king." There was a sharp intake of breath among the assembled company. The king, hardly able to contain his anger, put the question to her one more time. Her answer was the same. With a flick of his hand the king motioned her away. She had sealed her fate. She was immediately escorted to the kitchens and was told she was no longer under the king's protection and must look out for her own safety.

Ada spent the rest of that terrible day huddled in a corner of the huge noisy kitchen. Servant boys and girls rushed about carrying and fetching, all the while trying to keep out of the way of the red-faced slatternly cooks. Late in the evening when the food had been served the kitchens began to quieten down. One of the cooks, a round faced jowly man, finally noticed her crouched under one of the tables at the far end of the kitchen. He kicked her with his foot and bellowed at her to come out. She stood before him, but the acrid smell of his breath near her face made her turn her head away. He took a handful of her hair and pulled her head back. "And who have we got here then?" he bellowed into her face.

When she didn't answer immediately, he drew his hand back and gave her a resounding slap across the side of her head. Once again, he asked for her name. "My name is Ada," she said, "I order you to fetch my brother to take me home."

When Brumo, the cook heard this, he threw his head back, let go of Ada, and roared with laughter. He clutched his enormous stomach and slapped his thighs as wave after wave of laughter convulsed his flabby body. He used a corner of his filthy apron to wipe the tears of laughter from his face, and turning to the other servants who had gathered round, he said in a mocking high-pitched voice, "Will somebody kindly fetch my brother immediately?" There followed a deadly silence as everyone stiffened. They knew what was likely to follow because each of them had been subject to Brumo's viciousness from time to time. Despite his enormous size, he was quick on his feet. With a single swift move, he swung round to face Ada. He grabbed her by the hair again and shouted into her face. "Listen to me well girl. You will never leave this place. Nobody ever leaves this place. Nobody will come to fetch you and from now on you

Time After Time Before Time

belong to me." He flung her against the wall like he would a rotten cabbage, and immediately lost all interest in her.

Ada lay for many hours unable and afraid to move. Every time she tried to sit up her head began to spin and fresh blood seeped from a deep gash on the side of her face. She lay as still as she could because every part of her body was sore and aching. Hunger finally forced her to make another effort to sit up. After several attempts, her head began to clear and she managed to prop herself up against the wall. The huge table which ran the length of the kitchen, kept her hidden from view. She need not have worried because by this time, everyone had gone to the sleeping quarters. She knew the night was well advanced because she could see stars through the grill opening in the end wall of the kitchen. She heaved herself up off the ground and holding onto the edge of the table she managed to remain upright. She slowly and painfully began to make her way along the room heading to where she supposed a door might be. She was halfway along when she heard soft footsteps behind her. She slumped to the floor and crawled under the table. Expecting another assault, she covered her head with her arms and shut her eyes tight. When the blows didn't come, she opened her eyes and saw that two blue eyes set in a grimy face were staring back at her. A young lad, no older than twelve or thirteen, held out a piece of meat pie to her. She snatched it from him and devoured it in a couple of mouthfuls. He disappeared for a short while but came back with a beaker of cold water for her. While she drank, he crept in and sat alongside her.

Revived somewhat by the food, Ada, asked him his name and why he was helping her. "My name is Towah. My father is the man who kicked you and hurt you. He has supreme authority down here and that is why everyone is

Time After Time Before Time

afraid of him. He can make your life hell on earth if he so wishes. He beat my mother almost daily because she was the only person here in the kitchens who ever dared stand against him. For a while he tolerated her remarks because he liked to bed her every night. That is until the day he began to lash out at me. It was some years ago now when he began to turn his anger against me. It started with small but regular cuffs around the ear, then the kicking's began and soon he was dealing huge punches to my face whenever I did something wrong. One day last winter, I dropped a platter of meat which was meant for the king's table. The kitchen dogs were upon it immediately. He rushed at me like a mad foaming bull showering punches down on my head. He backed me into the far wall and the punches got stronger. I don't remember anything further because I must have lost consciousness. What I tell you now was told to me by some of the other servants. My mother, seeing what was happening to me, jumped on his back and started clawing his face. He wheeled round and because he is such a big man, he shook her off, and flung her across the kitchen. She hit her head against the stone trough and lay perfectly still. When I regained my senses, I was told that my mother was dead. From that moment, I vowed to kill Brumo but I am not strong enough yet."

    His story gave Ada her first tiny ray of fragile hope. She gripped his arm and locking her eyes onto his she said, "Please help me. I need to leave now before the day returns and my fate is sealed. Can you show me how to get outside? Come with me and I promise, that when we reach my father's house he will look after you for the rest of your life."

    "I cannot come with you," he said immediately, "Because I have vowed to remain here until I kill Brumo.

Time After Time Before Time

But I will help you. There is only one door from here that opens into the outside and only one key. All other openings simply take you into passages that lead further up into the palace. Brumo keeps the key safely hidden. I am the only person who knows where it is. Don't move until I come back." Without another word he crawled out on all fours and without a backward glance he was gone.

    As soon as he left her, a rolling wave of sadness and loneliness swept over her. She closed her eyes and thought of her home by the river's edge. She imagined her parents strolling together in the garden at first light. She tried to remember their faces in detail as her own face contorted with fear and pain. She waited for what seemed like a very long time, drifting in and out of consciousness as memories floated up to the surface and still there was no sign of the lad returning. A sudden sound pulled her back into the present. Her heart beat wildly as soft footsteps echoed along the stone floor. "Thank God, he's come back," she muttered half aloud. The lad slumped to his knees, stuck his head under the table and showed her the key.

    "We must be quick," he exclaimed, as he helped her out from her hiding place. She tried not to yelp in pain as she crawled out and tried to stand. He put his arm around her waist to steady her.

    Very slowly and painfully, they made their way along the length of the kitchen and up the steps leading to the outside door. Each step was agony for Ada. Blood streamed from her lips where she was biting down hard to stop herself from screaming with pain. She collapsed against the bottom step leading up to the door. The boy turned the key in the lock but the door refused to open. He pushed hard against it, until finally it began to give a little. For several long minutes he continued to heave and push until he judged the gap was large enough for them to squeeze through. As he turned back to help Ada to her feet, he froze where he stood.

The huge shape of Brumo was almost at the bottom step brandishing an iron bar. In the split second before the weapon cracked open his skull, he found Ada's eyes and smiled. She turned her face towards the dawn light streaming through the opening in the door. As her life energy faded, her soul was released into the fields beyond the door. She smelled the air and felt the warmth of the first rays of the rising sun. She heard the call of the buzzards as they circled overhead. Memories of tending sheep on an island home flooded her mind. Her consciousness travelled further back into memories of sacred waterfalls, wide open skies and healing ceremonies. She heard her grandfather call her by her ancient name Solasa. He held out the ceremonial healing cup to her as he had done so many times in that other life. Even as Brumo delivered his final fatal kick to her bleeding body, she raised the cup to her lips, and her soul began to journey home once more.

Time After Time Before Time

Chapter Ten

    From his vantage point at the top of the hill, Tadhg spotted Máire Beag crossing the stream in the valley below. It was a warm sunny day in April and he knew from the careful way she placed each foot that she didn't want to risk slipping on the crossing stones. He was puzzled by this because normally she would cross like a mountain goat and be on the other side in two or three strides. Her red shawl was wrapped tightly round her shoulders and tied securely at her back. He also found this strange because the day was very warm and it was unusual to see her wearing her winter shawl in such fine weather. When she had crossed over, she made her way further upstream along the opposite bank. The river meandered along the floor of the valley for several miles. It was bordered on one side by the oak forest and on the other by limestone cliffs. These cliffs were mostly covered in moss and ferns with tiny waterfalls cascading down at intervals. Over time the water had carved small caves into the rock. Tadhg watched her slow careful progress until she finally disappeared from his view.

    Máire Beag was so named because when she was born she had been so tiny or beag, that nobody expected her to live. Her mother developed an infection soon after Máire Beag was born and passed it on to the baby in her breast milk. The new-born developed convulsions. It was pitiful to watch her tiny frame going rigid. Each time she fitted, her father or one of her older siblings immediately prepared two small baths of water, one warm and one cold. The child was first plunged into the cold water, followed immediately by immersion in the warm water. Her screams were frightening coming from such a tiny fragile body but the water treatment cured her. Because of this rocky start in life, and her survival, Máire Beag was regarded as a miracle child. Prayers were offered in gratitude for her continuing good health, and most adults liked to pat her on the head whenever she passed them by.

    Her family were small farmers and generations of her family had lived and farmed in *Gleann na Coille*. The farm was at the head of the valley, in a remote spot hidden from view by the side of the mountain. Very few visitors ever made the long and arduous journey up to the farm even in the summer months when the snow had cleared and passage under foot was more stable. For Máire Beag and her family, the isolation of the farm helped them to stay loyal to their faith because there was nobody nearby to spy on what they were doing.

    This was the time of the penal laws which aggressively sought to rid the country of Catholicism and papist loyalties. The native Catholic aristocracy were disenfranchised. They couldn't hold public office, land inheritance was prohibited, and their traditional practice of sending their sons to Europe to be educated was also prohibited. Some of them, rather than lose their wealth, swore an oath renouncing their faith. Others however, paid lip service to the oath but secretly continued to practice their faith. The laws also affected the majority of the Catholic peasant population who were not allowed to celebrate mass, or teach their children Catholic doctrine.

    Máire Beag's family were loyal and devoted Catholics and on more than one occasion had successfully hidden a priest or travelling schoolmaster from the authorities. On this bright April morning, Máire Beag had

Time After Time Before Time

been sent on a mission. Several months before, not long before Christmas, word reached the farm that Father Murphy was on the run from the authorities. He was one of the outlawed priests who refused to take the oath of allegiance.

Earlier in the month he had been invited by the Talbot family of Teach Mór Cnoc to come and celebrate mass for them. The Talbot family had taken the oath of allegiance to the new conformist religion but everyone knew this was simply to pacify the authorities. They remained secretly loyal to the old religion and had continued to harbour priests who needed to lie low for a while. All precautions had been taken to ensure Father Murphy arrived safely and without the authorities knowing of his whereabouts. Father Patrick Murphy was not a man in the first flush of youth and the constant travelling from place to place to evade capture had begun to take its toll on his health.

On this occasion as he was being escorted on foot along the valley head and upwards onto the mountain side; he frequently had to pause for breath. Two of the local men who knew this valley well, walked with him. They felt the urgency to get the priest to his destination and out of sight as quickly as possible, but they were concerned for him when they noticed his laboured breathing as they began the ascent. "We'll stop here for a while sure," said Dónal and he lowered the sack he had been carrying. He knew how precious were its contents so he placed it gently at the priest's feet who was already sitting on the mossy earth trying to recover his breath.

"Will you be after havin' a bite of bread and cheese Father?" said the younger man. The three men sat in companionable silence eating and resting until Fionn, the younger man, asked why the law had been made to ban the celebration of mass and why Catholic beliefs could no longer be openly spoken about. Father Murphy put his hands on Fionn's shoulders and said, in a voice leaden with weariness, "Fionn, my lad, if they could wipe us off the face of the earth they would. Those men in parliament who make the laws want to rid our country of all us Catholics. They believe that by forbidding us to celebrate our religion openly we will do as we are told and turn our backs on the life we have always known. They want us to conform to the new protestant religion. They take away our land inheritance; the sons of our landlords can no longer send their sons abroad to be educated, and the catholic teachers have had to resort to sitting by the hedges to teach the children. But remember this Fionn, our faith is our life. Nobody can take it away from us. The authorities destroy our churches and our schools but what they cannot take away from us is what is in our hearts."

"It makes me so angry!" said Fionn in a voice filled with hate. "If only I had a gun!" The elderly priest again placed his hands on Fionn's shoulders and said, in a gentle voice, "But that is what they want my son, they are simply looking for an excuse to kill you. Live your faith Fionn, do not die for it, because one day somewhere in the future we will openly throng to our chapels and churches once again."

They gathered up their things and this time Fionn was entrusted with the sack and its precious contents. As the day wore on, the three men slowly made their way up towards Teach Mór Cnoc. As the house came into view, Dónal went on alone to make sure the coast was clear. Some twenty minutes later, he returned and all three made their way up to the house. They were greeted warmly by Lord Talbot himself and offered refreshments and a room to rest in. Father Murphy stretched out on the bed and was asleep

Time After Time Before Time

within a few minutes. Dónal and Fionn sat on chairs either side of the door, like two sentries guarding their charge. Within the hour a gentle knock on the door signalled that everything was now ready for Father Patrick to do what he had come to do. He was escorted into the parlour, closely followed by Fionn carrying the sack.

Without a word Fionn handed over the sack and quietly left the room. The priest removed his vestments from the sack. The alb stretched down to his feet and he tied it at the waist with the cincture. He then kissed the purple stole before placing it round his neck. He was now ready to hear the confessions of the family and all those who worked for them. About twenty people, young and old queued quietly outside the parlour door and waited their turn to go inside to make their confession.

When the final confession had been heard, Father Patrick came out carrying the sack and was taken along the corridor to the dining room. Here, all was ready for the celebration of mass apart from the sacred vessels which the priest had in the sack. The chalice, ciborium and paten were taken out and placed on the dining room table which had been transformed into a temporary altar. All was now ready. The last person to come through the door was an estate farm worker. He was known by the name of Peadar Óg and had a reputation for drunkenness and brawling. His clothing was ragged and farmyard dirty and unlike everyone else he had made no effort to clean himself up in honour of the sacredness and solemnity of the occasion. He skulked at the back of the room and Dónal and Fionn kept their eyes on him.

The congregation stood with bowed heads as the familiar words of the liturgy filled the room. Whatever fears Father Patrick might have felt for his personal safety, he now pushed them aside as he stepped into his role as celebrant of the ritual of the mass. The soft cadences rose and fell as all those present murmured the Latin responses. The light from the altar candles cast a warm glow on the raptured faces as each man, woman and child present walked up to receive communion.

When the mass was over, everyone simply walked away quietly and melted into the night. The family would keep the priest overnight and make sure he had a good breakfast before setting off early the next morning. The doors were securely locked and the household settled down for sleep. The night was dark and - apart from the night calls of the owls - all was quiet.

Just before dawn, everyone was startled from sleep by loud thunderous knocking on the front door. Soldiers on horseback were pacing outside and the household dogs were barking loudly and adding to the sense of confusion and mayhem. Upstairs, Dónal and Fionn wondered what might be going on outside. They roused the priest, told him to dress as quick as he could, and all three of them made their way down the back stairs and into an anti-chamber leading off the second sitting room. Lord Talbot was waiting for them. He knelt for the priest's blessing before he pressed a stone knob underneath the large marble mantlepiece. The heavy mantlepiece swung outwards revealing a hole behind it big enough for a man to crawl through. Dónal went in first, followed immediately by the priest and Fionn.

They crawled along on hands and knees in utter darkness for what seemed like miles but was in fact a mere quarter of a mile. Eventually they saw a pinhole of light ahead and within a few minutes cautiously emerged into the back of the ice house. The three men stood perfectly still against the back wall, waiting like cornered animals for any new threat to show itself. They waited until they heard the horses move off. Father Patrick knelt down and began to pray. Dónal took Fionn aside and whispered, "Stay with him. I will be back before nightfall." Without another word he left the ice house and moved with the stealth of a preying animal in the undergrowth.

Dónal quickly headed down into the valley and by mid-morning came into the village of Roon. He quickly made his way to the ale house where he knew the man he was looking for would be lavishly spending his bounty money. Sure enough, as soon as his eyes grew accustomed to the dim interior, he spotted Peader Óg sitting by himself in the far corner of the room. Dónal ordered a mug of ale for himself, and sat down opposite Peader Óg. As Dónal raised his cup to his lips, he looked the other man in the eye and muttered softly "Priest hunter."

Peader Óg stood up, knocking over his stool and spilling his drink. He crossed the room and went into the street. He hurried out of the village, and for a man who had consumed several mugs of ale, moved quickly. He made his way along the river bank and up into the woods. Because of the drink he had taken, he made a lot of noise, falling down several times. He saw no sign of the other man and decided that he had given him the slip. As the fright of the confrontation and of being pursued left him, he grew more confident and slowed his pace. Crossing the foot bridge at the bottom of the valley he didn't see Dónal way above him on the other side. Peader Óg left the river behind, and began to make his way up the side of the mountain to his cottage, but growing more and more tired he eventually lay down to rest.

He was awakened by a choking sensation in his throat and a voice whispering in his ear, "Priest hunter, bounty hunter." He looked into the eyes of the other man and the hatred he saw in them sealed his fate. He pleaded for his life, saying the money came from the sale of one of his pigs. Dónal tightened his grip even further and spat in the man's face. "You got the money last night, when you told the authorities that Father Patrick was up at the house to say the mass. Shall I tell you how I knew it was you? You came to the mass without making the slightest attempt to clean yourself up. Your greed to get your hands on the money made you forget that we never ever attend a mass without being washed and dressed in clean clothes as a mark of respect."

"Please don't kill me," begged Peader Óg, "You can have the money, I've only spent a little of it." As he tried to reach into his pocket to get the coins, Dónal plunged the knife in deep. When Peader Óg finally lay still, Dónal dragged him feet first down towards the river. As he rolled him into the water, Dónal muttered, "May God have mercy on your soul and on mine."

As he watched the body being carried downstream by the fast-flowing current, he heard a pair of buzzards calling overhead. They dipped and dived and their plaintive cry pierced Dónal's heart. He dropped to his knees and begged his God to forgive him for the crime he had committed. He stayed on his knees for a long while, regretting deeply what had happened, yet at the same time glad that justice had been done. When his emotions had quietened, he began to make his way up the bank and into the woods. He had to plunge his hands into his pockets to stop them shaking. Until a few minutes ago he had never harmed another human being. Now he had condemned his immortal soul to eternal damnation.

Taking a different route back, Dónal at last made his way towards the ice house. As he got near, he flattened himself in the long grass and gave a low call. To the untrained ear, it resembled the cry of the buzzard. He lay still and waited. Sure enough, a few seconds later he heard another buzzard call coming from the direction of the ice house. All three men were happy to see one another. However, one look at Dónal's face and both Fionn and Father Patrick knew what he had done. "*Tá brón orm, tá brón orm*," [5] the words of regret and sorrow escaping in a convulsive torrent from Dónal's lips.

"May God forgive you for what you have done," said the priest as he made the sign of the cross in front of the crying man. When Dónal had calmed himself sufficiently, he told the others the details of what had happened.

"Won't someone in the village wonder what has happened to Peadar Óg?" asked Fionn. "Indeed they won't," replied Dónal. "We've known for quite a while now that someone in the area has been passing on information about the dates and times of where mass will be celebrated. Word will spread about the betrayal and nothing will be said about his disappearance. Now we should try to get some rest, because we have a long way to go tonight before we reach safety."

The men settled down against the hard rock wall but the intense cold meant that very little sleep was had. Finally, when night came and the sky was inky black, the three men left their shelter and began the long arduous journey down the mountain, into the valley and on upwards into the mountains on the western side of the valley. This journey was hard going and long at the best of times in daylight, but

---

[5] I'm sorry, I'm sorry

now it was treacherous because of the dark. As the possibility of being pursued and captured was very real, they took many risks on the descent, trying to help the priest move faster than he was capable of.

Two or three hours later, Father Patrick stopped and said to his companions, "I'm sorry lads, I simply cannot go on." The others looked at each other and a decision was made without a word being spoken. "As you wish, Father. We'll rest here a while until you feel recovered, then we must carry on. It's important we reach safety before daybreak. The authorities may come looking for you for a second day before they finally give up."

Dónal had some bread and cheese which the landlord of the ale house had passed over the counter to him that morning, just before he followed the faithless Peader Óg outside. The landlord kept his eyes and ears open and was keen to help the Catholic cause in his own quiet way. He had known Dónal since he was a young lad, and once or twice he had saved Dónal from falling into the clutches of the authorities. Dónal knew that aiding and providing shelter to priests incurred extreme penalties, but that didn't stop him from doing what he felt called to do. When word got around that a priest had made his way into the area, it was Dónal who usually set the wheels in motion for a mass to be celebrated. This took a lot of careful planning and extreme caution.

Within the hour they had set off again. They had crossed the river and were beginning their ascent up the far mountainside when they heard the first bird calls of the morning. Time was not on their side, so despite his protests Dónal took first go at carrying the priest on his back. Father Patrick had been on the run now for many months, sleeping rough a lot of the time, never knowing when he was going to get some food, so when Dónal lifted him, he was surprised how little the older man weighed. Dónal and Fionn each carried the priest in short bursts and made good headway.

They finally came within sight of the farmstead at *Gleann na Coille*. Máire Beag's father and Máire Beag herself came down to meet them. The extra help with Father Patrick meant they were quickly within the walls of the farmhouse. Máire Beag and her mother began to rake up the fire, so they could warm some goat's milk for the travellers. All three men sat down and were asleep in their chairs before the milk was brought to them.

"I'll go on down the mountain a short way to make sure all is clear," said Pádraig, Máire Beag's father. He let himself out, closing the door softly behind him. He knew every inch of the mountain and valley. He had farmed this land for forty years now, as had his father and grandfather before him. His eyes were like eagle's that could zero in on anything that appeared different in this deeply familiar and deeply-loved landscape. He had no sons to carry on after him, but he had Máire Beag who loved this land even more perhaps than he himself did. She it was who taught him to sit and look and listen to the land. From the time she was a small child she would run to find him in the fields. She would beg him to stop work and instead simply sit with her in the long grass. Oftentimes, although he had an urgent need to finish whatever job he was doing, he downed his tools and gave into her wish. His reluctance to leave his work was soon recompensed by the soft feel of her small hand in his as they lay side by side in the long grass. Máire Beag particularly loved to watch the buzzards circling overhead as they taught their young the finer points of flying. Round and round they flew, circling and swooping

Time After Time Before Time

and calling to each other. Máire Beag would close her eyes and begin to make a sound deep in the back of her throat.

"What is that noise you are making *mo mhuirnín*?" [6] her father asked her the first time he heard her. "Oh Dada, don't you know, that is the sound we must make to let the birds know we will not harm them." Her father smiled indulgently into the uplifted shining face of his young daughter. He sometimes called her his fairy child because she seemed to take exquisite delight in all aspects of the natural world. As a very young child she would wander outside to say hello to the clouds and the trees and the grass. She especially loved the sound of running water and told her parents that the river told her stories. She drew pictures of a beautiful young girl standing in the river and an old man sitting some distance away from her. She drew this same scene many times. The first time she was asked about the story and the young girl she had drawn, she replied matter-of-factly, "That is me in the river. I was very cold, but my grandfather looked after me." The adults smiled indulgently.

Over the years, due to Máire Beag's influence, he noticed his own relationship with the land begin to soften. He continued to plough and plant his small acreage and tend his sheep, but oftentimes now, he would sit down at the end of his day's labour and wait for his daughter to join him, which she did most days.

Pádraig remembered those days now like they were yesterday, as he hunkered down in the yellow gorse inhaling its sweet aroma. He looked to the sparkling river water way below in the valley, ribboning its way, turning twisting and tumbling like a silver sinuous creature. He knew each and every curve of this body of water like he knew the feel of his

---

[6] A form of endearment

own flesh. He sat hugging his knees, and the rising heat of the day cast a shimmer over the greening earth. He listened for human sounds in the distance but in the stillness of the late morning he was lulled by the sound of the worker bees and the mothering call of one or two of his sheep to their lambs. All was as it should be. He knew every inch of every field, every round on the mountain side, and every mood of the river below him. Not a square inch of it would he have changed even if he had the power to do so. He was never happier than when he lay on his back among the mountain grasses with no other human beings to disturb his stillness. He loved his homeland with a fierce burning love, his people, his language, his faith, and the ways of his ancestors. The new laws that were being forced upon his people would destroy them if something wasn't done.

    Being around people made Pádraig feel uncomfortable. He wasn't given to making conversation so he rarely found pleasure in the trips he had of necessity to make to the village every few months or so. Normally, as he approached the houses tucked together like babies sleeping, Pádraig would feel his skin begin to tighten around the muscles on his face. Even before he got down to doing some buying or selling, he would be already itching to be on his way home again. He was not an unkind or sullen man but if truth be told he much preferred to be on the mountain than sipping ale with the townsfolk.

    Rousing himself from his musings, he swept with his eyes to make one final scan of the land below him. Satisfied that the three men now sleeping under his roof hadn't been tracked, he made his way back up to the farmyard.

    He carried on with his jobs like it was an ordinary day until the darkening hour approached and his belly told him it was time to go inside to eat. As he lifted the latch his nostrils were assailed by the smell of freshly baked bread. The two younger men were sitting at the table dipping chunks of bread into their bowls of hot stew. Máire Beag was reading by candlelight at the far end of the table. Her mother was busy preparing more food. It was a peaceful homely scene.

  The priest was still sleeping by the fire. He noticed that he was covered with his wife's outdoor red shawl and his shoes had been removed. After he had eaten, Pádraig drew up a chair opposite Father Pat and studied the features of the sleeping man. The priest slept with a slack jaw, his hands crossed loosely on his belly. Lines of weariness and despair were etched on his face, and the looseness of his coat and trousers told of his weight loss. Pádraig knew that the sleeping man was more than a celebrant of the rituals of the people's religion. In these harsh penal times, he, and many more besides, was a beacon of hope to a suppressed people. His rejection of the restrictions on his sacred duties and his continued non-adherence to an authority which sought to destroy them gave courage to everyone else to do the same. While the outlawed priests were still prepared to risk their lives or long terms of imprisonment if caught celebrating mass, the people knew they hadn't been abandoned. Pádraig knew that if this priest, right here sleeping by his fire, were to be found sheltering in his home the consequences for himself and his family would be severe. Yet he was prepared to take such a risk and would do it many times over because the priest was the embodiment of all that was sacred to them. He was their spiritual leader who filled the longing in their souls.

  Máire Beag brought her low stool and sat beside her father, resting her head in his lap. He absentmindedly stroked her long black hair as she began to hum a low plaintive melody. Perhaps it was the song itself reaching his ears or the proddings of hunger that woke the priest up a moment later. He started up in fright until he realised that he was safe. He sank back down in his chair and bowed his head towards Pádraig and Máire Beag.

"Will you be after havin' some food father?" said Pádraig. "I will indeed, and God bless you for sheltering me." Pádraig's wife Brighid told the priest to rest easy by the fire and she would bring the food over to him. While he ate, he told them how everywhere he went in the province, a secret place outdoors was usually found for him to celebrate mass. "Is there any spot hereabouts? I don't want to risk any more lives."

Máire Beag and her father exchanged glances and the girl immediately spoke up. "I know a place. It's a hidden cave in the cliffs on the far side of the river. It's behind the waterfall and can't be seen. The waterfall acts as a natural barrier, so you would be safe to celebrate mass there."

"Right you are then," said the priest, "We will need to get the word out, and quickly. I cannot stay too long in any one place."

"Leave that to me, father," said Pádraig, "I have some lambs to take to the sale tomorrow. I will pass the word to the landlord of the pub. That is all that is needed. He will make sure everyone knows before the day is out."

Dónal and Fionn made ready to leave. "Will ye not stay here the night?" asked Brighid.

Dónal was quick to answer. "No, it's best we leave now. The moon is full, and God willing, we can be back in Talbot lands before daybreak." The priest stood, raised his hands in a blessing over their bowed heads, and without a backward glance they were gone. Máire Beag watched them from the window until they were swallowed by the night.

Time After Time Before Time

The following morning, while Máire Beag and her mother prepared breakfast, Pádraig took Father Patrick aside.

"Probably best if you stay here for a few days. You can renew your strength and Brighid will no doubt try to fatten you up." Pádraig had a twinkle in his eye as he joked with the priest but secretly, he was wondering how Father Patrick could possibly survive for much longer being hunted day and night from place to place. "Sure, the poor man, God bless him, is a bag of bones, with an awful grey colour on his face," he mused to himself. He could only stand by helplessly as the older man bent double with a fit of coughing. When he had regained his breath, Pádraig motioned him to the chair by the fireside. "Rest easy here by the fire Father," said Pádraig, "Máire Beag and myself will see to what needs doing for the mass."

And so it was that on this bright April morning Tadhg the shepherd watched Máire Beag carefully crossing the stream wearing her red woollen shawl despite the warmth of the day. What Tadhg couldn't see was that the young girl way down below him in the valley was concealing something very precious in that shawl. All of the local people were used to seeing Máire Beag walking the hills and valleys day in and day out. Indeed, she was known as something of a wild child, and some of the less kind folk sometimes referred to her as 'That young *amadán* [7] who lives up the mountain'. But an amadán she was not. She was bright and intelligent but what made her seem odd to those who didn't know her well, was that sometimes she would be seen to stop dead in her tracks and stare into the middle

---

[7]   Fool, half-wit, simpleton

distance with a huge smile spreading across her face. She would oftentimes as well be heard having conversations with someone that only she could see. When questioned she would always refer to her unseen companions as her 'other people'. The hill shepherds like Tadhg and several others knew Máire Beag from when she was a little girl. They had grown used to her strange ways and usually left her to her own devices. So apart from wondering why she was walking carefully and wearing her shawl, Tadhg continued on his own path and thought no further about her.

She was tall for her fourteen years, slender with the first budding of her nascent womanhood, suggested in the slight stretching of her dress across her chest. Her long black hair accentuated the paleness of her face, and hung loose down her back. Her eyes were set wide apart and often had a startled expression like someone roused suddenly from sleep. Her long legs showed strong calf muscles developed from her daily roamings in the mountains. She was completely unaware of how untamed and striking she would have appeared to somebody coming across her for the first time. She could walk all day without tiring and only rested when she needed to eat or when she stopped to gather medicinal plants. Her knowledge of the healing properties of plants was deep and her remedies were usually found to be beneficial. No one had taught her how to make up healing balms or rubs for aching joints and muscles, but Máire Beag instinctively knew just what was needed. If a stranger happened to ask her how she knew so much about medicinal plants she would invariably answer, "Oh, I've always known." Her mind was quick and inquisitive and until the introduction of the penal laws, one of which forbade catholic children to go to school, she had been a regular pupil at the small valley school. She had always been eager and quick to

Time After Time Before Time

learn and despite her tender years she was one of the brightest pupils that the schoolmaster had come across. With the closure of the school, the master started up his own school which met for classes either in the open air in the warmer weather or in a small derelict outbuilding during the milder part of the winter.

Máire Beag and two other children paid for their lessons with food. The tiny hedge school, as it became known, continued for a few months until the master finally had to accept the painful truth of his situation. He was barely surviving on what he earned from his small number of pupils. He now faced the choice of teaching as an undermaster in a protestant school or finding some other type of work. He was a man who was addicted to the pleasure of opening young minds to the wonders of learning, so to give up teaching was not really a plausible choice for him. Before he left, he counselled Máire Beag never to stop reading and learning and he made her a parting gift of one of his books. It was the story of '*Diarmaid agus Gráinne*' [8] and their pursuit by Fionn, leader of the *Fianna*.[9] Máire Beag read about their hapless love story over and over until she could recite the whole book by heart. It became her single most treasured possession.

But now on this April morning as she made her way along the river bank, concealed under her shawl she carried something infinitely more precious than her book. Because her daily wanderings made her a familiar sight and wouldn't arouse suspicion, she had been entrusted to carry the sacred mass vessels to the cave. She wrapped them in a soft shawl which she had knitted for herself during the winter months

---

[8] Diarmaid and Grainne – a legendary love story
[9] A warrior tribe in Irish mythology

and then tied the bundle under her heavier red shawl. Now as the morning began to warm up and the sun drew the river out of the shadows, Máire Beag quickened her pace. She knew that from every direction people would be converging on the cave, silently and stealthily.

She was the first to arrive. Letting her outer shawl slip from her shoulders, she reverently opened the inner shawl and removed the chalice and ciborium. She laid them on a flat rock at the back of the cave and waited. She stretched out on the floor and sat with her back against the damp rock. She looked at the silver vessels which now seemed to shine in the muted light inside the cave. The light from the chalice grew brighter and brighter, drawing her closer and closer. As she stepped into the path of the light, she slipped through the gates of time and place. She had been taken back hundreds of years to witness again a ritual which aroused no fear in her.

She found herself standing beside an elderly man who was raising a ceremonial cup to his lips. She was by his side holding a smaller cup containing the same potion. This was the solstice ritual to awaken true knowledge and leadership. At a given signal, the old man raised his cup and drank. He then turned to the young woman beside him and nodded. She raised her cup aloft and then quickly drank. He took her free hand and raised it aloft, as he said in a strong voice of authority, "I give you Solasa." A roar went up from the onlookers and Máire Beag heard the cry, 'Hail Solasa'.

Without warning, she was pulled back into present time. The cup was roughly snatched from her hands and her father's voice said, "What on earth did you think you were doing holding up the chalice like that?" Máire Beag looked at him but didn't see him. Her gaze was fixed on the chalice which still beckoned to her. She made a move towards it but her father gripped her arm tightly. "What in God's holy name has got into you?" he shouted at her, "You know only the priest can handle the chalice." Father Patrick, who was standing behind Pádraig, placed a restraining hand on Pádraig's shoulder and said to Máire Beag in a kindly voice, "It's all right, my child, no harm done." She slumped to the floor, cradling her body as silent tears ran from her eyes. She turned her gaze to her father's stricken face and said in a tiny voice, "It was so beautiful on the hilltop father. I drank from the cup and I was named for the sun. They were my people from such a long time ago. Seeing the chalice made me remember the ancient ceremony."

    She turned, walked out of the cave and stood under the waterfall. The shocking coldness allowed her to put the ancient memories back into their right and proper place within her. A part of her knew instinctively that her knowledge of her own past lives was not to be shared, so she contained the ache that sat deep inside her, a longing to live those times again. For now, she needed to bring herself back into the present moment and keep her attention fixed on the ceremony of the mass that was shortly to take place. As she turned to go back inside the cave she heard quiet voices below her as the first of the congregation began to arrive. At strategic points around the mountain she knew that several men would be keeping a look out.

    About fifteen people had crammed themselves tightly into the cave, waiting for Father Patrick to begin. Men and women stood side by side, some fingering their rosary beads. Father Patrick kissed his stole before placing it round his neck and the mass began. The low murmur of voices mingled with the sound of the waterfall outside and the dripping of the roof water inside. The lilting cadences of the Gaelic swirled around the cave, sometimes soft and sometimes strong in response to the liturgy. Everything that these people held sacred had been forbidden to them by law, yet they were not cowed. They obeyed the laws in everyday life because they had to, but in matters of their faith, they clung with a fierce determination to their ancient customs. Each man, woman and child in that cave knew the risk of being caught at a mass. However, as the most solemn part of the mass drew near, each person gazed at the rough stone that was their altar and saw only beauty and strength.

The tiny bell, hidden until now in someone's pocket was rung three times to announce that the most sacred moment of the mass had arrived. As one, all heads bowed low, as the priest raised the chalice up high. From her place beside her father, Máire Beag once again saw within her mind's eye the circle of people gathered on a hill top in ancient times. In that moment she understood that what linked ancient past lives and the lives of those around her now, was a deep abiding reverence for the sacred rituals. She bowed her head to the ancestors. The quiet murmuring of voices hushed in prayer continued for some time until at last, everyone sank onto their knees as they waited to receive the final blessing. Father Patrick raised his right hand and made the sign of the cross over their heads, murmuring softly, "*In nomine Patris et Filii et Spiritus Sancti, Amen.*"

It was finished. People left quietly one at a time and quickly disappeared. Dónal and Fionn who had been watching from a spot hidden by the bend in the river, now appeared at the mouth of the cave. They nodded to Pádraig and Máire Beag but were anxious to get Father Patrick away as quickly as possible. Goodbyes were quickly said as the priest made to leave. He turned to Máire Beag and looked deep into her eyes. "I know that you can see in a way that is withheld from the rest of us. This is your special gift. Guard it well, and use it only to serve the light." He placed his old hands on her head and a shot of joy burst her heart wide open. His touch conveyed what no words could. Was it possible his soul knew hers from long, long ago? Was it possible he knew her as Solasa? Was it possible he was her beloved grandfather who had stood vigil with her as she pierced the veil while standing in the freezing river waters? Was his soul that of Naduree who had died while listening to the call of the buzzards above him?

    The old priest saw the questions in her eyes, He withdrew his hands, gave her a big smile and quickly left. She stood at the mouth of the cave watching him and the two young men as they made their way along the river bank. She followed their movements until they were hidden from sight. While her father made a final check of the cave for anything incriminating that might have been left behind, Máire Beag began to head out for the river. She had not gone more than two yards when she noticed a pair of buzzards circling overhead. One of them was spiralling, twisting and turning in a rapid series of movements which Máire Beag knew was meant to impress its mate. Its mewling call was a thread drawing her back to all she had known in other lifetimes. Her ability to look back in time was a gift as Father Patrick told her, but it also made her lose her footing in her present life. She knew that she appeared dreamy and distant to those who knew her. As a child she was constantly being told to stop daydreaming. Over time, she had learned to anchor herself in present time. One of her strongest anchors was the call of the buzzard. This beautiful mewling voice both brought her back to her current life or opened the door for her when she felt herself being drawn back into a previous life. She had also learned to accept she should never speak about her other lives. Who would believe her if she did? She knew that her gift ran contrary to the church's teachings on life after death. So she simply withdrew from people and immersed herself in nature.

While she waited for her father to join her on their journey back up the mountain to the farm, she followed the flight of the two buzzards as they continued their courtship in the thermals above her.

Time After Time Before Time

Chapter Eleven

Nothing in his military career so far had prepared Lieutenant Robert Evans for the lassitude of the men and the squalor of the barracks when he first arrived in Kilbrona to take up his commission.

He had been sent from the capital to restore law and order to these remote western lands. Reports of looting and rioting had been an embarrassment to the high commissioner, who was determined to re-establish law and order by whatever means it took. Lieutenant Evans, unmarried, a seasoned soldier and excellent horseman was the obvious choice. He was given full authority to do whatever was needed to restore military authority to the Kilbrona area. Although he hated to leave the city and its varied pleasures, he accepted the commission without grumble.

Inwardly, however, his heart sank at the prospect of living in a god-forsaken hole, somewhere in the bog lands of the west of Ireland. His first sight of what would turn out to be his home for the following three years, shattered any remaining illusions he might have had about what was in store for him. He had been travelling on horseback for two days and as he neared his destination he mused on the prospect of a hot bath and a clean bed. As he slid down from his horse outside the barracks, he was struck by the absence of sounds. The eerie silence hung heavy in the air, punctured only by the feeble barking of a mangy dog that looked more dead than alive. The stench of decay, mingled with the acrid

Time After Time Before Time

smell of wood smoke, filled his nostrils. "God almighty, what have I let myself in for?" he muttered aloud.

Tired and saddle-weary as he was, he drew himself up to his full height and strode to the door of the barracks. He threw it open and was shocked and sickened by what lay before his eyes. Several men, wearing the remnants of the king's uniform, lay sprawled around the room. They were obviously drunk and hardly noticed the stranger who stood in the doorway. As his eyes became accustomed to the thin light in the room, he noticed two women, dressed in rags, huddling together in a corner. As their eyes met his, they slunk further into their corner. He noticed the sores on their faces and their matted hair and the filthy rags which barely covered them. As he took a few steps further into the room, the men continued snoring unaware of his presence. He made a silent gesture to the women to leave. As they scurried past him, he took his pistol from its holder and fired a shot into the air, the bullet lodging deep into a smoke-tarred oak beam. "Whass goin on?" grunted one of the men as he opened his eyes and made to sit up.

"I'll tell you what's going on!" roared Lieutenant Evans, as he kicked the man viciously in the ribs. He fired another shot and then another until all of the men were trying desperately to get to their feet, terrified for their lives. Two of them, putting their hands in the air, were pleading for their lives. Evans pushed the pistol into the face of the man nearest to him and shouted, "Shut up, you stupid lazy bastard, or I'll finish you off!" Who's in charge here?" he roared at the now-wide-awake men.

"Nobody Sir," volunteered one of the men finally. "You see sir," the man went on, "Lieutenant Montgomery, who was in charge, died these three weeks past now. He had the scurvy and the sores on his body were spreading. We helped him as best we could but nothing helped him in the end. We don't have enough to eat a lot of the time, and sometimes the food is rotten by the time it reaches the barracks. None of it's our fault," he continued in a voice that was snivelling and whining.

"Enough!" shouted Lieutenant Evans, as he banged his fist on the table in front of him. "Judging by the state of every single man in this room, I see that you have no shortage of whisky or filthy sluts to keep you company. What I'm now going to say, I will say once and once only and I expect to be obeyed. I'm going outside again to clear my nostrils of the stench in this room. When I return I expect to see this room cleaned up and each of you wearing your full uniform and ready for inspection." He turned on his heels and left the room, slamming the door behind him. He leaned against the outside wall and tried to calm his emotions. He had expected this place to be without many creature comforts, but the state of the barracks was filthy beyond anything he had ever witnessed before and no doubt the men themselves were disease-ridden.

He inhaled the night air and as his mind settled, he set out to walk along the road away from the barracks. The night was calm and in the darkness it was easy to believe that all around him lay beautiful fields and hills. Indeed, there were hills nearby and fields aplenty but all beauty had been long since sucked out of the landscape like marrow from a bone. This was the time when the deep hunger of the people was echoed in the barrenness of the land, as if the fields and the hedgerows were also sucked dry. As he continued his walk, Lieutenant Evans knew nothing of this. He liked the silence of the night around him and was so lost in his personal revelries that he didn't notice a strange shuffling sound coming up behind him, until something

Time After Time Before Time

touched his sleeve. He heard a child's voice say, "*Tá ocras orm, tá ocras orm.*" [10]

A thin arm reached out and clutched Lieutenants Evans jacket. "Please sir, give me food." Evans shook the child off like he would a speck of dust. The tiny boy fell to the ground and looked up with the blank wide eyes of hunger. "Go away," said Evans, "Go home." The child scuttled under a nearby hedge, curled up and was swallowed by the darkness. Feeling annoyed by the encounter, Evans turned on his heel and made his way back to the barracks.

Even as he neared the building the stench was almost overpowering. He took the steps up to the door two at a time and flung open the door. The men immediately stood to attention, forming a line on both sides of the room. He walked between them and his heart sank with every step. Standing in front of him for inspection were twelve filthy, debauched men, none of whom was wearing a complete uniform. "How am I going to bring this lot back into some semblance of military discipline?" was his only thought as he finished his mockery of an inspection. He noted the sullen expressions, the lack-lustre eyes and above all the unshaven faces and strong body odours. He stood before the men and bellowed out, "From tomorrow morning, things will change around here. At first light I want fresh latrines dug, well away from this barracks. The present latrines, which judging by the stench are just behind this building, are to be filled in and covered. This room I want stripped of all bedding and furniture, so the walls and floor can be washed down. Is this clear?" He turned on his heels to leave. As he reached the door, he turned and in a deathly quiet voice said, "One last thing. This is a barracks, not a whore house. If I

---

[10]   I'm hungry, I'm hungry

ever catch one of you with a whore in this building, you will be flogged."

Outside, the night sky continued to shine its brilliance, weaving through the darkness like silvery seaweed. Dragonflies danced across the bog, enchanting and alluring. The night was indeed beautiful, but something was not quite right. Once again, he was struck by the absence of sounds. Apart from the occasional hooting of a distant owl, there were no animal sounds to be heard. How was he to know, coming from the city and bringing his ignorance of the true state of the land and its people with him, how was he to know in God's name, that all the animals had long since died? Not from disease or neglect, but from something much more harrowing. They died from starvation. Hunger was sweeping the western land and the animals were the first to suffer.

The land was producing plenty of grain but none of it fed the bellies of man or beast. It was delivered up as rent for the miserable hovels that the people called their homes. The rich fed well and turned their eyes away from the spectre of suffering humanity all around them. What did a well-fed landlord know of the supreme effort it took a man who was already weakened by hunger, to go into his fields, harvest his crop of wheat and see that very same crop taken away from him when his family was starving? Most of these families in the west had always known hunger to some degree or other. But not like now.

Each family had a small patch of land for growing potatoes and a cow or two for milking. The women knew how to make a bowl of potatoes sitting in warm milk feed a family of ten. Sometimes a small patch or two would be cleared for a few cabbages or turnips. And in the days before the small famines, a few hens could provide some extra food. Before the spirit of the people was broken and the beauty went from the land itself, most families managed to survive. Despite the misery and grinding poverty of their daily lives, they survived. They survived because of the music, which was like food to them. It didn't fill their bellies but for brief moments it ignited a fire in the soul. Their traditional music and their songs formed a thread which had remained unbroken through countless generations. The sound of the fiddle was a clarion call to the soul of an oppressed and humiliated people. When the fiddler took up his bow and the first notes washed over those listening, each man, woman and child present knew they belonged. As the jigs, reels and hornpipes bounced off the walls of the thatched hovels, the people could allow themselves to remember their deep ancestral roots. Their ancestors had been kings at Tara. They carried within their blood the faith of Patrick, the courage of Colmcille and the silver tongue of their filid.[11]

When the music had raised up their spirits, an opportunity would arise for the voice of the Seannachies [12] among them to speak of home and hearth, of mountains and heather, of cows and grass, of freedom and beauty, of living and dying, and perhaps most importantly, to tell the stories of the great legendary heroes of old. Heroes, who once trod this very same land, at least in the imaginations of the people. The Fir Bolg, Fionn Mac Cumhaill, and Cu Cúchulainn for a brief imaginary moment, once again roamed the land and fought for honour and glory. When the music started up again, some of the older men would take turns to dance the sean nós.[13] Aged feet and legs keeping

---

[11] Wandering poets in ancient Ireland
[12] Storytellers
[13] Traditional solo dance

Time After Time Before Time

time to the music of the fiddle and bones. Momentary pleasures for all those present. A few brief hours in which to slough off the degradation and despair of never having enough to eat and of watching their children die almost as soon as they were born. Watching the beauty of the women drain away as they clung to the vain hope that this year, or next year, might be better. But it never was. Hunger continued to stalk the land.

    The potato fields delivered up their blighted crop year upon year and the stench of despair was everywhere. Men and women clawed at the rotten tubers. When it was clear that every single potato had turned to black mush in the ground the women began to *caoin* [14] right there in the muddy diseased patches of earth. The poor laws, introduced to alleviate some of the suffering did very little. How can a man who is so emaciated from hunger be expected to use a shovel or pickaxe for eight hours a day in return for a handout of gruel? The starving men fell down where they worked, and were immediately replaced by other starving wretches.

    The women tried, mostly in vain, to suckle their newborns with dry empty breasts. They barely had the strength to dig for the roots of the silverweed which, when boiled up, tasted almost like the potato. Soon there was no more silverweed to be found near their lands. Although weakened by extreme lack of nourishment, some of the women walked vast distances each day searching for edible roots. They would often eat them raw, there and then in the fields and suffer the griping pains not long after. They watched their babies die the quiet voiceless death of the innocent and

---

[14]   Lament (Gaelic)

buried them with the last remaining vestiges of private dignity. The older children roamed together, like a pack of animals turned mad and savage from hunger. They looted whatever and whenever they could from the landlords' houses, always looking to fill the hole in the belly. They created fear among the landed gentry, who felt isolated and neglected by the authorities in the capital. These well-fed landlords asked for help to be sent to bring some order back into the province and to curb the actions of the roaming mobs.

Towards the eastern edge of the village of Kilbrona, the manse stood tall and four square, a potent symbol of power and wealth. Its orchards had long been stripped of all fruit by the starving youngsters. Arrests had been made but in truth Sgt. Thomas hadn't the heart to arrest the skeletal boys who daily clambered over the walls of the orchard hoping to find among the long grass some piece of overlooked fruit. Sgt. Thomas was sent for almost on a daily basis to arrest yet another child who had been caught stealing a crust or an egg from Lord Perry's kitchen.

In the days before the potato failure, when most of the surrounding small farmers could feed themselves, Lord Perry was not a bad landlord. He owned every cottage for ten miles in all directions and his deputy meticulously collected the rents in cereal crops after each harvest. Although the farmers hated the deep injustice of this, they knew they would always have enough to eat as long as they had a goodly potato crop for themselves. All this changed however when the potatoes failed year after year. There was nothing left to eat for man or beast. For many years Lord Perry had wanted to remove most of the tenants from his land and the famine disaster gave him an opportunity. If families gave up their cottages they could be housed and fed in the poor house. Most families were so desperate that they readily availed of the opportunity and abandoned their homes. The landlord was so keen for them never to return that he instructed his men to raze the hovels to the ground as soon as they became emptied of their occupants.

Some families however, like the O'Halorans who lived two miles out on the road towards the sea, refused to leave. For several generations the O'Halorans had been tenant farmers eeking out a living on the same few acres of poor bog land. Michael and his three sons supplemented their potatoes with fishing. Each season brought its own rhythm of work. Every spring time Michael, with his two sons Seán and Seamus, could be seen preparing the drills to take the seed potatoes. A small acreage of oats and barley was also sown at the same time so that they could be sure of paying their rent at Michaelmas time. Noreen, Michael's wife, saw to the house and the milking of their only cow. Her day started when the first light crept into their single-roomed cottage. Hot milk and *boxty* [15] was the daily fare for the whole family especially during the winter months when fishing was poor and nothing much was growing on the land.

Michael was a powerfully-built man and knew how to forge a horseshoe as his father had done before him. He had a small smithy to the side of the cottage and until the time of the great hunger he had lived well on the food which he earned in exchange for shoeing his neighbours' horses. Indeed, even Lord Perry had on occasion turned up with a lame horse to be shod. Michael had learned a few phrases in the English tongue so that he could pass the pleasantries of the day when Lord Perry happened by.

---

[15] A flat bread made from grated raw potato

Time After Time Before Time

One morning, not long after Lieutenant Evans had arrived at Kilrona barracks, Michael was awakened by a shout from outside his cottage. When he opened the door, he was astonished to see a smartly dressed soldier on horseback with three other soldiers on foot standing two or three paces behind.

"*Dia dhuit,*" [16] said Michael, "*Conas a tá tú?*" [17]

"For God's sake man, speak English can't you!" was the immediate gruff response. "Are you the blacksmith?"

"That I am sir," said Michael.

"See to my horse immediately, he's thrown a shoe." He slid from the horse and handed the reins to Michael. While Michael was dealing with the horse, Evans paced backwards and forwards impatient to be off. Even so, he noticed the air of neglect and decay all around the cottage. He noticed the surrounding fields empty of animals, except for a single scrawny cow tied up alongside the gable end. The animal looked more dead than alive with its entire rib cage visible through the thin stretched skin. "Why don't these people learn to take care of their animals?" he muttered. When his horse was led back to him, he turned on Michael and pointed towards the cow with his whip. "That animal is a disgrace, give it something to eat man!" He flung a coin down towards Michael and rode off.

Michael stood still, burning liquid anger flooding the entire length of his body. Sweat broke in droplets on his forehead with the effort he made not to scream aloud. His knees gave way and he fell face down on the hard earth. Wave after wave of soul anguish seeped out through his pores in shameful remembrances. "Why does he not see that

---

[16] Hello (literally God be with you)
[17] How are you ?

we have nothing to eat ourselves?" he repeated over and over as his fists beat the ground. "Why does he believe we would let our animals starve and die if we could help it? His kind have milked us dry until my country is haemorrhaging from empty bellies." He hunkered back onto his heels, his head between his hands, until the anger was replaced by the unbidden memories of how life used to be.

His mind took him to the hills beyond the bog lands, where he used to walk with Noreen before they were married. He could feel the smallness of her hand as it grasped his when they ventured up to the top of *Sliabh Mór*, in those early courting days, to collect the wild berries which grew abundantly among the heather. He never tired of hearing her singing as she worked, and the cadences of the Gaelic anchored into his heart. When she came to his bed after they were married, their delight in each other was spontaneous and deep. They had very few comforts in their life together, apart from the dancing at the crossroads and the singing and storytelling in neighbouring cottages during the long winter nights. Every man, woman and child who lived out here in the western lands knew grinding poverty from an early age, but that is how it was. They knew little of the riches and comforts of the ruling class who controlled every aspect of life in this land. Each family was too busy trying to survive from day to day to think about how unfair life really was. Each tenant farmer paid his rent in wheat and had precious little left for his own family. The system worked until the fields turned black with the decaying potatoes for the third year.

Michael finally raised himself up and went inside to speak with Noreen. He found her staring with the big blank eyes of one who is beyond hungry, at the small lifeless bundle in her lap. He crouched down beside her and stroked her face. *"Oh, grá mo chroi,"* [18] he muttered softly to her over and over. She lifted her face to his, and let out a single piercing sound. Her once beautiful face, gaunt with the blue veins showing beneath the stretched skin, contorted in grief, the words of despair spilling onto the lifeless baby. *"Tá mo chroi briste, tá mo chroi briste."* [19] He wrapped his arms around her, and wished that death would take them too. He took the bundle from her and together they silently walked down the boreen to the parish church. They approached the graveyard through the two giant yew trees and prepared to bury their tiny infant daughter. There was no priest now within the parish to perform the burial rites and no grave digger either. The progress of the great hunger could be seen in the dozens of newly dug graves, with their makeshift crosses.

    Michael found a stone and began to scrape out a hole. He took the baby from Noreen's arms and laid her softly down. He replaced the soil and they both dropped onto their knees. They prayed for her soul and when they were done, Michael found two small twigs which he laid in the shape of a cross on top of the tiny mound of earth. From that very moment, a cold determination gripped Michael's heart. He would leave this land behind him and join those of his countrymen who had already gone before him to a new life across the sea. He would not go to the alms-house and become a beggar. He had one thing of value that he would use to secure their passage to the new lands.

    His harp had come to him from his father and from his father before him and from several generations before that. It could possibly be traced back to the time of the great

---

[18]   Oh, love of my heart
[19]   My heart is broken

O'Carolan [20] himself. Indeed, Michael always referred to his harp as the *'Turlough'* which was how his father called it. He could remember as a small boy, when his father had come in from the smithy, and was washed and fed, how he would ask for the Turlough to be brought to him. Such was the beauty and mystery that he drew from those strings that Michael always believed that even the fairy folk might draw near to listen. On more than one occasion in better times, when Michael himself played the harp outside, of a summer's evening, Lord Perry, as he rode past, would dismount to listen. He would listen from a short distance away and nod his head towards Michael as the music ended.

As he sat in the house with Noreen on the night of the burial of his baby girl, he vowed he would give up no more children to the hunger. Later that evening when the family had eaten the few edible roots that their sons had managed to forage, Michael announced that tomorrow they would leave Kilbrona for ever. But first he had something to do. He pulled his harp from the corner of the room, covered it with some sacking and went out into the night. He walked the mile and a half down the boreen, through the village until he stood outside the heavy door of the manse. His heavy pounding was answered by Kathleen Murphy, a young woman from the village who had escaped the ravages of the famine because she lived and worked and ate in the big house. She smiled awkwardly at Michael and couldn't conceal her astonishment when he asked to see Lord Perry immediately. "*Téigh abhaile anois,*" [21] she whispered, just as Lord Perry himself appeared in the hallway. "What's going on?" he asked. "What do you want at this hour of the night?"

---

[20] Turlough O'Carolan was a famous, blind Irish harper
[21] Go home now

Michael took down the harp and began to play. He played the first few bars of the haunting melody '*Tabhair dom do Lámh*' [22] which he knew was one of Lord Perry's favourites. Then he abruptly stopped and said, "I am leaving Kilbrona in the morning and I need money to get my family across the sea. I will exchange my harp with you for ten guineas." Lord Perry, who had no musical talent himself, knew that a harp in his drawing room would be an attraction for the ladies of the house. He quickly said to Michael, "I'll give you five, and not a penny more." Michael nodded and Lord Perry rummaged in his pocket and thrust the coins into Michael's outstretched hand. With the coins in his left hand, Michael ran his hand over the strings for the last time. He abruptly turned and walked away.

Early next morning the O'Haloran family with their few meagre possessions stood by their door as Lieutenant Evans and his men arrived to make sure that the vacant house would not be immediately occupied by another dispossessed family who had discovered that life in the alms house was worse that life in their own hovels. Evans, who by this time had been in the district for six months, had a deeper understanding by now of the plight of the people. He would personally have turned a blind eye to a family taking refuge where they could. He had seen enough bloated dead bodies under hedges, the line of sepulchral figures walking the boreens daily looking for food; whole families huddled together under sacking behind the burnt out remains of their house waiting for death. Each and every day his humanity was pitched against his sense of military duty. Most evenings when he arrived back at the barracks, where a warm fire and hot food awaited him, his feeling of

---

[22]   Give me your hand

impotence made him quarrelsome with the men. To his surprise he had bonded deeply with this small band of men, and fully understood their sense of lassitude and slovenly habits which had so appalled him when he first arrived.

He himself was now as worn down as they were, and he felt his own life force being eroded. The barracks had a regular supply of food delivered, and on every occasion, there had been a riot as the starving crowds had tried to take the food. Several times his men had shot one or two of them. Lieutenant Evans had tried distributing a small amount of food which he kept in his saddlebags when he was out on his travels, but even this caused the children to fight and tear at one another in an attempt to get a tiny morsel of bread from him. His soul had grown weary from the suffering he witnessed and he used the whisky bottle to dull the images. Even in sleep he got no relief as hordes of emaciated figures peopled his dreams. He had been sending regular reports to the capital, describing the pitiful state of the inhabitants and asking for increases in the poor relief. His missives were duly answered with cold dismissal.

He had been a frequent dinner guest at Lord Perry's and had come to appreciate that, although Perry was not a bad man, he had no sense of affinity with the tenants on his land. As far as Perry was concerned, they had brought the hunger on themselves. He had also been sending regular missives to the authorities, stating his loyalty to the Crown and airing his grievances. Lieutenant Evans, on the other hand, by nature, always looked for solutions and this was reinforced by his military training. From his years spent living in the capital he knew first-hand about the shiploads of grain exported almost daily. This was grain which had been grown in the western lands. His most recent report to the authorities called for a ban on the export of grain and suggested it be distributed among the starving in the provinces; a temporary measure until a healthy potato crop was grown once more. His was a lone voice in the wilderness.

Michael's family had not gone far along the road when the smell of burning thatch filled their nostrils. They had no need to look round for the source of the smoke. Their cottage had been put to the torch as those of almost all their neighbours had been. There and then Michael spoke out loud his resolve never to forget this moment. "They have taken our land, our houses, our livelihoods, our dignity and our children from us, but they will never take our heartlands from us. All that we are and have been and will be again, is locked safely inside each one of us. This is our priceless jewel and it can ever be taken from us."

The family walked all day until they reached the bridge which had always acted as the gateway to and from their homelands. They could see solitary figures and groups of twos and threes coming down off the hills and heading for the bridge. Some of these people, like Michael's family, were hoping to make a new life for themselves in a new land. Others were seeing their families off as far as the bridge. Those choosing to remain were hoping that life might, just might, by the grace of God, get a little bit better for them once again at home. As those who were leaving crossed to the other side of the bridge, the wailing and cries of those staying behind ricocheting off the mountains and blanketing the land. The sorrow circled round and round like the cries of the parent buzzards when they are calling to their young in training flights. Except here, at the parting of the ways, there would be no returning home. When, finally, the last of those departing had crossed into the next valley and could no longer be seen on the far horizon, the cries of those left behind turned into soft moans, like the low murmuring sounds of the confessional.

As Michael and his family rose to go, a woman wrapped in rags, who had stayed behind when the rest of her family had left, came up to them and said, "May God look after you on your journey. Live a long time. Live for all of our dead. I will pray for each and every one of you, as long as I have breath left in my body." She clasped the hand of each of them and turned to retrace her steps. Michael begged her to go with them but she walked on and paid them no further heed.

As the family headed further west toward the port, Noreen grew visibly weaker with each passing day. She showed no interest in eating the scraps of food which Michael and her two sons managed to scavenge on route. When her legs could no longer support her own weight, the men took turns in carrying her on their backs. Although it was summer time, Noreen's body shook with cold. Her struggle for breath and the pitiful moans which escaped her lips were like branding irons on Michael's soul. When it was obvious that she was close to death, he laid her down on the side of the road. Their two sons looked on helplessly as Michael wrapped her in his arms and began to speak softly to her. "*Gra mo chroi*, you can rest now," he repeated over and over. He promised that he would lead their sons to safety and a new home. He closed his eyes and rocked her shrunken body as a mother cradles her new-born. When the breath finally left her body, they straightened out her limbs and wiped her face clean. They didn't have the strength to dig a hole to bury her. They plucked the heather from the bog and covered her up. They placed her body to face the rising sun and prayed for her eternal soul. Michael didn't want to leave her. Go on without me, he urged his sons, go without me. They knew it was the grief talking in him, so they got hold of his arms on either side and dragged him to his feet. When Michael got up from his knees, he had become an old man. All the fight had gone out of him and his sons had to continuously urge him to put one foot in front of the other.

At mid-morning on the fifth day they reached the port, where they were plunged into a world of bewildering and frightening chaos. The plight of hundreds of desperate starving men, women and children all begging to be allowed on an already overcrowded ship, was unimaginable. Those who tried to go aboard without a ticket were pushed unceremoniously aside despite their pleas for mercy. This hellish scene was made even worse - if that were indeed possible - by the rain and sea mist which engulfed the harbour. All around emaciated figures moved aimlessly in the mist like the risen dead. Despite the fact that hundreds of people were wandering around, there was very little noise. Most of those who had reached the harbour were in the final stages of starvation and too weak to waste what little energy they had left on useless talking. Not even the children made a noise. The eerie silence was only punctured by the long low wail as yet another poor soul died, or the rough loud voice of a sailor ordering someone off the ship.

Before they had even reached the queue to buy their passage, Michael and his sons had been pulled to the ground several times by starving hands asking for mercy. Michael knew what it had cost most of these people to travel as far as the port and now all hope of salvation had been snuffed out. Unlike his two sons who roughly pushed aside all who got in their way, Michael gently disentangled himself from the grip of the people who were doomed to die there on the docks.

Michael himself wanted to lie down among them to die. His sons however, had secured their passage.

Finally, out of the unbelievable chaos all around, the ship began to cast off. As it slowly inched away from the sea wall, some of those left behind threw themselves into the water in a futile attempt to get aboard. It was a sight that no human eyes should have to witness. Some of those who flung themselves into the water either got crushed between the ship's sides and the harbour wall, or were sucked under. The gates of hell were well and truly opened on this day.

The heavily overladen ship made its way out into the open seas and the nightmare for those on board only intensified. More than half the passengers, weak from starvation and disease, died well before the journey's end and were simply thrown overboard. The 'coffin ship' was a floating mortuary with the dead and dying and diseased all lying side by side in the filthy stench and heat of the airless hold. There was very little food for the number of people on board and most of it was unfit for humans. Some people who had started the voyage in reasonable shape now succumbed to severe bouts of diarrhoea and vomiting. In the over-crowded conditions typhus and other diseases spread rapidly, and the daily death toll rose sharply. On the fifth morning at sea, it was clear to his sons that their father was not far from death. Michael asked his sons to help him up onto the deck. Held upright by their strength, he turned his gaunt face up to the early morning sky. As the air filled his lungs, ancestral memories of rivers and standing stones, heather and bog land, ancient pathways and horses, rituals of love and medicine, all took shape in front of him. He heard the sacred bird calling him home. His sons gently lowered his lifeless body into the watery depths.

Time After Time Before Time

      Many weeks later when the ship finally sailed up the St. Lawrence river, less than a third of its passengers were still alive. The two brothers Seamus and Seán, weak with ship fever, supported each other off the ship as best they could. Seamus, the older of the two, reached down, touched the soil of this new land and swore in his heart he would never forget what had happened to his family and to the people of Ireland. Although they were allowed off the ship, they were too sick to continue their journey by steamship. They had been briefly assessed by the chief medical officer who placed them in quarantine. The makeshift hospital was woefully inadequate to deal with the number of diseased and dying passengers who were taken off the ship infected with typhus. For many days the two brothers lay side by side on straw pallets and drifted in and out of delirium. The medical staff did their best to treat the patients who might recover, in time, with adequate food and care. The dying were simply left to die, alone and unclean. Mass graves were dug to cope with the number of corpses. Seán and Seamus were among the few who survived. As their strength returned they were advised to keep themselves apart from the sick and dying to prevent re-infection. As more and more ships came up the river with their cargo of starving, disease-ridden famine victims, the two brothers looked for ways they might be of assistance. Their hearts bled for the plight of their fellow countrymen and women. With the memory of the unburied dead back home in Ireland still fresh in their minds, they asked if they could be in charge of burying the dead. Day after day they dug holes in the ground and placed ten or more bodies in a single hole. They were careful to cover their mouths and noses with clean cloths steeped in pungent herbs. When each burial was finished, they brothers knelt down together and prayed for the souls of those whom they had just buried. This then was their work for several weeks. Bone-tired and weary at the end of each day, they would make their way down to the river where they had made a sleeping and cooking place for themselves. At first, they sat and simply stared at the river flowing past. As they grappled with the horrific images of their daily work etched forever on their minds, their brokenness would spill out in heart-wrenching moans.

Away from the hospital and the main camp, they could give expression to their sense of degradation and grief. They would often talk together of their mother and father and the life they had left behind in the West Country. They would sing the Gaelic songs which their mother had sung to them and the very softness of this did much to restore some semblance of human dignity to them. Most nights, Seán, the younger brother, would scream in his sleep as the night terrors gripped his mind. Seamus would soothe him back to sleep, oftentimes cradling him until he quietened. Many a morning as Seamus woke from sleep, he would mistake the sound of the river for the gentle sounds of his father's harp playing. A momentary happiness would flood his body, before the realization of another grisly day's work ahead took its place.

First thing every morning, the bodies of those who hadn't made it through the night were piled in a cart outside the quarantine sheds. Seán and Seamus would drag the cart to the burial site and begin digging. They were by no means the only gravediggers, as the number of dead increased with every new ship that came up the river. Imperceptibly, the cool spring days turned into summer and the brothers were advised to secure their passage on a steam ship as soon as possible. Once summer ended, no further ships would make it up the St. Lawrence until the following spring. They were now certified disease-free. Their passage was paid for with funds from the emigrant relief society and the chief medical officer who had noticed how tirelessly they worked, gave them a small amount of his own money to get them started in their new life. They looked with surprise and astonishment as he placed the small leather purse in their hands the night before they were due to leave. He shook their hands and said, "I wish you well, and I hope your children thrive and never have to suffer like you have done."

    Seamus replied, "We cannot thank you enough for this. We will not forget your kindness to us. We can promise you we will live. And we will never forget what happened to our people."

Chapter Twelve

Even now after so many years, ninety-year-old Seamus O'Haloran thought of his brother Seán as soon as daylight touched his eyes every morning. His longing for his brother ran deep in his veins and coloured his thoughts with memories of Ireland. Now it was Seamus alone who carried the living memories. Although he was surrounded by the love of his sons and grandchildren, he felt a deep inner emptiness. Sitting in his rocker on the porch late into the evenings, he would regularly recall how sometimes he and Seán would look at each other, and the deep river of suffering and horror they had shared before they left Ireland would flow between them. Whenever the memories threatened to engulf either of them in those early days after they settled in Canada, a simple touch on an arm was enough to reassure. They were each other's witness to an almost unbearable pain, which they rarely spoke about. Each of them locked up those memories and tried to get on with the business of building a new life together.

His youngest granddaughter Saoirse was a frequent visitor to the farm from her home in the city and loved to sit with him in the evenings in companionable silence, watching the sun go down, until it was time for bed. Sometimes however, Seamus would talk about how he and his brother had bought this land and built up the farm together. He was a good storyteller and Saoirse was a keen listener. She loved her grandfather with an intensity which often surprised even herself and she wanted to know everything that had happened in his life. When she was a small child and he rocked her on his lap in the hot summer evenings, she would always ask him to tell her a story, each time insisting he start at the beginning. And so, over the years, as she grew, she began to really understand what life had really been like for her grandfather and his brother when they first arrived in this place.

"Well, me darlin," he would begin, "this is how it began. When your great uncle Seán and myself came to this land we knew immediately this was where we wanted to settle and build a new life. We had only a very small amount of money, but by the grace of God we secured this land. When the land became ours according to the law, we kissed the ground beneath our feet, and prayed that we might never know hunger again. We need not have feared, because our needs were small and easily satisfied. We made our camp right down there by the river and fished for our supper every evening. The daily routine was very tough as we needed to erect some sort of permanent shelter before the winter snows came. Your great-uncle Seán, although not of a strong build, wielded the axe like a man possessed. Within a short time we had enough trees cut to begin to make our cabin. Slowly, day by day it began to take shape, but the work was exhausting. At the close of each day, we washed in the river and shared some food. Seán would sing some songs from the old country or play his battered old *feadóg stáin* [23] which he had managed to keep hold of all the way from Ireland. The songs would unsettle us but we needed to stay connected with our homeland until such time as this new land felt like home. So, every night we sat by the fire and we sang the ancient songs telling of the warrior kings and the fairy folk."

---

[23]   Penny whistle

"By mutual unspoken agreement we never talked about what had happened to our parents and our neighbours and the terrible hunger that blighted the land. We never mentioned the sea voyage which brought us here because that too held many horrors which we tried to forget. During the daylight hours the physical work of building our cabin and land clearance left us no room for dwelling on the past. But when night fell upon us, the horrors which we had successfully reined in during the day broke loose. Night after night when we lay down to sleep, Seán would wake screaming and convulsing with his nightmares. As I struggled to stem up the same remembrances in myself, there was nothing I could do for him apart from holding him and singing soothing words, as our mother used to do. Sometimes he would drift back to sleep in my arms. On the really bad nights, he would leap up, eyes wild with terror and run. He would run until he dropped from exhaustion; arms, legs and face bloodied and bruised from crashing through the trees and undergrowth. Usually, when I eventually caught up with him, he would allow me to lead him back to our camp. Sometimes he would lie down and sleep peacefully until dawn. Other times, he would sit hugging his knees, rocking backwards and forwards, his unseeing eyes staring into the black distance, finally falling into a deep sleep just before daylight."

"Seán's accelerating nervous exhaustion and disturbed nightly sleep began to take its toll on him. He began to help less and less with the physical work. Mostly he would spend hours of each day walking through the woods, or he would sit for hours by the river quiet and peaceful. I knew that the balance of his mind was becoming more and more fragile, so unless there was a job I really needed him to help with, I mostly left him alone during the day."

"Time passed. The final days of autumn merged into winter with the first snows arriving stealthily one night. We were by this time secure in our cabin, and I was confident we could survive the winter on the stores of dried fish we had saved from our summer bounty. The almost continuous snowfall and the sharp biting wind kept us confined to the cabin during that first winter, sometimes for a week or more at a single stretch. Seán didn't take well to spending such a prolonged time in the cabin. A terrible crippling apathy engulfed him. He sat all day long staring into space, muttering words that made no sense. I couldn't rouse him to come outside and help me to bring in wood or clear the snow from the doorway. I'm ashamed to say that I preferred it when he was screaming in terror from his nightmares and running from unseen horrors. Most mornings, while I was busy outside shovelling snow to clear a path to the woodpile, he would sit on the edge of his bed, muttering under his breath and staring straight ahead. Despite my encouragement and assurances that he had nothing to worry about he was very reluctant to leave the cabin. He was losing weight as he oftentimes refused to eat. He became childlike in the way that he clung to me and I knew he was really frightened when I had to do some chores outside. He didn't want to be alone in the cabin, and at the same time he was scared of the outdoors. I could guess what shadows and terrors were lurking in this mind waiting to pounce on him. They lurked in my mind also."

"One morning during the darkest time of that first winter, he began to beat his head against the wall of the cabin. When I tried to stop him, he brushed me off, arms flailing wildly as he continued to beat his head. When I eventually got him to stop, there was blood running down his face from a deep gash on his forehead. As I led him over to the bed, he looked at me with unseeing eyes. In that moment I knew I had lost him forever. I was powerless to make his unfathomable mental pain go away, the very same pain that stalked my own days. But I had used the sweat and toil of my daily chores and the effort to keep us both alive, to distract me from my internal life. I shut the pain down deep and gave myself over to working so hard physically, that each night I fell into an exhausted dreamless sleep. But not so for Seán. He lacked the mental and emotional resilience to bury the horrors of our early life and what we had had to endure. He sat on the bed where I had left him, holding his head in his hands, making soft animal noises."

"I cleaned the blood off his face and wrapped my arms around him. He was my link with everything and everyone I had known and loved and I couldn't let him drift away, because I would be alone with my own brokenness which he only could possibly understand. I cradled him until he became calm. I laid him down on the bed and made him as comfortable as I could. When I was satisfied that he was asleep I went outside to get on with the chores while the light was still good. I went around the back and began to chop some wood. The river behind the cabin was in full spate and was making a deafening roar. I chopped enough wood to see us through for another few days."

"As I made my way back with the logs I knew that something was wrong. The door to the cabin was wide open and a trail of footprints led across the fresh snow. My pounding heart hurt inside my chest as I frantically called out his name. I found him curled up against a snow drift. He had finally found his peace. I carried him home and said the rosary for the repose of his soul. I sat with his body in the cabin for three days because I knew when he was gone from me, then I would be truly alone. On the fourth day I buried him down by the river."

"Everything that had once given meaning and identity to my life was wrenched from me that day and buried alongside my brother. He had been my last living connection with our ancestral land. Where once there had been shared memories of our home and family, there was now a black beast opening its jaws to devour me. I was lost, lost to myself and to my past. I was without hope, without identity in this vast wild land. Everything that could be taken from me was gone."

After Seán's death, during the remaining winter months, Seamus managed to do the daily chores that ensured his survival. His pounding grief and loneliness were manageable during the daylight hours but they ambushed him as soon as darkness fell. One particular night when the snow was falling thickly and the world was wrapped in silence, his mind strayed into thoughts of oblivion. He tortured himself with the idea of walking out into the night and simply lying down in the snow like Seán had done. He was beyond pain, beyond pity, no longer caring that he couldn't call up the faces of his dead parents or brother. He could remember without any effort the scenes of horror and human degradation he had witnessed, yet why couldn't he now recall the quiet soft faces of his mother and father.

His God was keeping from him the images of the faces of his beloved family. He was consumed with burning bitter rage against this God who would play such a cruel trick on him. He turned his huge roaring anger on everything that wasn't nailed down in his cabin. He smashed and hurled everything his hands touched, until finally he collapsed, utterly spent among the debris. The bitter bone-chilling cold of the morning woke him. It was a bleak scene which met his eyes. While he was clearing up the worst of the carnage, he came across Seán's *feadóg stáin* and once more he was plunged into unutterable grief. He cleaned it up with the tail of his shirt and very tentitively began to play. He was hesitant at first but gradually the sounds began to soothe his soul. He closed his eyes as his fingers and breath made the music. As he played, his fingers gathered speed and a familiar haunting tune took shape. Entwined within the sounds he began to hear the voice of his father as he lay dying aboard the coffin ship.

"You have to survive. You have to tell your children what was done to us. You have to tell how we were starved out of our homes, and country. You have to remember how our language and music and culture were ridiculed." And Seamus remembered. Once again, he heard the urgency in his father's frail voice. It gave him the strength he needed. Out of the depths of his brokenness, he knew in that moment that he would never again think about killing himself. He had a sacred duty to give meaning to all those destroyed lives. He would live for them. His continuing life would be their monument.

When the thaw came the occasional tradesman or trapper came by, en route to the trading post. Seamus had secured for himself some knives and a good axe in exchange for his blacksmithing skills. Amongst the trappers, he earned himself a reputation for making a good horseshoe. He had, from the time he was a very young lad, helped his father in his makeshift forge in Ireland. He was confident of his skills with the hammer and tongs. He had bartered for a rifle in exchange for treating a lame horse of a trapper and replacing two of its shoes. The trapper refused to part with any of the furs he was taking to the outpost, but he was happy to unwrap his bundle so Seamus could have a look. Never before had Seamus touched anything as soft as the beautiful silver fox pelts which now lay before him. Something inside him longed for this tenderness of touch. It had been so many years since his own body had been caressed, not since he had been a young child before the famine destroyed his life. As he stroked the soft supple fur, he was soothed almost as if a golden healing balm was being poured directly into his soul. His hitherto unacknowledged need for beauty and tenderness threatened to overwhelm him. His memories of the starving ragged spectral figures walking the famine-ridden land of his birth had driven out any kind or humane memories he might have had.

Try as he might, he could only very vaguely conjure up images of the landscape of Ireland as it had been when food was plentiful and its people were generally happy. He tried not to search for the faces of his family among his memories. These were now sealed deep in a place inside him where he could never go again. He had managed to get himself through the months of winter since Seán died by working himself into an exhausted state every day and falling into a dreamless sleep every night.

But now that Spring was spreading across the land he began to look forward to the very rare opportunity of passing company. His cabin became a halfway resting place for the independent trappers and mountain men, all journeying to the trading post to sell their wares. He listened to tales of hunting and fishing and tiny seeds of hope began to attach themselves to Seamus. As the days grew hotter, he began to really look at his land for the first time since his brother's death. Although he was used to the wide-open flat bog lands of western Ireland, his blood now quickened at the sight of the hills marking the eastern boundary of his land. He had come to love the forest sloping gently down towards the cabin. He had also grown to love the sound of the wind as it sometimes hurtled down the mountain and almost come to a full stop when it hit the trees. He sometimes, during the long summer nights, took his sleeping roll and curled up under the trees to sleep. The sound of the swaying, groaning trees became his lullaby. He settled into this land and became, if not happy, at least content with his own company. He fished the river, tilled a small portion of the land nearest the cabin to supply him with some vegetables. He knew where the summer and autumn berries grew in abundance and where the wild apples were. He continued to work each day from dawn till dusk and his body became hard-muscled and strong. His cabin had few luxuries but it held everything he needed.

      Most evenings he sat on the porch and simply rested his eyes on the distant hills. He developed the capacity to sit in stillness and silence. Gradually his inner wounds began to heal. The natural beauty which surrounded him helped the hard places in his heart to soften. Sometimes a trapper would drop by, and once food had been eaten, a bottle of liquor would be offered. The softening effect of the alcohol lifted the veil on some of those memories which Seamus had tried to bury. He allowed himself to see in his mind's eye the wide long view of the heather-covered bogs where he had come from. He could almost smell the sea salt carried on the wind and he could hear the soft lilting voices of his neighbours and family. Then usually, as the effects of the alcohol wore off, the familiar pain brought on by remembrance would seep up and strangled him all over again. He could still allow huge bouts of fiery destructive anger to consume him.

In truth, he was afraid if he ceased feeling angry he would become an empty shell, a shadow of himself. He needed the anger in order to carry on living.

In the spring of his fourth year living alone he decided one day to head off towards the trading post. Up until now, he had been reluctant to visit the trading post and the tiny settlement which had grown up around it. Whenever a trapper stopped by, Seamus would ask for some goods to be bought for him on the trapper's return journey. This service was usually in exchange for a bed for the night and horse shoeing. This system had worked very well for Seamus. Until now that is. Something had shifted inside him. He told himself he had very sensible reasons to make the journey. He hadn't been visited by a trapper for quite a long while now and he was in sore need of seeds and household goods like coffee, sugar and salt. But in truth he was feeling lonely for the first time since his brother Seán had died.

The night before he was due to leave, he made his preparations. He brought out from the bottom of the wooden chest the only clean shirt he possessed. He polished his boots till they shone and he heated enough water to give himself a hot wash. Next morning, he saddled up his horse early and set off just as the sun was coming over the tops of the faraway hills. As he rode away it was hard to tell he was the same young man who had arrived at this place just four years ago. Then, he was skinny, troubled and unsure of himself in every way. The furtive look in his eyes gave an indication of a soul in trouble. His voice had been quiet, hardly above a whisper except when he spoke with his brother. He'd had a habit of looking behind him whenever he walked about. As if he felt there was something or someone stalking him. The ghostly scenes of human suffering and degradation were indeed following him at that time, threatening to grind him into pulp at any moment.

    Now those same memories were no longer pursuing him. The daily hard physical work had hardened his body and the regular food he put into his belly had filled out his skin to fit his bones. He ate what his own land yielded up. He ate the small animals he shot on a regular basis. He knew how to prepare the land to grow vegetables because this knowledge ran with the blood in his veins. His vegetables thrived and Seamus fed himself well. Although he enjoyed the cornmeal of his new land, he still preferred the flat potato bread called *boxty,* which had been the staple part of his family diet in Ireland before the hunger times. Remembering the *boxty* cooking on the griddle on the hot embers of the turf fire was a good memory, a memory he wanted to hold onto. He never tired of making this for his evening meal. He was now a fine figure of a man. He was excited as he rode the trail, and for the first time since he was a very young child he was free of worry. He rode at a leisurely pace because he was in no particular hurry to reach his destination. He was slowly with each mile he covered preparing himself to engage with the outside world again. For four years he met only the few trappers who had passed through his land. And they were usually men not given much to conversation. Seamus was excited and nervous about being among company after such a long time alone but he needed the slow pace of the journey to prepare himself. He rode that first day until the sun began to dip below the horizon. He made his camp by the edge of the stream which he had been following for most of the day. He quickly got a fire under way and cooked up his supper. He lay on his back looking at the night sky, listening to the sound of the night creatures and the river.

Next morning, he was in the saddle early. As he drew closer and closer to the trading post he began to regret his decision. Twice during this second day out he nearly turned the horse's head for home. But he talked out loud to himself, "Look here Seamus, you've survived situations which most folk in these parts have no idea about. If disease and famine haven't killed you, surely you can survive mixing with a few unknown folks for a few days." And so it went on for most part of the second day, the third day and indeed the fourth day. On the fifth day, he had run out of reasons to turn back so he resigned himself to the inevitable.

He arrived at the trading post towards evening, when the families who lived nearby were cooking up their evening meal. Young boys ran about shouting and playing with hoops and sticks. Men, mostly older, sat together in the evening sun drinking and smoking. They looked without curiosity at the tall handsome stranger as he approached. By the time he reached the trading post, he had a long gaggle of young children following him. Seamus noticed the torn filthy clothes these children were wearing but their voices were crisp and bright as they tried to catch his attention.

"Hey mister, where you come from?" one of the smallest urchins asked as he ran alongside Seamus's horse. Seamus laughed but continued riding down the muddy street which was strewn with empty liquor bottles. After the pristine wilderness he had travelled through during the past few days, he found his senses were assailed by the air of neglect and stupor in this place. As he approached the trading post he again had to stifle the desire to turn his horse's head around and gallop off in the direction he had come from.

He dismounted, tossed a coin to the oldest child, and told him to feed and water his horse. He slung his heavy saddle bags over his shoulder and climbed the steps into the store. He was momentarily dazzled by the array of goods lining the shelves. It seemed every available space, not just on the shelves but on the floor as well, was filled with goods of all sizes and colour. There were jars and cans, salted and cured meats and fish, guns and bullets, fishing tackle, buckets, furs and boots, bolts of brightly coloured fabric, sewing cottons and silver buttons. Coffee and tea were stacked on the shelf behind the counter. Lamps of all sizes were hung from the ceiling and in the far-right corner next to the sacks of corn meal, he noticed a huge box of tallow candles and soap mixed up together. As his eyes adjusted to the extravaganza of colours and shapes before him, he was greeted by the man standing behind the counter.

"What can I do for you mister?" said a kindly voice. The storekeeper was a man of fifty years or so, wearing a large white apron. He had the pale unhealthy skin of someone who spends the most part of each day indoors. His eyes, however, were kindly and bright as they swept over Seamus from head to toe.

"I will need to buy quite a few items from you, but for now I need a bed for the night and a hot meal."

"Well now, let me see," said the storekeeper as he scratched his bald head. There's widow Carney's down by the river, but if its sleep you're after, you likely won't get much there as she has all sorts of men getting drunk and shouting most of the night. There's also Eliza's place just up from here but the girls who work for her would rob you blind. I can offer you a room out back of the store and my daughter would have no objection to setting another place at table."

"Thank you kindly," said Seamus, "that sounds just grand."

"That's settled then," said the older man. He stretched out his hand. "I'm Sam Maxwell. I'll show you where you can wash out back before we eat."

Seamus followed his host through the curtain which separated the store from the living quarters of father and daughter. He was shown his room which was clean but sparsely furnished. There was a narrow bed against one wall, a chair and a looking glass hanging on the far wall. Seamus went outside, stripped to the waist and splashed his face and upper body with cool refreshing water. He immediately felt better. He used the cloth hanging alongside the water barrel to dry himself. As he buried his face in the cloth, he smelled the unmistakable sweet odour of a woman's cleanliness. He sucked in the smell, deep into his lungs. He sat down on the bench next to the water barrel and waited to be called for food. For the first time in a very long time he felt softness towards the outer world. He couldn't name what he was feeling but he didn't want for anything else in that moment. He was startled from his reverie with a call to supper. He walked inside and found himself in a large room where a young woman with her back to him, was juggling a series of pans on top of the woodstove. The smells which filled the room were delicious.

"Lucy, my dear, come and meet our guest for the night." She turned around and Seamus felt his insides dissolve into liquid. The woman who came towards him with her hand outstretched was the most beautiful he had ever seen.

"I'm Lucy Maxwell, and I see you've already met my father."

Seamus took her hand and managed to splutter, "I'm Seamus O'Haloran."

Her green eyes smiled into his, as she said, "You're welcome, I'm sure. Please sit down."

Seamus continued to hold her hand. She laughed as she pulled away and turned back to the stove. Seamus took his seat awkwardly and as Lucy busied herself putting the food on the table, Seamus tried to concentrate on the conversation with her father but all the while he was wishing he was any place else apart from being in the same room as this young woman who had thrown his emotions into chaos. He felt like a skittish horse who wants to be given his head. He was not used to being in company, especially not the company of women. Also, he was certainly not used to the refined domestic ways of a household run by a woman. He remained almost tongue-tied for the greater part of the meal and felt his heart bang loudly against his chest whenever Lucy passed him a dish and caught his eye. Finally, when the meal was over, the two men sat outside in quiet companionship. Sam puffed contentedly on his pipe.

When the time came to retire for the night, Seamus felt an unaccustomed sense of peacefulness, despite his confusing emotions. He lay in his bed thinking about Lucy. He found everything about her appearance pleasing to his eye, from the way she flashed her wide smile to the way she seemed to glide across the room, her long dress creating a soft swish as she passed by his chair. He also felt a strange and unfamiliar feeling that he had somehow known Lucy before today. The absurdity of this notion kept him tossing and turning for what seemed like hours. He was unable to calm his emotions until finally he fell into an exhausted dreamless sleep.

He woke to the aroma of fresh coffee and the sounds of quiet voices. Lucy and her father were already seated having breakfast. Lucy rose and poured him a cup of coffee.

He now felt less shy and tongue-tied around her as he bid them both a good morning. He took a seat opposite Sam and nodded his thanks to Lucy as she brought him his breakfast. After he had finished eating, he seemed reluctant to leave the table.

"I have to see to our horses now," said Sam as he took his hat off the peg and headed out the door. "Lucy will see to your purchases."

Seamus drank a second cup of coffee while Lucy cleared the table and swept the floor. When she was satisfied that all was in order, she invited Seamus to follow her through into the store. Once again his eyes were bedazzled by the array of goods lining the shelves. He chose coffee, sugar, a sack of corn meal, salt, candles, nails, ammunition for his rifle, and lastly a soft red blanket. He filled his saddle bags with most of the smaller purchases. The bigger items he strapped across his horse. When everything was ready, he surprised himself by asking Lucy to take a walk with him around the settlement.

"I'm afraid there is very little to see, but I will accompany you nevertheless."

She turned back into the living room to fetch her bonnet and shawl. No sooner had they descended the steps of the trading post when they were joined by a group of young children, all clamouring for Lucy's attention. She knew each child by name and had a soft and kind word for each of them. Seamus noted how the eyes of several children lit up when she tousled their hair or allowed them to hold her hands. Their walk didn't take very long because there was, in truth, very little to see. A few makeshift cabins were sited on the far side of the river. These were lived in by trappers and their families. An air of total neglect hung like a mist in the air. Everywhere he looked, Seamus sensed that life was suspended for those living here. They had reached the end of their road, a road going nowhere. By the time they had finished their walk and were heading back to the store he had seen enough to know that the life he lived on his land, although a lonely existence, was still preferable to rotting away in a settlement. As he saddled his horse and prepared to leave, Lucy stood on the steps of her father's store and waved him goodbye.

The months passed from spring into summer and into autumn. Seamus continued his life on his homestead as he had been accustomed to doing. Yet everything had changed for him. Since his meeting with Lucy he found it difficult to rein in his thoughts about his life, past or present. He was constantly engulfed in a sea of terrible loneliness. When his brother had died and he was truly alone he had survived by pushing his body to its physical limit each and every day. This left him no time for thinking, as he worked non-stop until sundown every day. His overwhelming bodily tiredness meant he fell into a dreamless sleep each night. But now he was being engulfed by a sense of his own isolation and solitude, which made him constantly restless and unable to work. He did the minimum amount of work needed to sustain his life. The rest of the time he would ride for miles into the mountains - almost every day. His heart was sick with longing. He had seen so much horror and human degradation which had caused him to create a hard shell in order to protect himself from further pain.

But now he was cracking open. Simply being around Lucy had begun the process of peeling back his armour. He was scared and conflicted. He mustn't allow himself to love another human being because loving meant pain and intolerable grief and loss. Yet he longed for the softness of Lucy. He was shrivelling from lack of human comfort, human touch. For months he worked himself into a daily frenzy where he told himself that his life was fine as it was. He was safe now, he had survived. He would not risk loving again, because everyone he had ever loved had died horrible deaths - deaths he was powerless to prevent. Invariably this inner dialogue was punctuated with images of Lucy and how her generous smile made him feel alive, truly alive again. He had not thought it possible to ever feel that sort of happiness.

The winter snows blanketed the land once more and all thoughts of making the journey to the settlement again to see Lucy had to be put aside. But he had resolved that when the Spring came around again he would make the journey to see her. During the long winter nights, he kept himself busy playing reels and jigs and hornpipes on his *feadóg stáin*. He never tired of playing this music, because it lifted his spirits and connected him with his ancestors. Sometimes he would speak out loud in the Gaelic language just so he could hear the mellow sounds of his mother tongue. He also began carving some very fine animals from wood he had saved for this purpose. He spent weeks carving a beautiful tiny Celtic cross. He replicated in exquisite detail the cross that stood near the church where his Irish home had been. He carved tiny triple knots, swirls and serpents. Several times while working on it late into the night, he felt a connection with something or someone more powerful than himself. He came to believe that a hand more ancient than his own hand was guiding the work.

When it was finished, he was amazed that he had actually made this thing of beauty. He polished it until the patina of the wood was as fine as any silken thread. He wrapped it in a piece of cloth and placed it for safe keeping in a box under his bed. For days he wondered how he could have fashioned the cross. In the end he came to understand

and accept that something mysterious had happened and perhaps there was no need for him to understand the how or the why of it. With the making of the cross he seemed to have crossed over a threshold into a state of inner peace.

He patiently waited out the rest of the long winter season as he laid down his plans for visiting Lucy when the warmer weather arrived. He no longer felt caged or lonely. He began to make some pieces of furniture to add a bit of comfort to his still-spartan cabin. He developed the knack of looking at his surroundings as if he were looking through Lucy's eyes. He even managed, albeit with great difficulty, to persuade one of the passing trappers to part with one of his silver fox pelts and a deer skin. Seamus only shot an animal for food, never simply for its skin. He had no objection to others doing so, but he himself had seen too much death to take the life unnecessarily from any living creature. When he tried explaining this to the trappers, they shook their heads in disbelief. Consequently, his cabin had very few skins to add warmth and comfort.

With the coming of the warmer weather he turned his attention to the area immediately surrounding the cabin. He spent long days felling trees which were close by and were casting too much shade. He replenished the wood store and lastly, cleared a path down to the river.

As spring began to give way to early summer, he knew the time had come for him to visit the settlement again. This time he had no doubts or misgivings, but he still had feelings of nervousness and anxiety. He wanted to see Lucy again so very much but he hadn't allowed himself to think that she might not have similar feelings for him. But he wasn't going to let thoughts of failure get in his way. He felt that the fates had placed them in each other's path. How else was he to explain to himself the tremendous pull she made on his heart? He felt he had always loved her. At night he dreamed of her. The same dream, over and over. In his dreams of her he always saw water, and upon awakening he often felt a terrible sense of betrayal. He knew this didn't make sense but it gave him the courage he needed to pursue her.

On this second journey to the settlement, he rode hard during the days and was back in the saddle again before dawn. As he rode into the trading post, on the surface everything looked exactly as it had on his first visit, but something was different. There was no raggle taggle group of children running alongside his horse. There was not a living soul out and about. There was a much deeper sense of inertia and lethargy than he had experienced on his previous visit.

He mounted the steps of the trading post two at a time and burst through the door. The store was exactly as he remembered; a cornucopia of goods needed by every homesteader. He pressed the little bell on the counter which would summon either Sam or his daughter. Although he waited for a couple of minutes, he already knew that something was wrong. He drew aside the curtain and let himself into the living quarters. He could smell death. He recoiled in horror as a terrible fear wound itself around his heart. He could hear the laboured breathing coming from the bedroom. He did not want to open the door because he never again wanted to see the helpless beseeching look in the eyes of the dying. However, he steeled himself and opened it. Sam was lying on the bed, the death rattle filling the tiny room. Kneeling beside him, fast asleep with her head resting on the bed was Lucy. Even in sleep, she still had hold of her father's skeleton hand. Her breathing was soft and easy. He gently touched her arm and she was instantly awake. She looked at him with startled eyes.

"Please help us," she begged as she quickly stood up, and fell into his arms. He noticed how thin she was and how there were deep hollows in her cheeks. He told her to make herself some food and he would sit with her father. She did as she was bid. He sat with Sam until she called him for food. While they ate, listening all the while to the laboured breathing from the sick room, she told him what had happened in the settlement.

"It's the black cholera" she said. "First the youngest children died and then the adults succumbed. It spread quickly from one cabin to another. Those who were not immediately affected left, and now the settlement is nothing more than a ghost town. My father helped to bury the dead until his strength gave way. He seemed so strong that I believed he would not be stricken down. But five days ago he couldn't rise from his bed. I don't know how to help him any more."

Seamus reached across the table for her hand and gently said

"Lucy, your father is on the point of death. He will not live to see the morning." He could see the pain spreading across her face as she struggled to accept what he said.

"How do you know?" she asked him, in a high voice, full of panic, rising from the table and knocking over her chair. He caught her in his arms and held her as she sobbed and beat at his chest.

"Let us sit with your father, and together we can pray for him."

He led her gently back into the sick room and they knelt on either side of the bed. She was calmer now. She gently laid her head on Sam's chest and muttered soft words that Seamus couldn't understand. Beads of sweat appeared on Seamus's forehead as he struggled with the urge to flee. Pictures of starving faces with taut skin drawn back from the bones flooded his vision. Images he had tried so hard to bury, now galloped towards him and there was no way he could stop them. The blood began to drain from his face as his stomach lurched and churned. He just about made it out of the room when the contents of his stomach hit the floor. Such was his pain on remembering all he had seen before he left Ireland and the horrors of the boat crossing, that he flung himself onto the floorboards and curled up like a baby. He rocked his body backwards and forwards, his arms wound tightly round his body as if he could give himself some comfort. Each time he rocked forwards he banged his head hard on the floor in a vain attempt to make the images go away. He was jerked back into reality by a loud cry from Lucy.

"My God, what are you doing to yourself?"

The floor beneath him was splattered in blood as was his face and shirt. He looked up at her as his body began to convulse with sobs. She knelt beside him and gathered him into her arms, muttering into his ear, "What has been done to you?"

She rocked him backwards and forwards until he became quiet. She helped him up and said that her father was gone. There was no need for further words. Lucy went into the bedroom to prepare her father's body. Seamus went out back in search of a shovel. When he had dug a hole deep enough, they carried Sam to his grave. Lucy shed no tears. As they walked back to the store however, all her strength seemed to leave her and she had to cling tightly to Seamus's arm. They ate a simple meal together, each locked in their own thoughts. Although the evening was warm, Seamus built up the fire in the stove and during the hours of that long night, he spoke to Lucy of the pitiless horrors he and his family had endured. He spoke in the soft tones of his native land, only pausing when the telling of the scenes of degradation he had witnessed became too much for him. As his story unfolded, Lucy realised there was something about Seamus, something vague and totally ungraspable, but it was pulling at her consciousness. Seamus, exhausted from the telling of his life story, fell asleep in his chair. While he slept, Lucy studied his face, and time stood still.

Afterwards, she couldn't really tell whether she too had fallen asleep, or whether her intense sorrow at her own loss and those of Seamus, had lifted a veil between worlds. She dreamed she was standing in the prow of a boat. Her brother was with her. Dark things happened which resulted in her death. Her brother could not save her as she lay dying. She reached for his hand and was startled to find that Seamus was kneeling in front of her holding both her hands and telling her everything was alright.

"What happened?" she asked.

"You had a bad dream."

"Yes, I remember. It was horrible." She told him of the brother in her dream who could not save her. She paused, stood up, pulled Seamus to his feet and told him with tears in her eyes that he was that brother. She believed they had a connection together that had spilled over from other lifetimes. He nodded.

Neither of them said another word, as they clung to each other.

"Leave this place and come back with me," he said softly. "We can make a new life together, and this time I will not fail you."

Time After Time Before Time

From her father's house, they collected all the things that would be useful for their life together and loaded them into the wagon. They took most of the dry foodstuff from the shop, but at Lucy's insistence they left some behind for those few souls in the settlement who might survive the disease. She carefully folded the two beautiful brightly coloured bed quilts which were the only link Lucy had to her mother. She gathered up her own sewing materials and before she joined Seamus on the wagon, she removed the large family bible from its alcove above her father's bed. She closed the door behind her and went to join Seamus who was already seated on the wagon and ready to go. His own horse was tied to the back of the wagon.

They pulled away from the settlement without a backward glance. The spring sun was warm enough on their skin as they sat side by side in companionable silence. They made slow but steady progress. The wild, untamed beauty of the prairies stretching all around them as far as the eye could see in any direction, intoxicated her with joy. After several hours they stopped by a river to rest and water the horses. Lucy wandered a little way downstream and quickly and without embarrassment removed all her clothes. She was already in the water when Seamus caught up with her. He sat on the grass enjoying her naked elegance as she lay on her back gently floating. He couldn't quite believe that this wonderful woman was going to share her life with him.

"Come in," she said, "It's lovely!"

He quickly pulled off his clothes and ran down into the water. He pulled her towards him. She gave no resistance as their bodies became entwined. She curled her arms round his neck and he swept her into his arms and carried her up onto the grass. Their kisses were greedy as if neither of them could satisfy their hunger. They were both totally inexperienced in love making but their hunger for each other overcame any hesitation. They revelled in each other's body. Seamus kissed every inch of her nakedness over and over until he was so filled up with her softness that he cried out in joy. Lucy's unusual lack of coyness or embarrassment made their love making feel like the most natural thing in the world.

Afterwards they lay, with their arms tightly wound round each other. Nothing broke the deep contented silence which surrounded them apart from the natural sounds of the river and the cry of birds. When the late afternoon heat began to lessen, and the breeze felt cool on their bodies, they reluctantly put on their clothes again. Seamus held Lucy's flushed face between his hands and felt her breath quicken.

"I will never leave you," he promised, and I will let no harm come to you."

Her eyes said everything. She kissed his lips with such tenderness so that he too could feel safe in her love.

"I can never undo the pain you have suffered, or take away the awful images you have in your mind. But I will love you with all my heart and together we will create new memories for ourselves."

They reached the homestead after several days. The nightly camping was a true bonding time for them. They got to know one another at a level which might not have happened if they had plunged directly and immediately into daily living. As it was, being on the trail became a period of time when all the usual constraints on behaviour were abandoned. They disregarded the normal rules which governed the behaviour of men and women. They were so at perfect ease in one another's company such that anyone observing them might be forgiven for thinking they had known each other a very long time. There was an aura of peace and contentment surrounding them which, in part, stemmed from their sexual intimacy. But it also arose from the deep trust they had in one another.

On seeing the location of her new home for the first time, Lucy's heart skipped a bit. They approached the homestead from the mountain ridge high above the cabin. The sight of her new home, nestling in the valley below, with the river running alongside, dispelled any doubts that she was doing the right thing in choosing to live far away from any settlement. They made their way slowly and carefully down the mountain, and along the way Seamus pointed out the various landmarks that had become important to him.

"See that line of trees to the north of the cabin? Those trees give us all the firewood and building materials we need. They also shelter the cabin when the storms are blowing down on us from the north. You may find this strange Lucy, but they also give me a sense of peace and security. When I was at a very low ebb after Seán died, the only place I found any comfort was in amongst those trees. Many a time, when the walls of the cabin were crowding in on me and fury and desolation were at my heels, I would take my sleeping roll into the woods and I found I could sleep like a baby. I think it was the sound of the wind amongst the taller trees which soothed me. I didn't feel alone. But there was something else. The trees felt solid and strong, rooted and unmoving, and I knew that I too needed to put roots down. Those trees helped me to keep going at a time when I simply wanted to lie down and die."

Lucy turned and looked with admiration and respect at this man she had come away with. Apart from her father, Lucy had only ever been in the company of trappers and traders. Rough men, prone to fighting and bouts of hard drinking. She had no idea that a man could contain within him the softness and mysterious soul qualities that Seamus had showed her. She knew then, deep in her own soul that life had given them this chance to find each other.

However when she stepped inside the cabin her heart sank. For Seamus's sake she tried not to show her dismay. The place was bare of any comforts and clearly had never had any care lavished on it. But Lucy was a woman of strong heart and limbs and glancing around she mentally told herself that she would turn it into a comfortable home without too much effort. And she did.

They lived and worked the land for over forty years together, and they thrived. Seamus had a way with horses and over the years he built up a reputation for himself as an excellent stud breeder. He built a forge some distance from the cabin and honed his blacksmith's skills. He continued to provide a service for the horses of the passing trappers. In time he became known simply as the horse man. With Lucy's help he prepared some of the land for growing crops for their own use and to barter for goods they couldn't provide for themselves. He still refused to use his gun to kill animals for food but he didn't object to Lucy doing so. They were never without meat of some kind or other because she became an expert shot over time.

When their first son was born their happiness was complete. They named him Michael in honour of Seamus's father. Two years later baby Sam arrived and with the arrival of Aidan some years later their family was complete. The three boys grew strong in mind and limb and loved to follow Seamus around the farm. They loved to hear the fairy stories of Ireland which Seamus used to tell them almost every evening before they went to sleep. As they grew older, he told them what it was like to live in Ireland when he was a young child. He only spoke of the happy times and he never mentioned the famine. Some nights as he watched his three fine sons sleeping, he felt a deep sense of completion. He himself had survived and his own sons would never go hungry and would never be driven off their land. This was his legacy.

      Seamus became a contented man. Lucy made their home a place of beauty and comfort. She was loved with a fierce love by all three of her sons as well as her husband.

Chapter Thirteen

Aidan O'Haloran and his daughter Saoirse arrived in Dublin after a long and fraught sea journey from New York. This trip had been Saoirse's idea. Ever since she was a little girl, during the annual visit back west to see her grandparents, she had listened with avid attention to the stories of Ireland which Grandpa Seamus had loved to tell her. His stories came alive for her and she developed a deep desire to visit the land her ancestors had come from. She would sit on his knee when she was no more than four or five and ask for the same stories to be repeated over and over. Her favourites were those tales of the *Fianna* warriors and the fairy folk. With her wild, unpolluted imagination she began to weave an image of Ireland which her grandfather did nothing to dissipate and actually positively encouraged. The Ireland of Saoirse's young imagination was a place of wild and beautiful landscape, where fairies hid behind every rock.

Her father Aidan had left the family farm many years earlier to make a name for himself in New York. He loved the huge open spaces surrounding his parents' homestead but unlike his two older brothers he didn't share their love of working on the land. While his brothers and father were out riding, mending fences or working with the animals, Aidan was usually to be found curled up in the hay loft reading. He was a thin sickly child and Lucy argued for him to be released from his share of the farm chores. His brothers by no means resented him for this. They were happy to do the work they loved and while they themselves had absolutely no interest in reading, they fully accepted that their younger brother was different. As their father aged and became less able to help with the heavy work, the older boys began to shoulder more and more of the responsibility for the everyday running of the farm. Aidan was called on to lend a hand at the busiest times of the year. He tried his best but he usually made a pig's ear of whatever job he had been given to do. Initially his brothers laughed at his paltry efforts but over time their frustration grew. They began to resent Aidan's presence around the place. Lucy and Seamus tried to keep the family together but one night in early December things finally came to a head. Aidan himself knew that it was now impossible for him to remain living at home. He loved his parents with a fierce love, and his brothers also, but he now felt he was a complete misfit in the family.

After supper one evening, he announced that come the new year he would be leaving to make a life for himself in New York. No amount of persuasion by his parents made him change his mind. The decision was particularly hard for Seamus to accept. He felt he had failed to make his son feel safe. Feelings of fear that had lain dormant for many years inside Seamus's heart now resurfaced. He felt his son was being driven from his home just as he himself had been driven out of Ireland all those years ago. He kept these feelings to himself, but the day before Aidan was due to leave, he arranged some time to be alone with him. After supper, he asked Aidan to come outside with him. It was a cold winter night. The sky, filled with the light of a trillion stars reflecting on the deep snow turned the ground into a jewelled carpet. They leaned over the porch, each revelling in the austere beauty in front of them. The white silence wrapped round them, until Seamus finally spoke.

"I never wanted you to leave my side son," he began. "I only wanted to make you feel safe."

"You and your brothers made sense of my life. You gave meaning to all the pain and suffering my parents and my brother had to endure. I made a vow, long before you were born that my children would survive and prosper and be a living memorial to all of my dispossessed ancestors. So when you said you wanted to leave, I found this difficult to understand when everything you ever needed was right here on the farm. But now, I've come to realise that you are making a free choice. You are listening to a call somewhere within you that knows that your destiny lies elsewhere. So you have my blessing on your journey. But before you go, I have something I want you to have."

Seamus reached inside his shirt pocket and took out a tiny object wrapped in a faded piece of cloth. He held it out to Aidan and said, "I made this a very long time ago. I would like you to have it. It holds all my memories of my homeland, its faith, its culture and language. Keep it safe."

Aidan unwrapped the parcel and, nestling there in the palm of his hand, was the most exquisite miniature wooden Celtic cross. He looked from the cross to his father and back again with a thousand questions racing through his mind.

"I made this at a time when I had no hope left," began Seamus. "I worked into it everything I could remember about what was great and beautiful about Ireland and its people. This tiny cross is my record of a nation."

"Thank you father, I shall treasure it always."

Father and son embraced, each of them with tears spilling down their cheeks.

Aidan lay in bed not able to sleep on that final night before his departure. He was deeply moved by his father's gift and found himself having doubts about his planned course of action. He was hardly more than a boy really at age twenty-one, and he hadn't let on to anyone in the family that he was actually feeling quite scared about leaving. He had no experience of city life. The furthest he had travelled was to their nearest small town. Like the rest of his family he rarely visited the town except to collect quarterly supplies and to sell their own surplus goods. While the rest of the family dealt with the buying and selling, Aidan would head for the mail house to collect any parcels and letters waiting for the family. Usually he would be rewarded with a large parcel for himself containing several books he had ordered from New York. He had eclectic taste in reading but lately he had been drawn to books about the history of ancient man. He became fascinated with how the history of a certain race could be traced through the everyday objects they left behind. At times, the ancient past seemed more real to him than the actual living present. He became increasingly interested in reading about the burial rituals of ancient peoples.

    At supper most evenings, the family talk centred around matters to do with the farm and the livestock. Aidan usually took no part in this. He was happy with his own company. However, on this, his last night under the family roof, he wished he had picked up some practical skills that might come in useful in his new life. He had never experienced the rough and tumble of normal life as his brothers had. He had never been in a fight, drunk beer or kissed a girl. Even though he had been raised on a very successful stud farm he was not all that comfortable around horses. When he was a small boy, he had liked to watch his father working the bellows in the smithy, but not once did he ask to have a go himself. It was almost as if all things physical scared him. He lived in his mind and the make-believe world of his favourite books.

He was not physically strong like his brothers but he was well formed and cut quite a dash. He had not been immune to the shy glances of several young ladies in his direction whenever he visited town. Due to his extreme shyness, he managed to side step any attempt at conversation or involvement with the opposite sex. Whenever he found himself in female company he found himself completely tongue-tied.

As he tossed and turned through his last night at home, he was overcome with fears. He would miss his family and the farm but equally he longed for a life that could give him the stimulation of the mind he longed for. He wanted to go to New York, not so much to earn his fortune but to have the opportunity to immerse himself more thoroughly in books and the world of learning. His father had gifted him a small amount of money but the farm and the land would be shared by his two brothers. This meant Aidan would not be living the easy life in the city. He would most certainly have to find employment in order to augment his inheritance and to cover his annual living expenses.

Next morning, saying goodbye to his parents and brothers was harder than he could have imagined. His youthful heart longed to be free and on his adventurous path. The part of his heart which loved and cherished his home and family was full of natural sorrow. However, as a young man of twenty-one years, the whole world lay before him.

Time After Time Before Time

Chapter Fourteen

Aidan O'Haloran lay resting on his bed in the Shelbourne Hotel. He was delighted to discover that their rooms overlooked a beautiful green space known as St. Stephen's Green.

He had found the sea crossing from New York more tiring than he had anticipated. This was caused in part by being cooped up with the same people for almost a week. Meals were a particular irritation to him as he was forced to socialise with those others sharing his table. Despite living in New York for over forty years, he had never lost his shyness around people. He still found it difficult to make small talk. He was never rude to those seeking to talk with him but he certainly never encouraged confidences. The exceptions were his two children. He never tired of being with them, and in their company he became truly animated.

In his department at the university where he was associate professor of ancient history, all of his colleagues considered him dour and unfriendly. He was considered to be a man with a fine mind who could ignite a passion for his subject in his students. But outside the lecture theatre he was considered to be totally socially inept. He never accepted invitations to dine out with colleagues, or visit their homes. After a while the invitations ceased. Opinions were formed as to his testy character and he was left to his own devices after working hours. Aidan liked it this way. Since the time when he had left the farm back west, he had found solace in his own company. In the early days, he was far too busy working and studying to give any time to personal friendships even if he had wanted to.

When he first arrived in New York, he surprised himself by taking everything in his stride. When he had sorted out a place to live, he then walked the city streets to orientate himself. He located every bookshop and library within walking distance of his lodgings. He quickly found employment tutoring children of wealthy families. The income from this allowed him to buy the books he needed to study in order to gain entrance to the university. He became a well-known figure in the local bookshops. He was supremely happy when he was surrounded by books. He loved everything about bookshops, especially the smell. He inhaled the smell of knowledge like it was the most beautiful perfume. He often found himself stroking the binding on an especially beautiful tome in the way that other men might caress a lover. Although he might be considered a dreamer, he also had a fierce determination to learn as much as he could about the history of ancient man. This was his passion and he pursued it with a single mindedness that filled every waking moment.

When he finally presented himself for interview at the university, his lack of formal qualifications was overlooked by the examining board. They had never before come across a young person so deeply steeped in his subject. He was awarded a full scholarship which immediately removed the need to carry on his tutoring work. From the beginning of the course his ability was recognised. He graduated with due honours and went on to do further study. He quickly and easily climbed the academic ladder and at the young age of thirty-two was awarded a professorship.

During the ten years since leaving the farm he had made the trip back home only once to attend the funeral of his mother. He rarely thought about the life he had left behind apart from when he sat down to write his dutiful yearly letter to his family. When he arrived for the funeral, he was shocked to see how much his father had aged. His mother had fallen from her horse while out shooting, and her neck had been snapped by the fall. After the burial, he walked round with his brothers to look at all the changes that had been made on the farm. He could see that they were immensely proud of all the work they had done and he was genuinely happy for them. Neither of them had married. They seemed to be very close to Seamus, and the old man relied on them for everything. They asked about his life in New York but when he began to tell them something of his work, he could see it didn't really interest them. He understood then, that in order to fit in with his family he would have to suppress parts of himself. He could do this because he loved his brothers and father. He also recognised that he had lost something very valuable. He knew he would never belong amongst them again. He had thrown that away like a worn-out coat.

    One night he sat outside on the stoop with his dad. He was reminded of the night before he had left home. They sat in silence for a long while before Aidan asked of his father, "You will miss Mom?" Seamus turned, his eyes ablaze with incomprehension toward his youngest son.

    "Miss her, you say? I wanted to die with her. She was my life, my heartbeat, my very breath. Do you know what it is to love like that son?"

    Before Aidan could reply, Seamus turned his face away and continued. "She made my life whole. Until I met her, I was a living dead-man. I walked and ate and slept and worked but I was dead. Dead inside where it matters. She really saw the man behind the pain and the anger and the memories and she healed me with the strength of her love. She touched my soul and with her I became whole."

He paused to look once more at Aidan. "You have built a good life for yourself son. You are a fine city man now but you have buried your soul. Your books cannot hold you when night terrors take hold. Can they touch your body with hands like velvet or silk? Can they bring you to ecstasy? Can your books take away your deepest fears? Can they soothe your brow when you are raging with fever? Do not let your work fill up all the spaces in your heart and soul. Leave a space for human warmth. When everything is taken away, all that remains is love."

This outpouring from his father left Aidan in a complete spin. His father had shown Aidan a glimpse of what a life with love as its foundation could be like. His own life seemed like a very pale glimmer by comparison. After his father had retired to bed, Aidan sat out late into the night. He wept for what his selfishness had done to him and how he had felt driven to achieve. He had reached the pinnacle of his profession but he had nobody to share it with.

Back in New York life continued much the same for Aidan as it had always done - with one notable difference. He began to exchange pleasantries with staff and students. People were astonished at first by his new behaviour but rather liked it. He began to receive invitations to dinner parties and he accepted some of them. He found this quite a challenge but he persevered because he now wished to be liked for himself and not just tolerated because of his outstanding research.

One winter evening, several years after his visit home to bury his mother, Aidan received an invitation to a dinner party. He tossed the invitation aside because as was his custom he would rather spend the evening sitting by his own fireside reading. The day of the party was a particularly cold and snowy day. The snow had been falling since before dawn. When Aidan set off for the university that morning the city lay quiet and hushed. As he walked across the campus to his department, he was struck by the stillness and the stark beauty of the trees that lined the avenue. He felt a huge upsurge of goodwill and joy and there and then he decided he would attend the dinner party after all. He surprised himself by this sudden change of heart. He wondered where it had come from. As he walked on, he realised that the beauty of the snow had touched him in a way that he had not experienced before. It was as if for the first time in his life he was allowing beauty and joy to weave their magic on his spirit. His day continued as normal except that he actually found himself thinking about the party from time to time. He realised he was actually looking forward to it. Classes ended early because of the weather. Aidan stopped off on his way home to buy some chocolates for his hosts and despite the freezing cold he was in a happy mood when he turned the key in his own front door.

    He was not known for his sartorial elegance, but tonight he made a bigger effort than usual getting ready. When he looked at himself in the hall mirror on his way out, he was quite pleased with what he saw reflected back. Age had not robbed him of his handsome good looks but had overlaid his features with a steely determined look which was most attractive especially to the ladies. Aidan of course was totally oblivious to this. When he arrived at the party, he was quite surprised to find he felt quite excited. He was ushered into the sitting room where a large open log fire was burning. He recognised everyone present apart from one young woman who was engaged in earnest conversation

Time After Time Before Time

with another guest. When they were called in to dinner, Aidan was seated next to the young woman. Her name was Kitty and she was an art teacher. They fell into easy conversation. She listened attentively while he described how the burial rituals of our ancestors had always fascinated him. His enthusiasm for his subject normally blinded him to the glazed look which usually crept into the eyes of whoever was on the receiving end of his preferred topic of conversation. Kitty was the exception. She asked timely and appropriate questions and her avid attention caused him to blush once or twice.

"I'm boring you," he said.

"Oh, not at all," she quickly replied. "It's fascinating to learn about the customs and rituals of those who have gone before us. How our ancestors lived must surely have shaped how we live and think in our own time. I'm a painter. I especially like to paint trees, dead ones as well as those thriving. The dead ones are very beautiful to my eyes, because they have been stripped of everything but their bare form. Sometimes I wonder about all the experiences and lives that the ancient trees have borne witness to. They have secrets within them and I would love to know what they have seen. Don't think me crazy, but I love these trees. You are the first person I've told about this. Painting the trees gives me an excuse to sit in front of them for hours at a time. People don't think it odd to see someone sitting in front of a tree painting. However, if I were to simply sit and stare for hours without an easel in front of me, it would be considered very odd behaviour indeed."

Aiden looked at her wide eyed with astonishment. He continued to stare at her until Kitty blushed and lowered her eyes in embarrassment.

"Oh, I'm sorry," he finally blurted out, "It's just that I've never met anyone quite like you." As he had always shied away from female company, he had never mastered the social graces exchanged between men and women of his generation and social standing. Tonight however, in the company of Kitty, he felt he could be completely himself. "I would love to see some of your paintings."

"And so you shall," she said without hesitation.

They were each aware of the attraction between them. During the remainder of the evening while they were engaged in conversation with the other guests, Aidan found himself glancing in her direction more than once. He found he didn't want to talk with anyone else apart from her. Once when he glanced towards her, she happened to catch his eye and smiled broadly at him. His heart thumped in his chest and for the second time that day he experienced a surge of joy. When the evening drew to a close, he helped her on with her coat and asked if he could see her to her home.

Over the following months a deep and passionate love blossomed between them. They seemed to have the capacity to tap into each other's soul. In loving Kitty, he finally understood how his father had loved his mother. They married within the year - much to everyone's surprise. Aidan and Kitty had found in each other the perfect companion who could accept and even glory in the other's quirky personal traits. Aidan absolutely blossomed in the marriage like a thin straggly plant finally getting the correct nourishment and conditions for optimum growth. Kitty never tired of listening to the details of his work and various projects. He often asked her opinion and he was always eager to invite her on the most exciting of his field trips. For his part, Aidan loved to watch Kitty at work. He especially loved the way her brow wrinkled in concentration as she worked on a painting. She introduced him to the art of seeing not just with the eyes but with the whole body.

Sometimes at weekends, they would take a picnic basket and head off into the countryside immediately after breakfast. Kitty would set up her easel and she would encourage Aidan to sit with her and simply look at what was in front of him. He made tentative attempts to paint, mainly to please Kitty. She introduced him to what she called the 'whole body way of seeing'. She explained that when we simply look with our eyes, we tend to ignore all the different nuances which our other senses are showing us. So sometimes, when she noticed that he was getting particularly frustrated with his attempts to paint, she would ask him to lie flat out on the grass beneath the trees. Then she would encourage him to look up into the tree from below until he felt enveloped within the leafy branches. Other times she would take his hand and rub it along the bark of the tree encouraging him to feel the texture. She also encouraged him to close his eyes and listen to the sounds within the branches, which Kitty called the voice of the tree. Kitty insisted that he needed to form a personal relationship with the tree he was trying to paint.

Under any other circumstances Aidan would have found this extremely trite and irritating, but Kitty made everything plausible and acceptable to him. Initially, because he loved her and wanted to please her, Aidan went along with her theories. But as time passed, he found he really looked forward to their painting trips. He also found, to his own astonishment, that he now considered himself to be a lover of trees. This love affair with trees broadened out to include rivers and mountains and meadows.

In the third year of their marriage, Kitty gave birth to a son, Thomas, and a daughter Saoirse twenty months later.

Time After Time Before Time

When the children were robust enough to travel, the whole family made the long journey back west to the family farm. Seamus was delighted to meet his daughter-in-law and his two grandchildren. The visit was a happy time for everyone and the children thrived. Most days one or other of Aidan's brothers could be seen walking round the farm with little Thomas perched on his shoulders. Saoirse, on the other hand never strayed far from her grandfather's side. The two of them formed an immediate bond. The presence of the children brought a deep healing into all the family relationships.

Following on from that first visit, the children were taken to visit their grandfather and uncles every summer. Saoirse loved to sit with Grandpa Seamus as he was affectionately known. He often sang some of the ancient Gaelic songs to her as she lay snuggled against him before bedtime. As the years passed and the children grew into young adults, Saoirse never missed her annual visit to grandfather Seamus with her parents. Her brother Thomas began to make excuses for not accompanying them some years, until he finally stopped going altogether. Saoirse more than made up for his absence with her ebullient personality. She adored her grandfather and he in turn cherished her with a love that felt timeless.

Many an evening when he had rocked her to sleep on his lap in the hot balmy prairie night, he had a strange feeling that he was reworking something from way way back in time. He felt a connection with her that was missing from his relationship with his three sons. She loved to hear his stories about Ireland. By the time she was fifteen her knowledge of Ireland, its customs and its people, was extensive. The first time grandfather Seamus told her about the great hunger, she sat in absolute silence by his feet, afraid to move in case he stopped talking. She encouraged him to talk until she sensed that the memories he was trawling were still painful for him. He spoke to her of the suffering of the famine in a way that he had never spoken before, not even to his beloved Lucy. When he told her about the rotting corpses on the sides of the roads of Ireland, and the hellish scenes on the coffin ship that brought him to this new land, she felt her heart would break. She held the frail sobbing body of her grandfather in her strong young arms. Together they wept. Him for the loss of his parents, brother and neighbours; her for the sheer ruthlessness of the political and social system that had starved and dispossessed a nation. She wondered how her grandfather had managed to stop the black memories from destroying his life. He told her he had taken a vow to survive. He had lived his life in honour of all those who had needlessly died.

"And I am part of that vow," said Saoirse. "I will make sure the whole world knows your story."

For the next three years, Saoirse spent all her holidays on the farm. She encouraged her grandfather to open up more and more about his memories of Ireland and the Great Famine. She also encouraged him to tell her about the happy times he had lived as a young boy. And so it was that she developed a deep yearning to visit the places her grandfather so vividly described for her. The years had not dimmed his memory of the dancing in his parents' house, of his father playing the harp on a winter's night with the neighbours gathered round. In her mind's eye she imagined she could hear the sound of the dancing feet on the dirt floor as the fiddlers played the jigs and reels faster and faster. So detailed were her grandfather's memories, that she could almost smell the sweet aroma of the turf fire and hear the soft lilting of the Gaelic language. She wrote everything down while it was fresh in her mind.

The summer before she was due to start her university course, she startled her parents by announcing that she wanted to visit Ireland before beginning her studies. Her father didn't approve but finally agreed to her going provided he accompanied her. And so it was that in the early summer of 1916, father and daughter found themselves staying in the elegant Shelbourne hotel in Dublin, with rooms overlooking St. Stephen's Green.

This was a small but beautiful park situated at the top of Grafton Street. Normally, during the hotter months of the year, the park would be crowded with office workers and shop assistants using their lunch breaks to avail themselves of fresh air in a peaceful green city space. Now it was pretty much empty at lunchtimes because it was barely three months since the failed Easter Rising, where it had been used to fire on the soldiers holding out in the Shelbourne Hotel opposite. The city centre had been reduced to rubble and the general populace was still reeling from the aftermath. Thousands of people had been arrested and the speedy execution of the leaders galvanised public opinion. There was a general outrage at such barbarity and the executed leaders immediately took on the status of martyrs. Songs and ballads about these heroic figures were circulated in the pubs and taverns. While the atmosphere on the streets was subdued and cautious, in the gathering places around the city there was impassioned talk about continuing the fight for freedom.

Of course, Aidan and Saoirse were blissfully unaware of this political unrest, and had no idea that only a few months prior to their visit the city of Dublin had been in such turmoil. They were extremely fatigued after their

Atlantic sea crossing and for the first twenty-four hours didn't leave their rooms. Over breakfast on the second day they gleaned from the national newspapers some idea of the recent insurgence. Aidan immediately became worried for their safety, but was reassured by the hotel management that the rebellion had been crushed and that there was absolutely no danger to them on the streets.

Although not completely at ease, Aidan gave his arm to his daughter, and the pair strolled down the length of Grafton Street. They noticed that several buildings had windows boarded up and some frontages bore the pock marks of gunfire. Normal city life seemed to be going on all around them though, so Aidan began to relax and enjoy the morning air.

As they passed the main entrance to Trinity College, Saoirse felt an unexplainable urge to go through into the quadrangle. As the day belonged to them and they were in no hurry to be any place, Aidan smiled indulgently at his daughter, and suggested they head straight for the old library where thousands of ancient books were housed. The high vaulted ceilings and wooden interior of the library elicits a hushed reverence from all who enter it. Students were hunched over research papers quietly studying. Saoirse was immediately drawn to a sign pointing the way to the area where the Book of Kells was on public display. She joined the line of people waiting to see the book and as she got near the top of the queue she began to feel hot and sweaty. She experienced the most peculiar notion that her life was about to be changed for ever. Waves of anxiety engulfed her and she almost turned away from the queue. But something inside her made her wait her turn. She controlled her breathing and felt herself settle. When at last she gazed on the magnificent ancient book laid out before her, her heart began to pound. She was overcome with emotion and was totally unaware of the silent tears running down her face. The assistant on duty asked her if she wanted some help, as he could see she was visibly shaken.

"Are you all right, my dear?" he asked her.

She turned her shining face towards him and replied, "Oh, yes. Thank you. I'm more than all right. I've never been more all right in my life so far."

With that, she quickly left the room and went in search of her father. She knew where to look for him. Sure enough she located him in the section devoted to ancient tribal customs. He had several books opened in front of him and was relaxed and totally engrossed in his reading. Almost like a camera shutter, opening and closing, Saoirse saw her father as she had many times before. A true academic, absorbed in his work, lost to the outside world. When she tapped him on his shoulder, he took a second or two to bring his attention back from the world of the ancients.

"Can we leave now please papa?" she said in a hushed voice. "I'm not feeling very well."

Aidan immediately stood up, knocking over his chair which drew frowns from one or two readers seated at the long table.

"What is it, my dear?" he asked anxiously, taking her arm.

"I just need to be outside in the fresh air."

Leaning on her father's arm, they left the college and went to seek refreshments, ending up in Bewley's coffee house. Over their lunch, Saoirse tried to explain to her father what had happened to her when she first looked at the manuscript.

"It's very difficult to explain what happened to me in the library," began Saoirse, almost as soon as they sat down at their table. "In truth papa, I don't think I can explain because I don't understand what happened in there. Even before I actually saw the manuscript, I felt as if something beyond my control was happening to me. When my eyes saw the beauty of those pages, I felt a huge sense of joy and warmth and a deep sense of belonging welling up inside me. And please don't think me crazy papa, but I could hear the sea, a wild sea crashing against rocks."

Saoirse paused and seemed to be lost in her own thoughts. Her father reached across the table for her hand and said in a kindly voice. "Saoirse my dear, perhaps you are still rather tired from our recent voyage. Why don't we go straight back to the hotel after lunch and you can rest for a while?"

Her father's obvious but unspoken anxiety and concern for her was enough to make Saoirse understand that she must speak no further. What had happened to her was for her alone to understand.

"You're absolutely right as usual papa, I am feeling a little fatigued."

She ate her lunch and ordered a rather large dessert to follow. This made her father laugh out loud. "Well my dear, I'm happy to see that the little episode in the library hasn't dulled your appetite."

When they returned to the hotel, Saoirse couldn't wait to retire to her room so she could think about what had happened to her. Removing her outer garments, she lay down on her bed and mentally retraced what had occurred in the library. For the second time that day she felt her life would never be the same again. Why would looking at that sacred manuscript generate such deep feelings of joy in her? Yes, it was very beautiful, but that alone couldn't account for the effect it had on her. She knew nothing about ancient

Time After Time Before Time

manuscripts, Irish or otherwise, but the Book of Kells had unleashed something in her which was both wonderful and deeply disturbing at the same time.

She was awakened from a strange dream by a knocking on her door. She sat bolt upright on the bed not knowing where she was for a second or two.

"It's time for dinner," her father's voice said from outside the door. I'll wait for you downstairs."

She looked at her watch and realised she had been asleep all afternoon and into the early evening. The dream she had been so abruptly awakened from had been so real. She recalled images of an island, and feelings of cold and hunger. There was also something about a precious book and a fire. The images were superimposed upon each other and were not particularly clear. There was one aspect of the dream though that was very clear and memorable. It was the sound of a bell.

As she got ready to go downstairs she couldn't shake off the dream. She knew without a shadow of a doubt that she had known the sound of that particular bell and that it had held great importance for her. She tried to rationalise these thoughts by telling herself that it was only a dream and not real. But it didn't work. The vividness of the dream images clung to her like a silk garment. As she joined her father in the hotel restaurant, she felt deep in her bones that she must not share her dream with anyone, least of all her father.

After her father had retired for the night, Saoirse decided to take an evening stroll by herself. She turned left out of the hotel and after a short walk she found herself in Dame Street. Once again she found herself outside the gates of Trinity College. She knew the library would be closed at such a late hour but she decided she would go inside anyway and stroll around the quadrangle, simply to be in the vicinity of the manuscript. She realised this made no sense but she went in through the gates without hesitation. She could hear Irish music coming from a second-floor room of the student accommodation. Standing in the deserted quad below, she was totally transfixed by the haunting slow sounds coming through the open windows. As the final notes faded away, and she was about to move on, the quick-fire notes of a Kerry hornpipe reached her ears. She remembered all the stories grandfather Seamus had told her about the liveliness of the music way back when he was a lad in Ireland. The music was like a key opening a door into a world she had no experience of.

A voice from the open window shouted down to her. "Why don't you come up? We don't bite!"

The voice belonged to a young man with a mop of black curly hair who was leaning out of the window at a very dangerous angle.

"Thank you very much, but it's time for me to get back."

Saoirse turned and made to leave the quadrangle. The voice from the window shouted down again.

"Why not come up for half an hour, and one of us will see you safely home afterwards."

He extended his hand towards her and made an imaginary bow and almost fell out of the window. Saoirse laughed and said

"OK. I'll come up for a very short while, but only if you please stop leaning so far out of the window."

"We're on the second floor, room 22."

Saoirse let herself in through the large oak door at ground level, and followed the sounds of the music. The door to room 22 was wide open and she was immediately ushered in by the same young man who had been hanging out the window. There were four musicians sitting together on hard-backed chairs in a semi-circle in the centre of the room. Others were sitting on cushions propped up against the walls. She was acknowledged with a slight nod of the head but nobody spoke. Everyone was giving their full attention to the music. Saoirse looked around her at the rapt young faces and felt a stab of happiness. When the music stopped, there was a spontaneous outburst of thunderous applause. When the room settled down again the young man who had invited her up introduced himself to her as Joseph. When she told him her name was Saoirse, a huge smile lit up his face.

"That's a wonderful Irish name you've got there," he gushed, "but you're American."

"How do you know that?" she said quizzingly.
Joseph burst out laughing, slapping his thighs in delight. He came up close to her, and whispered in her ear.

"Your accent my dear, gives you away."

Saoirse's eyes widened in delight and she began to giggle.

"Let me introduce you to everyone," he said as he led her by the hand into the centre of the room.

"Listen everyone," he began in a loud voice, "This is Saoirse and she's come to join us all the way from America. But we won't hold that against her, will we?"

There was a burst of laughter and everyone came over to shake her had. For the next few minutes she was inundated with questions about where she came from and what was she doing in Dublin.

Joseph stood apart, his gaze following every expression that flitted across Saoirse's face. He noticed her flushed cheeks and ready smile and from that moment

Time After Time Before Time

onwards his heart was no longer his own. She was very beautiful, tall for a woman, with a slender figure. What made her appear even more beautiful was her complete lack of affectation. She seemed to be totally unaware of her effect on almost all the young men in the room that evening.

When the musicians started to play again, Joseph came over and invited her to sit beside him. Once more the room was silent as the beautiful strains of the traditional music filled the night air. Saoirse closed her eyes and thought of her grandfather. Her reverie was interrupted by a very loud knocking on the door. Mr. Sullivan, the night porter, came in and immediately everyone began packing up their things.

"Sorry to break up the evening, ladies and gents," he said in a kindly voice, "but you know the rules. No music after ten o'clock." Saoirse felt a moment of panic as she hadn't realised the lateness of the hour.

"I really have to go," she said as she left the room and began to make her way down the stairs rather quickly. Joseph followed her down and fell into step with her as they went out of the college and into Grafton street. They walked in silence until they reached the Shelbourne Hotel. Joseph gave a low whistle.

"Is this where you're staying? You must be very wealthy."

Saoirse turned to face him, her cheeks reddening and her mouth set in a firm line. Joseph's regret was immediate, he made to speak but was stopped by the look on her face.

"That is none of your business," she replied. Thank you for walking me back!" She turned on her heel and had gone through the hotel doors before Joseph could say another word. As she approached the desk to collect her room key, she heard her father's voice call her name. He was seated behind her in the lobby, a glass of whiskey on the table in front of him.

"Come and sit with me," he said. Although she was very tired Saoirse sensed that this was not an invitation to refuse. Her father got straight to the point.

"Where on earth have you been? You went off without telling me. I came to your room to talk over some travelling plans only to find you had left the hotel without telling me." Perhaps because she was vexed with Joseph, she answered her father rather sharply.

"I'm no longer a child, and I don't need your permission to go out in the evenings!"

Her father swallowed his reply because the young woman he saw sitting in front of him was certainly no longer a child. In fact he acknowledged to himself for the first time, that she had blossomed into a beautiful young woman, strong-willed and at times very stubborn, but always generous with her love and affections.

"I'm sorry my dear, you're right. I simply worried about you being out alone in an unfamiliar city." Saoirse got up from her chair and hugged her father.

"Thank you, papa. But please don't worry about me. I'll join you for breakfast in the morning. Goodnight."

For the next five days, Saoirse spent as much time as she could in the library of Trinity College researching ancient Irish manuscripts. She was gripped by a passion that seemed to consume her every waking moment. From nine o'clock until well into the late evening she poured over the research papers which the elderly librarian handed into her care each morning. As her knowledge accumulated, she allowed an idea to take shape in her mind.

Time After Time Before Time

"What if I don't go home to university? What if I stay in Ireland and do my degree here in Trinity College in ancient Irish History?" The more she thought about this, her sense of excitement grew and, like a beautiful secret, she nursed it inside herself until she was absolutely sure that this was the right thing for her to do. She made enquiries at the admissions office and an interview was set up for her. The panel of three men were very thorough in their questions. They were happy with her academic qualifications but were concerned about her reasons for wanting to stay and study in Ireland.

Was this not a whim? they gently suggested, and would she not feel very homesick after a few months away from her family?

For the next fifteen minutes Saoirse told them about her grandfather Seamus and how he had made Ireland come alive for her in her imagination. She spoke about her indignation and anger when she first heard about the Great Famine. She told them about her own father's academic research into ancient burial rituals and how she had grown up in a household where a sense of the past was almost like a living presence.

"The oldest of the three men, stopped her at this point and gently said, "What I would like to hear from you my dear, is why you are drawn to the Ancient History Department."

Saoirse looked at the kindly face of the man in front of her and decided she would risk telling him the truth.

"When I first saw the Book of Kells, something quite beyond my present understanding happened to me. I know it sounds absolutely crazy, but I felt a sense of deep connection with the people and places where such manuscripts were written. I feel profoundly affected and I would like to devote

Time After Time Before Time

the rest of my life to studying such ancient artefacts." She stopped because she began to cry.

"I'm so sorry," she said, "it's just that whenever I speak about ancient Ireland I feel deeply happy and sad all at the same time. It makes it hard to control my emotions."

With that she stood up and said, "I'm sorry gentlemen, for wasting your time." The older man stood up also saying, "Please be seated Miss O'Haloran." Saoirse sat down on the edge of her seat and waited. The older man, looked at each of his colleagues in turn and then, turning to face the young woman sitting nervously in front of him, he stood up and extending his hand towards her, he said with a smile, "Welcome to Trinity College Miss O'Haloran. We can offer you a place on the Ancient Irish History Degree course beginning this coming autumn. Please make yourself known to the admissions office to make the arrangements."

Saoirse stood also and her pleasure and astonishment spilled all over her face making her look very childlike. "Thank you so much gentlemen." She shook hands with each member of the panel in turn before taking her leave. As she walked across the quadrangle towards the main gates such was her excitement that she gave a little hop, skip and a jump.

A voice behind her mocked, "Very unladylike I'm sure!" She recognised Joseph's voice. She turned around to face him and looked at him with shining eyes. Her previous anger towards him completely evaporated. "You'll never guess what's just happened!" she blurted excitedly.

"You've fallen madly in love with me!" replied Joseph with a huge grin on his face.

Saoirse raised one eyebrow in disdain before she too found herself grinning. "Don't be silly," she said quickly,

"I've got absolutely no intention of falling in love with you. Something wonderful has just happened to me."

"What could be more fantastic than falling in love with me?" answered Joseph with a cheeky expression on his face.

"If you will be serious for a moment, I will tell you."

"Go on then, spill the beans," he said.

"Well, I've just been offered a place to begin studying here at the college in the autumn."

"Wow, that's fantastic news! Let's go celebrate."

Saoirse's hesitation was only momentary, but Joseph caught it nevertheless. "Will you come if I promise not to mention falling in love with me again?" he said in a very cheeky voice, which immediately melted her resolve to have nothing to do with him.

She linked her arm through his and together they left the college grounds and headed along Grafton Street. He took her into Bewley's coffee house where he seemed to know many of the customers who were already seated.

When the full telling of the interview was completed, Joseph asked what her father thought of the turn of events. The question threw Saoirse into a complete spin, as she hadn't given any thought to what might be the reaction of her family, especially her father.

The colour drained from her face and Joseph knew he had hit a raw nerve. He reached for her hand and looked deep into her eyes and said gently, "Be kind in the telling. But live your own dream. This is your time, so you must take it."

Saoirse looked at him with a new sense of respect.

"How did you get to be so wise?" she said. "That's exactly what I needed to hear. I must speak with my father right away because he has every right to know as soon as

Time After Time Before Time

possible." Before they left the coffee shop, they arranged to meet in the college quad later that evening.

Joseph watched her go, until she rounded the corner at the top of Grafton Street.

As soon as they were seated at their usual table for lunch Saoirse told her father about her future plans. Aidan received her news with a simple nod of his head. When she tried to probe him for his response, he gave her a steely look, stating, "We will discuss this after lunch in my room." Saoirse was quite familiar with her father's usage of cold calm detachment and single-mindedness. This was the reason he had very few close friends in his life as he had no tolerance for trivial conversation. He certainly didn't suffer fools gladly and many of his students over the years had suffered the brunt of his scathing tongue. They ate their lunch in complete silence, all the while Saoirse dreading what she expected was yet to come.

As soon as door closed behind them in her father's room, he immediately gave vent to his anger. "This is absolute nonsense. You will be returning to America with me in three weeks' time as planned, where you will take up your place at university. I know that your grandfather has filled your head with stories about Ireland, most of which have little truth in them. Ireland is a beautiful country, I'll grant you that, and the people are indeed very friendly and welcoming here in Dublin, but this is not your home. I'll not hear another word about staying on here to study. It's complete madness. You don't know anyone here in this city, you have no family here, and the Irish way of life is completely foreign to you."

"But that's what makes it so exciting. Don't you see papa, I want some adventure in my life. Everything back home has been mapped out for me which makes me feel suffocated. I need to stay here; I can feel it in my bones. I'm meant to be here."

Her father's voice cut through the air. "You will not stay here." There was a momentary softening in his voice as he continued. "You are my daughter and you will do what I feel is best for you. Forget all this nonsense and we'll say no more about it."

Throughout all the years of her growing up, Saoirse had hardly ever quarrelled with either of her parents. She loved her mother without reservation but the love she had for her father was mixed up with her desire to please him and make him proud of her. Yet somehow without fully understanding what was happening to her, she was now about to defy him for the first time.

"Papa, I really want to stay here and study. I feel really clear about this."

"Nonsense girl, you are hardly more than a child. You cannot possibly know what is best for you at this stage of your life. This discussion is over. We will not be changing our plans."

Saoirse would remember with absolute clarity for a long time, everything about that moment when time stood still. The grandfather clock in the hallway outside the room struck two o'clock. She noticed her father tap his fingers against his right thigh, a habit he had when he was either angry or very impatient. A woman's voice drifted up from the street below. The long white voile curtains ballooned in the breeze and Saoirse's hands became hot with sweat. She looked at her father and the strength of her love for him was almost her undoing. But she couldn't turn the clock back. She knew that something beyond her control had drawn her to this moment and she would take courage from this. Their eyes held each other's in silence and a cold finality brushed against her heart. The aura around her father was icy, she took a step towards him and stopped.

"I'm sorry to disobey you Papa, but I'm staying here in Dublin."

"Then my duty is done towards you. I will leave for home as soon as I can arrange a passage. I will leave you enough money to pay for your own passage should you change your mind. There is war going on in Europe, shipping is constantly being interrupted. Passenger ships have been sunk. As the war accelerates, you may not be able to make safe passage home. And I've been reliably informed that there are insurgents mobilizing all over Ireland ready to fight to further the cause for Irish freedom. You will definitely not be safe in this country. For the very last time, please come home with me." She shook her head and her father motioned for her to leave the room.

For the remainder of the day and evening Father and daughter each stayed in their own rooms. Saoirse spent several hours pacing the floorboards tormenting herself about her decision. She wasn't unduly worried about money as she had a sizeable amount in her name which had been deposited in a bank account for her the day she was born. Neither was she concerned about settling in a new country. She felt she was in a country which she knew very well from listening to her grandfather's stories. If she had been pressed on the matter, she would have said that she was nurturing a secret delight in reversing the process of the Great Famine. Her grandfather's family had been driven out of Ireland by a social system which favoured the wealthy. Now three generations later, she was choosing to make her life there. Moreover, she was listening to a deep silent voice which was directing her actions. She needed to know at the level of the logical mind what was drawing her to these ancient manuscripts, and how to make sense of the strange images that gripped her mind from time to time. Intuitively, she was simply following something that had its source in her soul and was showing her the way. She had to trust this process.

She fiinally settled down in a comfortable chair and allowed her thoughts to quieten as best she could. In her mind's eye she pictured grandfather Seamus sitting in his rocker, looking at the evening sky. From her heart, she sent out a silent plea to him to let her know that he approved of her decision to remain in Ireland. She slowed her breathing right down. She brought to mind his old weathered kindly face and speaking aloud she said, "Please give me your blessing Grandfather. I need your blessing."

When she walked into the dining room for dinner that evening, she felt apprehensive about meeting her father. However, as soon as he caught sight of her, he immediately beckoned her over. He stood up and embraced her and she clung to him in relief. She sensed a sea change in his attitude.

"Let's enjoy our last dinner together," he said. I've been able to arrange my passage home tomorrow for an exorbitant price, because it may be the last safe sailing for quite some time. Her father continued, "I've nothing further to add to what's been said already, but I want you to know that I will always love you and hope some day you will return to live with your family. I have something very special which I want to now give to you because it will connect you with all of us back home. It's very special and very precious to me but it feels right to hand it over into your safe-keeping at this time." He reached into his breast pocket and withdrew a tiny package. He passed it across the starched white tablecloth to his daughter. Saoirse felt her throat constrict and her eyes filled with tears. She knew what was in the package and it was the sign she had asked for. She slowly opened the package and nestling on a piece of blue silk was the tiny Celtic cross which grandfather Seamus had carved all those years ago. She reverently picked it up, held it to her lips and said a silent 'thank you' to her grandfather. He had indeed heard her call for his blessing.

"Thank you, papa, I will treasure it. I feel I have Grandfather's blessing now to guide me and keep me safe."

Her father reached over and took both her hands in his.

"Although I totally disapprove of what you plan, I have no hesitation in saying that your grandfather would probably wholeheartedly approve. You two are very similar in many ways, not least of which is you are both headstrong and inclined to get your own way once you've decided to do something. And now, let us enjoy the remaining time we have together."

Saoirse felt as if the bottom had fallen out of her world when she saw her father board the ship the following day. He stood on the top deck and waved his white handkerchief until he became no more than a tiny dot as the ship moved further and further away. She continued to wave long after there was any possibility that he could see her. Finally, she turned her back to the sea, and she felt an emptiness which would stay with her for some time to come.

On her journey back to the Shelbourne Hotel, her fingers constantly sought the reassurance of the tiny cross nestling in the front pocket of her summer dress. Once back in her room she felt a sharp spasm of loneliness come over her. She left the hotel straight after lunch, passed Trinity College and made her way straight down to O'Connell Street. She was astonished to see the degree of destruction the city centre had suffered during the recent insurrection. Many of the buildings surrounding the General Post Office where Patrick Pearse [24] had so recently proclaimed Irish freedom, had been reduced almost to rubble. She knew very little about recent Irish politics. Her knowledge of Ireland and its people had been entirely crafted by the tales of her grandfather, and was full of mysticism, longings for the homeland and a fuzzy understanding of the unseen worlds as represented by what he called 'the little folk'. She could repeat the stories of Cuchulainn, Fionn McCool, Tír na n-Óg and other legendary Irish heroes without faltering, as these had been told to her countless times by her grandfather. Now, she was seeing a land struggling to proclaim its identity and she realised with a degree of shame how very little she knew about the living, breathing Ireland that was here and now in her time. Her grandfather had left a land driven to its knees from hunger and oppression. Things were different now. The struggle for independence was gathering momentum and she felt she needed to be part of it in some capacity. She rounded the corner of the post office and walked into Henry Street.

    Halfway down she heard the Moore Street vegetable sellers calling out. The vegetables and fruit were nestling in wooden trays, which in turn were nestling on the chassis of old baby prams. This meant that at the close of trade each day, the hawkers simply had to wheel their goods away, and not have to bother with dismantling stands. She slowly inched her way along the line of sellers, buying some apples from one old woman whose poverty-lined face tugged at Saoirse's heartstrings. In fact, most of the women looked ill-clad and weary lines etched their faces. However, their

---

[24]   One of the leaders of the 1916 Rising

spirits remained high as they called out to the passers-by. When she found she was laden with far too many oranges and apples than she could possibly eat, she decided to retrace her steps and head back to her hotel. As she crossed O'Connell Bridge she offered all the fruit she had bought to a tinker woman who was sitting begging on the bridge. As Saoirse offered the fruit, the woman held out a begging hand and parted her shawl to reveal a small baby nestling at her breast. Saoirse was overcome with compassion and gave her all the money she had left in her purse.

"Blessings of God on ye," said the woman as her hand grasped the money.

"You're welcome I'm sure," replied Saoirse as she continued on her way. Further along the bridge, she paused and leaned over to look at the Guinness barges slowing making their way back up the river to St. James Brewery while they had the run of the tide. She had yet to try a pint of the dark national drink but no doubt this would come in due course. She continued walking along the south quays towards the small fishing village of Ringsend and further out to the red lighthouse. She had reached the point where the River Liffey merged into the Irish Sea. As she looked out over the water, she sent up a silent prayer asking that her father's ship be protected from all harm on its journey to America. For the second time that day she turned her back on the ocean and began her return journey. The sun was setting over the city as she finally reached the hotel.

Time After Time Before Time

Time After Time Before Time

Chapter Fifteen

There was a note waiting for her at reception. It was from Joseph with an invitation to her to come to the college Buttery the following day to have lunch with him. She smiled when she read his scrawled writing, unusually big and ornate for a man. Her spirits were immediately lifted and the sense of aloneness which had been with her all day no longer troubled her. She slept without interruption until eight o'clock the next morning.

She awoke from her dreamless sleep as the sun poured through the large windows to the right of her bed. She had left the windows open and the soft Irish voices drifted up from the street below. She was in no hurry to rise as she luxuriated in the comfort of the bed and the warmth of the morning. She looked at the photograph of her family on the bedside table and smiled. She would miss them of course, but all of her nerve endings tingled with the excitement of being on her own and making her own decisions. She glanced lovingly at her grandfather's cross which lay beside the photo, and she laid to rest any residual feelings of doubt about the turn of events in her life.

She enjoyed a leisurely morning during which she wrote a letter to her grandfather explaining what had been happening to her and telling him how much she loved him and thanking him for passing on his love of Ireland to her. At one thirty precisely she walked into the Buttery. Joseph left his table and came up to greet her. He planted a kiss on her cheek, an informality which still surprised but also delighted her. They lunched on bacon and cabbage, a dish which she found utterly disgusting in contrast with the fine foods of the Shelbourne Hotel. She finally put down her knife and fork with her plate still half full. Joseph burst out laughing and said, "Disgusting, isn't it? But it's cheap and satisfying."

They talked without inhibition with each other for several hours. She learned that he came from a large family and she delighted in the stories he told her of his three sisters and brothers. Unfortunately, two of his brothers had been involved in the Easter Rising, albeit only marginally. Nevertheless, they had been rounded up and taken to the Welsh internment camp at a place called Frongoch. They were still there now but there was talk of them being released any time soon. Saoirse sat with her head in her hands, her eyes never leaving his face as Joseph gave her a very brief summary of modern Irish history.

As he was talking, he couldn't help but notice what a charming picture she made sitting opposite him in her blue cotton summer dress, her young beautiful face framed by her dark curly hair. He knew he was falling in love with her but he was aware how much of a razor's edge this might be with her. He had an instinctive understanding that he would need to take his time. When they had been finally asked to leave by the waiting staff who needed to prepare for the evening meal, they strolled out into the street and walked up Grafton Street and into St. Stephen's Green.

They completed a slow circuit of the park then sat down on a bench near the pond. They sat in companionable silence, their bodies just touching. Joseph reached for her hand and she didn't pull away. He felt her quiver as their lips touched for the first time. He pulled her closer and was surprised by her response. She softened into him but then, as if she suddenly remembered where they were, she pushed him away. Before he could protest she said softly, "Not here, please."

He simply nodded and took her hand as they left the park, and by an unspoken agreement they made their way up the steps of the Shelbourne hotel. She unashamedly asked for her key while the young clerk on duty smirked as she walked into the lift with her young man.

The afternoon was warm as they lay naked together on the soft bed. They explored each other's bodies with a softness of touch which led to a deeper and more prolonged arousal of passion for Saoirse. Back home in America, she had had little experience of sexual activity apart from the inept fumblings of the boys at the annual school dance. With Joseph she experienced a whole new world of desire and pleasure which made her feel deeply alive. She had no idea that her body could give so much pleasure to a man, and that her own body could be awakened to such deep surging penetrating pleasure. Even though this was her first time to lie with a man, she had no fear, only a sense of wild abandon into the world of the flesh. They finally lay spent, arms wrapped round one another as they day lengthened into evening. When they awoke, the city around them was in darkness, and she recognised by the sounds around her, that the hotel was about to serve dinner. She shifted her weight and felt Joseph stir beside her. She planted a kiss on his back before showering and dressing quickly.

Old habits die hard and as she dressed, she realised with a giggle that she was very hungry and was not going to miss out on dinner. She tried to rouse Joseph but he was dead to the world. She went down to the dining room and enjoyed a three-course meal with a glass of good wine. When she finally returned to her room she was surprised and a little hurt to find that Joseph had left without saying goodbye. There was a short note on the dressing table saying that he looked forward to seeing her again tomorrow in the buttery at the same time. The lack of any indication of affection in the note left Saoirse feeling oddly distant from him.

Despite her newly discovered sexual pleasures, she realised that an entanglement with him would interfere with her plans. She wanted to spend the remainder of the summer visiting the West of Ireland in order to connect with the spirit of her ancestors. In a way, she would be going on pilgrimage to the land of her ancestors and she needed to make her preparations. She rang down to the front desk and asked that her bill be prepared as she would be leaving the hotel the following morning.

The Dublin to Westport train left Amiens Street station at precisely 10.30 am the following morning. Saoirse sat in a window seat and spent the long journey thinking about the life lived by her grandfather before the great famine. She remembered how sometimes he would stop suddenly in the middle of telling her a story about Ireland and a strange aura of bewilderment would come over him. When queried, he would laugh and say he was just an old man and his mind was becoming forgetful. But Saoirse knew that the remembrances of the horrors of those hunger years took root in a place within him where no other human being could enter. She had cried with him and shared his sorrow on many an evening on the ranch but even she dared not try to enter those hidden painful places. But within her own deep places she felt that grandfather Seamus and herself were like two ships who had been built from the same timber. She was so familiar with the story of the famine years that she could not bear to waste food or watch others wasting food. As the train hurtled through the Midlands, she felt a corresponding urgency within herself. She was on a journey to become more of her true self. Everything of depth and importance within her soul was waiting to be discovered. From her family, and especially from her grandfather, she had inherited a strong leaning towards personal integrity. She gazed out of the window and hardly noticed the flat rich land of the middle counties gradually giving way to the poorer soil of the west.

"What am I looking for?" she asked of herself several times during the journey. "What am I hoping to find?"

She really didn't understand exactly what was driving her but it was connected with not only her grandfather's home but also with a time in Ireland's past. A long-forgotten past perhaps, but a past that was creeping into her life now and infusing it with mystery and half-remembered feelings. She knew she had to hold on to the thread that was weaving itself around her bit by bit.

When the train pulled into Athlone station, Saoirse felt a sense of uncomplicated joy and happiness. This was interrupted by an announcement informing her that railway problems made it necessary to finish her journey by bus. She had no desire to stay in the city a moment longer than necessary. She knew she needed to go further west to fulfil the purpose she came for. She boarded the bus heading out to Westport - which was where her grandfather had embarked for America. As the bus journeyed further and further westwards, Saoirse became mesmerised by the passing landscape.

As far as the eye could see, the land was strewn with stones.

They filled the fields and made up the walls. They had a startling compelling beauty. Her eyes quickly became saturated with this wild beauty all around. The beauty of the rocks and the bogs gave way to the surge of the sea and the distant mountains which appeared and vanished with the rising and falling mists. The landscape of her grandfather's youth came alive for her. She was entering the homeland of her ancestors. All around her in the bus she heard the soft-spoken voices of the west and she had a flash of memory of a time when language was treasured as the soul expression of a people whose lives were harsh with poverty. How was it possible that she was remembering a time when the daily workload tore at skin and sinew? Were these the memories she had garnered from her grandfather? Or could it be that she also had been alive at that time in another body? Was it too difficult and outlandish to believe that her soul could travel from lifetime to lifetime and carry memories with it? A memory of an evening fire, where the song and the story flowed like honey from the lips of men and women, who, like the stony landscape, were also embedded in this place. These were the spirits of her people. She had come to engage with what they might have to reveal to her of the mysterious world that lies beyond the veil of everyday living.

      She was jolted from her reveries by flashes of yellow in the fields either side of the road. The beautiful yellow wild irises rooting into the damp places stood erect, bright and glorious. Fuchsia-covered hedges caught her attention as the fairy-red flowers dangled in the evening light. The sun was setting in the western sky, lightening up the patterned layers of the drying ricks of turf. The cows in the fields looked golden in the crimson light, and Saoirse was deeply happy to be part of all this wild beauty. All around her in the bus the soft voices continued. Her ears were awakened once again to the sounds which her heart and mind held in memory. To sit amidst her kinsfolk and hear the ancient tongue of her people was a precious gift to her. She closed her eyes and lay back in her seat and the sounds washed over her. She imagined she could hear the music of the pipes, the flute, and fiddle but most of all the sweet strains of the harp. Her fingers sought out the little cross that nestled in her pocket and her happiness was complete.

It was dark when the bus reached Westport, the final stop. Following the last remaining passengers, she walked towards the centre of the town. Sights, sounds and smells of early twentieth century Ireland assailed her senses, as she tried to imagine what this small port might have looked like all those years ago when her grandfather and thousands like him saw it as their gateway to the new world. As she continued along the streets, she traced her fingers along the stones of the buildings, knowing that they too held the memories of the terrible suffering they had been witnesses to. She finally reached the harbour. She sat down and her young unblemished heart burst wide open with compassion. As she looked across the expanse of water where her own homeland and family were, her sense of suffering was acute. Her grandfather had been here in this very place where she now stood and he was hardly more than a walking skeleton at the time. He had seen all that was dear to him stripped away and yet he held on to the thought that he would find a way to make a new life for himself.

Life had conspired to push him out of his own land and life had now conspired to pull Saoirse back into the same place he had abandoned. She could see clearly the interweaving of life from generation to generation and she knew that she too had no choice. She could not but be in this place now, given that she was the granddaughter of a famine emigrant. She too, in her own way was looking for sanctuary. She sat for a long while. She knew with a deep certainty that somewhere within this landscape, she would discover whatever it was her soul was searching for.

Chapter Sixteen

Leaving her lodgings early the following morning Saoirse made her way to the general store. She asked for a pair of strong walking boots and a knapsack. The proprietor of the store, in true Irish fashion wanted to know if she was going on a pilgrimage. When Saoirse told him that she was heading out to the village of Kilbrona he looked very bemused.

"What's a young lady like yourself going out there for?" he asked her. "Sure, there's nothing at all out there except a few old burned out hovels, the remains of a big house and an abandoned graveyard." He leaned closer to her as he said almost reverentially, "It was a famine village you know. Scarcely a soul survived."

Saoirse felt something tighten in her gut as she registered his words.

"Can you tell me how far it is from here please?" she asked quietly.

"Oh, let me see now," he said as he scratched his head. "Sure it's six or seven miles. You'll be needing a lift to get you there. I can ask Michael Murphy to give you a ride out if you like?"

Saoirse thanked him quickly but said she would rather walk. She paid for her purchases and left the store. Further down the street she bought some food for the journey. Leaving the town behind her she turned her face to the open road. She was going home. Home to the land of her ancestors. However, it wasn't long before life gave her a painful reality check. Her feet, in the new ill-fitting boots began to blister. Although they were causing her a great deal of pain, she was determined to continue. Thoughts of her grandfather spurred her on. If he could walk this same road in a state of emaciation, then she, a well-nourished young woman could surely do the same.

    She walked on slowly through the morning with her rest stops becoming more frequent. Not a single human being passed her on the road, which didn't surprise her. The land was poor and was mainly bog. Bog as far as the eye could see. There were a few isolated cottages situated some distance in from the road, their white-painted walls giving some stimulation to the eye after the miles and miles of the same flatness of the bog.

    Finally, she reached a bridge which she immediately recognised from descriptions her grandfather had given her. When her grandfather had told her about his home village in Ireland, he had frequently mentioned the bridge which marked the parish boundary. It was a small double bridge in need of some repair. A small stream gurgled underneath. She sat under its low arch and put her aching feet in the cool water. She lay back on the grassy slope, closed her eyes and she let the gentle sounds of the water wash over her. She began to doze. The sensation of the water on her feet catapulted her into another soul-time when she stood in agony in a river of initiation carefully watched over by the chief of the clan. Image after image showed up in rapid succession on the screen of her inner eye. The images of water were creating memories of betrayal and fear and despair. Someone was calling to her across a river, someone bright and beautiful. Someone from the world of the Sidhe. She reached forward and immediately the image faded and she woke with a start. She sat up, dazed and confused, not knowing where she was for a second or two.

Time After Time Before Time

"What is happening to me?" she asked herself. "Where are these dreams coming from? Are they dreams or remembrances? They feel so real." She stood up quickly, anxious now to be on her way again. A small group of buzzards were circling in the sky near her and their bright mewling cries felt soothing.

Within another couple of hours, she had reached her journey's end. The ruined village of Kilbrona lay before her. An eerie silence and stillness wrapped itself around the landscape as if nature herself wanted to shroud human eyes and ears from the awfulness and horrors that had happened here. She could just about make out the shape of what would have been the houses of the villagers. All around were the burnt-out remains of what had once been homes. The sense of desolation was in the very air. Saoirse knew from what her grandfather had told her that when the people were driven from their pitiful homes because they couldn't pay the rent, their houses were immediately set alight by the soldiers to prevent other homeless families from finding shelter.

Saoirse sought out the graveyard where many of the famine victims had been hastily buried. It was now completely neglected and overgrown. Somewhere among the briars and the nettles her grandfather's baby sister had been buried. She lowered herself onto the ground as the awfulness of what had happened here crowded her mind. It wasn't hard to imagine a line of skeletal starving figures leaving this village, abandoning the bloated bodies of their unburied dead on the side of the road. Images of women and children lying crouched together in the throes of agonizing death, their lips green from eating grass, flooded her inner vision. She covered her face with her hands as if she could obliterate the de-humanizing images that this landscape was revealing to her. When she could no longer bear to be shown such unimaginable suffering, she lifted her face from her hands and let out a blood curdling howl. She began to scream "Why, why!" over and over and over again until her voice was raw and hoarse. Her breathing became harsh and gasping, as wave of nausea made her retch. Her knees buckled as she fell forwards. Her whole body began to convulse with fear and pain.

    Somewhere, within the velvet fragility of her mind she was taking on the suffering of her ancestors. She made no effort to control what was happening to her body as the mental and psychic images created a corresponding reaction in her body. Finally she lay exhausted and quiet, as the images slowly loosened their grip on her sensitivities. She prayed for the souls of those who had lived and died in this place, for those who had left and died along the road. She prayed for all those who had died in the coffin ships while they clung to the hope of a new life. She prayed for her grandfather who had endured and survived the terrible suffering. Finally, she prayed for herself that she also might learn to endure.

    She stood and raised her hands in blessing, an action totally uncharacteristic for her. Her voice rang out loud and strong. She held her hands aloft, allowing the grace of the Divine to sweep over the land. She felt all the heaviness and sorrow leave her mind and heart and soul. Something had shifted inside her. She had completed her task. It was no longer part of her soul journey to take on the sorrows of her kinsfolk. She picked up her things and walked away with a lightened step. She covered the ground quickly and was back in Westport as darkness fell.

Her lodgings were above O'Donnell's pub in the town centre. That evening, while sitting in the back room of the bar, she listened to the town's folk discussing news of the escalating war in Europe, and how the struggle for freedom in Ireland must continue. She noticed an older man sitting alone quietly drinking his pint. He had an air of tattered elegance about him, even though he looked as if he had slept in the clothes he was wearing. He had a shock of thick white hair which curled behind his ears. This gave him a bit of a roguish look which was further enhanced by a pair of the palest blue eyes she had ever seen. It was his hands though which drew Saoirse's attention.

They were totally unblemished, long fine fingers curling round his glass, and were certainly not the hands of a working man or farmer.

"Why don't you come and sit by me so you can have a closer look?" he said with a wide smile on his face.

Saoirse blushed deeply as she realised that she must have been staring at him for some time. She left her own table and stood before him.

"I'm so very sorry. It was rude of me to stare at you in such a manner."

"Think nothing of it. Sit down here opposite me so that I can get a good look at you, then we can call it quits."

With that he laughed and Saoirse found herself responding likewise.

"My name is Mactus, a name which is unusual even in Ireland. It has associations with the fairy kingdom and I'm told by those who have the sight that it is the given name to the king of the fairies. I fancy my mother knew a thing or two about the other world to give me a name like that." He stopped in mid-sentence because all the colour had drained from Saoirse's face. He leaned over and touched her hand.

"What's the matter my dear?"

"Nothing really, it's just your name. When I heard you say it, it threw me into a bit of a spin. I think I've heard it before somewhere."

"Not to worry my dear, fairy names can have that effect on some people."

The barman brought over some drinks and asked, "Will you be giving us a few tunes tonight Mactus?"

"I will, and gladly." He reached down the side of the settle and brought up a battered fiddle case. As he prepared the bow, everyone in the bar turned in his direction and all talking ceased.

He began to play a slow haunting traditional air that filled the room with sweetness. When the last few notes faded away, nobody stirred for a moment or two. Then the applause rang out. Immediately, Mactus changed the mood by playing a set of three very fast reels. He played for thirty minutes or more without stopping, his eyes closed and his feet tapping out the rhythms. The atmosphere in the room was electric with the sense of heightened energy he had created with his music. When he finally put down his fiddle, the applause was thunderous. Saoirse's eyes were shining with appreciation.

"That was truly amazing!" she began. Mactus put up his hand to stop her saying anything further.

"Sure, 'twas nothing at all. Do you have music yourself?" he asked of her.

"Oh, no, but my great grandfather played the harp. He sold it to pay for his family's passage to America during the great Famine. My grandfather, who was a young lad at the time remembers that the harp even had a name. When

Time After Time Before Time

great grandfather wanted to play he would call out 'Can someone bring me the Turlough?' A bit strange, wouldn't you agree, to give an instrument a name and a very odd name at that?"

Mactus looked at her kindly and said, "Let me tell you a story, my dear."

"There was once a young man who was the most famous harper this country has known. He lived a long time ago and he was the last of the great Irish bards. He travelled around the country composing melodies, playing for his patrons to earn his keep. This harper was blind. He had been struck by small pox at the age of eighteen and subsequently lost his sight. His name was Turlough O'Carolan. So now you know why your great grandfather called his own harp the Turlough. He was honouring the great musician and composer who had gone before him."

Saoirse was delighted to hear this. She felt comfortably at ease, and over the course of the evening she told Mactus about her recent experiences of a somewhat mystical but troubling nature.

"There is nothing to be afraid of, my dear," he said to her in a fatherly way. "What you are experiencing are past life memories. Sometimes these flashbacks come to us in dreams, or in our waking moments when we are in a heightened state of awareness. They can be activated when we find ourselves in a particular landscape which has retained memories of what has gone before. In such landscapes, the veil between the seen and the unseen worlds is very thin. Or sometimes a particular object we come across can be the trigger which will part the veils for us. You have a strong ancestral connection with this land and from what you have told me, seeing the Book of Kells in Trinity College was the trigger which allowed your latent psychic abilities to come forward. Do not suppress these abilities and do not be afraid of them. They have been activated within you for a reason in this current lifetime. Your soul has carried over memories of significant events that occurred in some of your past lives. You are not going mad or hallucinating. In fact, you are blessed to be able to retrieve some of these memories. What you do with them is entirely up to you. You can either use them to further your soul's purpose within this lifetime, or you can distort this present time by trying to figure out intellectually what happened to you in past lives."

Mactus paused here and locked onto Saoirse's eyes. She felt she had dropped down deep into a warm pool of unconditional love.

He continued, "I want you to listen very carefully now. We have been brought together this evening for a purpose. We have met before in another lifetime. You don't have to believe this but what you should understand and accept is that you have the gift of 'sight'. You have spent a great deal of time in this lifetime listening to the stories of the fairy folk from your grandfather. None of these stories seemed strange to you at the time because you have an affinity with the beings of the unseen worlds from a previous lifetime."

Saoirse looked at him in total astonishment.

"How do you know this, and how can you be so sure of what you are telling me?"

"Because, like yourself, I too have had similar experiences. The only difference between us is that I have had many years to assimilate and integrate what I've been shown. I will tell you something else which you need to understand."

Time After Time Before Time

He leaned in closer, lowered his voice and said, "It's vital for your own personal safety that you learn to protect yourself from all unwanted influences. He noticed the immediate look of fear on her face. "Do not be afraid! I will teach you all you need to know to keep you safe. But not now. Can you meet me tomorrow morning just before dawn on the top of the hill? Take the path which leads up from the river. I will be waiting for you.

She nodded and asked, "Why are you taking such trouble with me? You don't know me and we only met for the first time this evening."

He flashed her a brilliant smile. "Ah, my dear, that's where you're wrong." He stood up, hoisted his fiddle onto his back, and was out the door before she had a chance to query what he had just said.

Time After Time Before Time

Chapter Seventeen

The rain was cold on her skin as she made her way up the hill. A pre-dawn mist swirled around the top and was steadily making its way downwards. The hill turned out to be far steeper and more challenging than Saoirse had expected. The town was silent and dark and few people were up and about at such an early hour. Even the birds were still sleeping. She crossed the river and slowly made her way upwards, regretting that she hadn't had something to eat before she left her lodgings. The mist grew thicker, making it almost impossible at times to see the well-trodden path clearly. Now and again she heard animal noises in the undergrowth which startled her. Not for the first time did she question the wisdom of agreeing to meet a man she hardly knew on the top of a hill at dawn.

Suddenly she was enveloped in an impenetrable dark cloud. She could feel a rising sense of panic pushing upwards from her solar plexus. She couldn't see the path in either direction but she carried on regardless for a few hundred metres. Just as suddenly as it came down, the mist cleared and she realised with horror that she was standing right at a sheer edge and would have tumbled over if she had taken another step forward. All colour leached from her face as she cautiously took a step back from the edge. The mist closed about her again just as suddenly as it had lifted and she startled as she heard a voice behind her, "Be still. Don't take another step. It is I, Mactus." His arms caught her as she sank to her knees. He knelt down in front of her and said gently, "Calm yourself. Control your breathing."

After a few minutes she felt sufficiently recovered to stand up. The mist had mysteriously cleared once again. She held his gaze for a long moment, then she lifted her hand and slapped his face hard. He laughed outright and astonished her by saying, "That's more like it. That's the sort of energy you need to keep yourself safe." He turned on his heels, saying, "Follow me."

She obeyed him without hesitation because she didn't want to be left alone again. They continued upwards without speaking. Mactus was a confident easy climber and at times she had difficulty keeping up with the fast pace he set. When she reached the top, hot, tired and largely out of breath, he was sitting cross-legged on the grass, calmly waiting for her. He beckoned for her to sit down opposite him. He waited for her to regain her breath. She realised that there was a sense of great personal power coming from him and she knew without fully understanding why, that he was someone she could trust with her life.

"Please close your eyes, keep your spine erect, and be still in your body. We will sit quietly for a while together and we will wait."

A deep velvet silence grew between them. Mactus began to hum gently. Saoirse became drowsy. As the sweet sounds entered her body, she began to dream. She saw herself in an ethereal domain where everything about her radiated exquisite light and beauty. The trees glowed, the rivers sparkled and jumped with life, the rocks were alive and she could hear the grasses growing. Amongst all this beauty she saw a tall man whom she knew to be her father. He came forward and took both her hands.

"You are a child of the Sidhe, you belong in the fairy kingdom with us. But because we love you, we can let you go back into the world of the humans. I will protect you through all your lifetimes. Take with you the gift of deep seeing. Use it well." He placed his cloak around her and vanished before she could call out.

She woke with a start to find herself looking directly into the eyes of Mactus. There was a radiance about his face which felt warm and tender. Tears slowly rolled down her cheeks as she said in a tiny voice

"It was you, wasn't it? You were my father in another place in another time."

He nodded his head. "We have been given the gift of being able to recognise one another. Fate has brought us together again for this brief moment in this lifetime so that you can learn another lesson. Your gift of far-seeing is now coming into its full power and I have come to teach you how to protect yourself from any untoward influences. Let's begin with your journey up the hill this morning. When you got lost in the mist, your first reaction was fear. This is not good. Fear leaves you vulnerable and allows your auric field to be penetrated. Anything that is not of the light will use fear as a gateway into your energy system. What you need to do whenever you become lost, threatened, or under attack physically, emotionally, mentally or spiritually, is to first take control of any fears arising. Then you need to make sure that your systems of protection are in place."

"Protection?" said Saoirse. "I don't really understand what you mean."

"I want you to give your full attention to what I am about to tell you. You are aware of the forces of light and love in the world, but you also need to be aware of the opposing forces of darkness and destruction. You are a very unique human because you have a deep knowledge of other worlds. You have seen beyond the veil which separates our world from the world of the Sidhe. You have carried this knowledge deep in your soul and the time has now come for you wake up to who you really are."

"Whatever do you mean?" quizzed Saoirse. "I know exactly who I am. I'm Saoirse O'Haloran. I was born in America, and in a short while I will begin studying at Trinity College Dublin."

Mactus raised one eyebrow. "That is merely a label attached to your persona. Tell me, how do you explain your reaction when you first set eyes on the Book of Kells? How come you can actually see and experience the horrors of what happened in this land during the Great Famine? How come you have visions of a beautiful light filled kingdom where everything is gentle and where everyone has special powers? I will tell you why. Your soul has safeguarded these memories until you entered upon a lifetime where you would have access to them. That time is now. Cherish your gift and let it guide your actions from here on out. It will not make for an easy life but I can teach you how to look after yourself so that you keep your energy pure and strong. But first let us have something to eat, because if I judge correctly you will not have had breakfast before you left your lodgings this morning."

He took a chunk of cheese and some bread out of his satchel and offered some to her. As they ate together, the rays of the rising sun filled the sky with ribbons of pink and purple. They watched in companionable silence until the whole sky was ablaze. When all the food was finished Mactus motioned for Saoirse to stand up.

"Look around you," he told her. "See and appreciate the glory and the beauty you see every day in the natural world. This world is alive with elemental forces who will work in partnership with us humans if we cooperate. You are fortunate to be able to see the energetic beings in water which give it its life-giving qualities. These undines love to jump and sparkle and without them we would not be able to sustain our own life force. Similarly, with the sylphs of the air, and the fire salamanders. And, of course, the earth spirits. You have brought into this lifetime a deep memory of how beautiful life was when you lived in close communion with the elemental kingdom. Most humans think these beings exist only in the pages of childrens' story books. But you know better. You know that when you get flashes of a beautiful light-filled world where anything is possible, that you have actually experienced this in another lifetime. You are not imagining this, or engaging in wishful thinking.

    Be grateful for this knowledge. Gratitude is one of the keys which help to keep the human heart open. Enter each day with the intention of seeing the very best in every person you meet. However, when you intuit that you are in the company of someone who is not filled with light and love, you must immediately protect yourself. Ask your higher self to wrap you in an invisible cloak of protection and all will be well. Set aside a time each day to sit in stillness and listen to the voice of your soul. Guard your gift from prying eyes and use it only in the service of love and light and the evolution of humanity. Never boast about what you can see and choose your companions wisely. Cultivate those friends who will become your spiritual companions. They will come into your life without any effort on your part. They will be your support in those times when you feel downcast or misunderstood. Go about your daily tasks but always remember that your soul is constantly steering you towards the work of the Spirit. May Divine Love be yours and may it guide you safely throughout your days. Mark this next phase of your life's work with a spiritually meaningful gesture to set your intention. Our work here is done. We shall not meet again."

    Mactus finally stopped speaking. He looked at Saoirse with infinite love in his eyes, then promptly turned and quickly began to make his way down the hill. She remained standing perfectly still resisting the impulse to chase down after him. She continued to look at him until finally he was lost from her view. She suddenly felt bereft as if an invisible cord had been severed between them. She sat down and tried to digest everything that she had been told. She felt incredibly tired and emotionally drained, and laid herself down on the grass to feel the heat of the sun warming her face, drifting into a dreamless sleep. She awoke two hours later feeling completely invigorated and full of determination.

Time After Time Before Time

Chapter Eighteen

Saoirse sat motionless next to the window in her small flat in Leeson Street, in the central part of Dublin, clutching a single sheet of paper.

She let the letter fall to the floor as the first shock waves crashed over her. In the two years since her father had sailed without her back to America, not once had she received a letter from him. Her mother had given her regular news of home and her grandfather had also written to her several times. As soon as she saw her father's handwriting on the envelope, she knew immediately that something bad had happened. He had written to tell her that her beloved grandfather Seamus had passed away peacefully in his sleep. She opened the small wardrobe where she kept her few clothes and pulled out the tiny wooden box where she kept her grandfather's Celtic cross. She ran her fingers tenderly over it as she prayed for his soul. She thanked him aloud for igniting in her the desire to walk the path of mystery and to seek out the numinous. She cried then as she remembered the horrors of his early life in Ireland during the hungry years.

Ever since her meeting with Mactus she had been studying hard at college and tried to keep herself grounded in everyday life as he had suggested. As she sat quietly grieving, her mind drifted back to the pilgrimage she had made to the summit of *Croagh Patrick* [25] just before her first term at college. Mactus had told her to undertake a journey

---

[25] Ireland's sacred pilgrimage mountain

Time After Time Before Time

as an outward expression of her inner intention. Croagh Patrick was the most sacred mountain in Ireland and thus felt well suited to her purpose. She began her ascent quite early in the morning and was surprised to see that she was not alone. The going was tough and she paused frequently to slow her breathing down. She was amazed to see quite elderly people walking alongside her. She drifted into conversation with some of them and discovered that many people who climbed the mountain did so as a penance for sins committed. They believed that reaching the top of the holy mountain would give them absolution. She heard stories of how at special times of the year some people ascend the mountain on their knees as an extra penitential gesture. She noticed that at certain points on the path, her fellow walkers made a circuit around cairns of stones which were known as 'the stations'. There was a set ritual to be performed at each station which finished with a decade of the rosary. Saoirse had no idea what was going on but she decided to join in nevertheless. She fell into step with an elderly woman who was walking alone. After they had circumnavigated the first station three times, the older woman introduced herself.

"I'm Kathleen McNamara" she said as she extended her hand to Saoirse. "And what's a young slip of a thing like yourself doing climbing up Croagh Patrick. Sure, you're far too young to have dark blots on your soul. Not like some of these old codgers," she said, nodding her head in the direction of the other pilgrims.

Saoirse laughed aloud and introduced herself in turn. It turned out that Kathleen had been climbing this mountain once a year for the last thirty years or more.

"But why keep on doing it?" asked Saoirse. "Surely once is enough?"

Time After Time Before Time

"That's where you're wrong my dear." Each time I haul myself up this mountain I edge a little bit closer to finding whatever it is I've been searching for all my adult life. Sometimes when I've come back down off the mountain, I can let go of certain frustrations that have blighted my life. Somehow this mountain teaches me about what is important, what I need to change, what I need to let go of, and what I need to forgive. You see, my dear, I'm not just climbing a mountain, I'm taking a clean hard look at myself with every step. Not in a chest thumping sort of way but I'm clearing myself out all the same. I can allow my broken places to come out for an airing. Ah, sure don't listen to me blathering on about broken places. What would a young woman like yourself know about brokenness, when you've hardly just begun to live."

Something in the look that Saoirse gave her stopped her in her tracks.

"Shall we sit a while, and give our legs a rest?" Saoirse nodded. The two women sat side by side, legs stretched out in front of them with their backs to the mountain. Saoirse gasped when she looked down at the view from her vantage position on the mountain. She could see, stretched out below her the whole of Clew bay and the hundreds of tiny islands sitting like jewels in the sea. For several minutes neither woman spoke. Saoirse could feel her consciousness begin to shift as she felt that strange but familiar bodily tingling which was signalling to her that she was about to have an out of body experience again. At the same moment she remembered what Mactus had told her about taking charge of her abilities. She took a few deep breaths and willed herself to stay totally in the present moment.

Kathleen pointed to the magnificent bay below them and said in a strangely quieter voice, "That is where so many of the famine people sailed away from these shores. That bay you see below you and this mountain hold between them, the memories of all that pain and suffering. When I climb this mountain, I can meditate on their suffering and somehow this places my own brokenness into its true perspective. That is another reason I make this yearly pilgrimage. Saoirse nodded and her eyes glistened with tears.

Kathleen looked hard at Saoirse and took her measure. She noted the quiet inner strength and the calm quiet exterior of this beautiful young woman with the American accent. She reached for Saoirse's hands.

"You are a long way from your earthly home but you are finding your way to your true home. Those who have gone before you are never very far away. They are always ready to help you. All you need to do is to ask for their aid whenever you need it."

"I'm not sure I understand what you are telling me."

"Yes you do," replied Kathleen, "you can hear the voice of your ancestors at any time of your choosing. But I can see by your physique that you need some bodily building up."

Reaching into her brown canvas bag which was lying at her feet, she dropped into Saoirse's lap a tiny phial.

"This will help you fall into a long dreamless sleep, whenever you need to switch off from prolonged exhausting visions."

"How do you know about my visions?"

Kathleen smiled and replied, "You can carry on up now by yourself. I would like to sit here alone for a while."

Saoirse took the phial and headed off up the path. After some time, she turned and looked at Kathleen sitting motionless in the same spot. An elderly woman with a mane of thick grey hair falling down her back. She had a blue scarf tied around her neck which was the same colour as the skirt she was wearing. Even from some distance away, she could see that Kathleen's back was ramrod straight. There was a thought itching away at the back of Saoirse's mind that told her there was something vaguely familiar about Kathleen but she couldn't grasp it. She carried on upwards sometimes leaning her hands on her knees as she struggled to get her breath. She had already slid several times on the loose scree and her knees were badly grazed.

"I hate this," she said out loud, as she lost her footing yet again and slid back down a couple of feet.

"Don't try so hard and you'll be all right," a familiar voice said beside her. Kathleen was standing next to her and she reached down to give Saoirse a hand up.

"How on earth did you get up here? When I last looked, you were still sitting way down below where I had left you."

Hoots of deep throated laughter erupted from Kathleen.

"I know this mountain like I do my own body. You've got to take your time. Lift your eyes up now and again and you will find your feet will still know what to do."

They walked on in companionable silence for some time. They were soon cresting the shoulder of the mountain and the going became a little bit easier. Saoirse sneaked a sideways look at Kathleen and a sudden piercing memory flooded every cell of her body. She grabbed the older woman by the arm and pulled her round to face her. "I've had dreams of when I was a young child rolling down a hill on a warm summer's day and a beautiful woman catching me at the bottom and throwing me up in the air. Just now, you reminded me of that woman. I feel as if I really know you." A shadow passed across Kathleen's face. "Aye, said Kathleen, we are all connected. Nothing is ever lost or forgotten in the human psyche. Our souls retain all the memories of all the lifetimes we have ever lived. So, it is not strange after all that you and I find ourselves on this mountain together and feeling as if we know each other." Saoirse felt eerily calm and rooted to the spot as Kathleen continued.

"You see my dear, I too have visions like yourself and this morning I feel I have been sent to guide you. I have a memory and a picture in my head of a beautiful young child who was taken away from me long, long ago. It haunts my dreamworld. You remind me of that child."

The two women embraced wordlessly. Kathleen held Saoirse's face between her hands and in a soft low voice said, "Do not look to the past. Find your meaning and your love in this lifetime because this is what you are called upon to do. The past has taught us how to live in the present. As soon as we are born, all past experiences are forgotten so we can live in the present with freedom to choose. But some of us, like you and me retain memories which can be stimulated by meeting certain people. This is happening right now between us my dear. It is enough that we have met like this. We don't have to pursue anything further. Our souls have worked something out which was set in motion a long time ago. We are each very blessed and privileged to have some awareness of our past lives. But we must guard against letting the past infiltrate our lives now and so distort the present. Today, here on this sacred mountain, we have been granted a very rare numinous experience. We have been allowed to see beyond the veil separating the seen from the unseen and for that we need to give thanks. Making our pilgrimage feels like a fitting way to acknowledge our gratitude."

She planted a kiss on Saoirse's head and said, "Right, my girl, let's be carrying on, shall we?" Saoirse had to shake her head several times in order to bring herself back to her surroundings.

Kathleen reached into her bag and offered her an apple, saying, "It's always good to eat something after a change in consciousness, as food makes the body heavy and grounds it." She took another one out of her bag for herself and munched on it noisily. The two women walked on in companionable silence until they could see the summit not too far above them. As they neared the top a thick mist began to roll in making the air suddenly cold and damp. Saoirse sat down and leaned her back against the wall of the tiny chapel on the summit. Kathleen rested beside her, fingering her rosary beads. Saoirse tried to find the words to pray but her heart was too full. She sat with closed eyes and began to tune into her own internal energy systems. She waited while her breath slowed to its normal natural rhythm. She found that her mind was clear of all thoughts. She wanted for nothing; she was happy simply being quiet in that moment. She was totally at peace.

It was the cold seeping into her which caused her to rouse herself. Kathleen was nowhere in sight. Saoirse immediately understood that whatever had passed between them was over so she had no need to feel let down by the lack of a farewell gesture. Other pilgrims now joined her on the summit. Saoirse hung around and waited until they were ready to begin their descent. She followed closely on their heels because she felt suddenly very alone. When she finally left the mountain behind, she had a strong intuition that her fate was sealed. She knew from meeting both Mactus and Kathleen that her destiny lay in Ireland and that she would always be protected by the spirit of the ancestors.

Chapter Nineteen

During her years at Trinity College, the struggle for Irish Independence continued, culminating in the Civil War which set brother against brother. During those turbulent years Saoirse immersed herself in the world of ancient manuscripts with a single-mindedness which earned her the highest honours in her graduate studies. Her area of expertise centred around the period of Irish and Scottish history when the Book of Kells was begun. She continued to live in the same small flat in Leeson Street, and made the short journey on foot to the college every day.

Her need for solitude had steadily grown since her encounter with Mactus. She now understood that he was a great spiritual teacher and initiate and he had been the cause of a permanent change in her. She avoided all romantic encounters, which caused quite a lot of speculation among her colleagues. She was a startlingly beautiful woman with a soft rounded figure which drew admiring looks from the opposite sex wherever she went. However, Saoirse rebuffed all advances, and continued to go home alone to her flat each evening. Mostly she stayed late working in the department, always searching for that elusive piece of information, the golden key, which would open up the mystery of the ancients for her. She had several intuitive flashes over the years that the treasure she was searching for lay in the far western isles. During her long years of dedicated study her fascination with the Book of Kells and St. Colmcille of Iona intensified.

As part of her post-doctoral research work, she took herself off to Donegal. She wished to immerse herself in the landscape where St. Colmcille was born and where he had spent his early years. Her fascination with this saint went far beyond scholarly interest. She felt a very deep love for this saintly man who had lived many thousands of years ago. She actually felt at times that she known him, had broken bread with him, had travelled with him and had been by his side at his passing. On one of those rare occasions when a glass or two of good red wine had loosened her tongue, she let it slip to a colleague that she believed she had known St. Colmcille in a previous lifetime. Her colleague laughed outright at such a preposterous notion but stopped when he saw the look of pain on Saoirse's face. "Surely you can't actually believe such nonsense? It's a crazy idea," he said. Immediately realising she had made a cardinal error in speaking of her inner world to sceptics, Saoirse laughed and said, "Of course you're right. It is a crazy idea. I was really just pulling your leg. It must be the wine speaking." But was it a crazy idea? In her daily meditations and quiet periods of reflection she felt an almost visceral connection with St. Colmcille. She had read everything that had been published about him. She had carefully picked her way through all the material relating to his younger days before his departure for the sacred Isle of Iona. But she was experiencing an ever-increasing inner connection to him which no amount of reading or study could account for. Now she needed to physically walk in the same landscape where he had spent the early part of his life.

And so it was, that during the Christmas holidays while most people were celebrating with family and friends, Saoirse found herself alone in Glen Colmcille in West Donegal. Arrangements had been made through the

Time After Time Before Time

university before she left Dublin to make contact with Professor Seth O'Neill, one of the foremost authorities on early Irish Christianity. He was to be her guide and mentor in the next stage of her research. Saoirse had initially turned down his generous offer to put her up in his own home. But when he explained that at Christmas time in the Glen, every house would be full with returning relatives for the Christmas holidays, she accepted his hospitality. Now however, as the train hurtled towards County Donegal she wondered how she would cope working with the professor and living in his house. She was met at the station by a middle-aged woman, who introduced herself as Sinead, the house keeper at *Carraig Fada*. In no time at all Saoirse, together with her single suitcase and satchel, were quickly loaded onto the buggy. The light was beginning to fade and the wind was getting up as they set off. Sinead handled the horse and buggy with an experienced hand and they made steady progress. Conversation was almost impossible because of the wind which was rapidly gathering momentum. By the time they reached the farm, it was completely dark. The house lights were a welcome relief and it wasn't until she had alighted from the buggy that Saoirse realised how tired and hungry she was. Even in the dark, the house appeared rather large but a very welcome sight.

The large wooden front door was thrown wide open and a middle-aged man appeared on the doorstep. He stretched out his hand to Saoirse.

"*Fáilte go Carraig Fada!* [26] You are very welcome indeed. Come away in out of the cold," he said as he picked up her bag and satchel leading the way into the house. She followed Professor O'Neill into a high-ceilinged sitting

---

[26]   Welcome to Carraig Fada

room and was practically knocked off her feet by the advances of two friendly large Irish wolfhounds. Responding to a mere click of his fingers, the two dogs went back to their customary places by the side of the fireplace. "Please come and warm yourself," he said indicating a large comfortable armchair. "I will go and check on tea."

While he was gone, Saoirse gazed around the room and was surprised at the colourful, rather feminine furnishings. The floor-to-ceiling sash windows were curtained in heavy, beautifully embroidered curtains which immediately drew her eye. Similarly, the chairs were comfortable and upholstered in equally sumptuous material. The light from the fire reflected off the highly polished side tables and the overall effect of the room was comfort and beauty, and definitely arranged by a woman. She settled herself deeper into the chair and was startled awake by the clatter of cups and saucers. Saoirse was mortified to realise that she had fallen asleep even if only for a short while. As she began to stammer an apology, the professor stopped her short.

"Please don't apologise, you have had a long journey and you must be very tired. After our tea, Sinead will show you to your room. Dinner will be served at eight o'clock."

Alone in her room at last, she unpacked her few clothes and lay down on the bed. Sleep didn't come but waves of loneliness did. She hadn't seen her parents or her brother since she first visited Ireland. Her life had been so consumed by her studies and her own inner developmental work that she rarely allowed herself the time to dwell on their lives. But tonight, in this house, where a woman's touch was evident in every nook and cranny, Saoirse was flooded with memories of her own childhood and family home in America. Her body ached for the comfort and touch of her mother's arms around her. She thought back to her first sexual encounter and how easy her passionate nature was aroused. How did she succeed in suppressing all that passion? Ever since the moment when she had first glimpsed the Book of Kells, she had accepted that her chosen path was indeed a hard, lonely and barren road. She had cauterised her own innate passionate and sexual nature in order to give herself wholly to her work. But tonight, lying on her bed in a stranger's home two days before Christmas, she was overwhelmed by a cruel longing for all those things which she had eliminated from her life.

"Why does it have to be this way?" she asked herself out loud. "Why can't I have it all? Why can't I have a man who loves me and who will grow old with me? Why has my work taken any hope of a normal life away from me?"

As soon as she heard herself saying the word *normal*, she felt better. She knew she would never be normal in the everyday sense of that word. Her raised consciousness had allowed her access into the realms of the extra-ordinary and her ability to glimpse the luminosity of rarefied energetic spaces had given her the strength to pursue her path. Tonight, however, her very fragile human nature was asking for attention. She had failed to love her own body and had viewed it as an entrapment which would ultimately pull her away from her spiritual path. She knew beyond a shadow of a doubt, that in previous lifetimes, especially the one where she dwelt with Mactus in the fairy realm, that she had not had free choice. Now in this lifetime, her biggest challenge it seems, is to be able to work with the power of choice. She had chosen to eschew romantic entanglements. Her train of thought was brought to a close by Sinead knocking on her door to tell her that dinner was ready.

The dining room was in-keeping with the rest of the house, tastefully decorated, with the same patterned embroidered curtains she had so admired in the sitting room. She sat opposite the professor and they ate their soup in companionable silence. While Sinead was serving up the main course Saoirse asked if Mrs. O'Neill would be joining them. She sensed the change in the atmosphere almost as soon as the words left her mouth. The silence that followed was relieved by the clock in the hall chiming the quarter hour. When the silence settled in again the professor cleared his throat noisily.

"My wife died several years ago."

Then he carried on eating, indicating that the subject was closed. Saoirse's ultra-sensitive nature immediately alerted her to the level of unspoken pain which was being radiated out from the man sitting opposite her.

"He has suffered greatly," she told herself, "over and beyond the death of his wife."

She carried on eating her meal which she found to be surprisingly good. But simultaneously she was working extremely hard to keep herself grounded and totally present. Her senses were on full alert mode. She could feel that familiar tingling sensation at the back of her head which signalled that she was about to enter an altered state of consciousness. She focused on not allowing it to happen. However, try as she might, the sensations all around her head were so strong that she was pulled into the current and entered a different reality.

Chapter Twenty

The woman was in a grass hut lying on a warm soft covering. Although she knew the ground outside was covered in deep snow, here in the birthing hut the air was stiflingly hot. The pains had been with her all through the night and still the child didn't come. Her screams could be heard throughout the camp. Her husband had prepared his special herbs to give her relief, but to no avail. He sat motionless outside the hut for the three days she laboured. Her agony tore at his heart. When the birthing women at last came outside to hand him his child, he knew by their faces that all was lost. Without even a glance at the child, he brushed past them and went to her. She lay on her back, her unseeing eyes wide open, her recent agony still etched on her once beautiful face. He gathered her in his arms and roared out his grief into the silent whitened world. He kept vigil with her all through that day and into the night.

Suddenly the scene shifted and Saoirse saw the same man in another lifetime where his skills as an herbalist were much in demand. He specialised in helping women who were having difficulties conceiving. He frequently travelled on horseback up into the mountain villages where he diagnosed illnesses and distributed potions to the young women to help them when their time came to deliver their child. He always travelled alone and this suited him very well. He had a deep love of solitude and wild open spaces. He was content with his own company. He liked to sit in the mountains and watch the buzzards circling overhead. Their mewling calls always reminded him of something which, try as he might, he could never quite grasp. Saoirse gave an involuntary gasp. She realised she was watching a past life of Professor O'Neill.

"Glad you're back with us," a voice in front of her said. "What happened?" she asked in a bewildered voice. "You seem to have fainted. Here, drink this," offering her a glass of water. She accepted gratefully and immediately lost the out-of-body sensation. She was back in the dining room but she retained the memory of Professor O'Neill's past lifetimes. When the meal was finished, they retired to the sitting room and the remainder of the evening passed without further incident.

The following morning the household awakened to a muffled world. There had been a heavy snowfall in the night, and large white flakes continued to fall. When Saoirse drew back her bedroom curtains, the world beyond her window was dazzlingly beautiful. Over breakfast, the professor announced that they might be cut off for a few days if the snow continued. Once the breakfast dishes were cleared away, he steered Saoirse towards his study where they would make a start on the research she had come to do. As it was Christmas Eve, she felt she ought to apologise for intruding on him during the holiday season. He looked at her with a raised eyebrow before replying.

"I have a feeling we are two of a kind. Christmas means very little to me. I have no family to celebrate with. My work is what matters. Shall we get started?"

He drew out a chair for her opposite his desk, crossed his arms over his chest and said, "Begin!" Saoirse was a bit taken aback by the bluntness of his tone but she obeyed. "Well, she began, I want to further my research into the life of St. Colmcille.

Time After Time Before Time

"Please stop there," interrupted the professor. "I know why you're here, but what I need to discover before we work together is who you really are."

"You know who I am." She quickly replied, "The university will have forwarded all my credentials to you."

"I'm not interested in your qualifications. You are not your qualifications. I saw what happened to you last night at the supper table. It was immediately apparent to me that you entered a strong altered state of consciousness and saw images and scenes from past lives, your own or those of others. Am I right?"

"How can you possibly know what was happening to me? Why do you not believe that I simply fainted?"

"Because, I too have similar abilities. I immediately recognised from your body language that you were struggling to stay in the present moment last evening. You shifted into a different reality as soon as I mentioned my wife. Can I ask what was revealed to you?"

Saoirse took a long hard look at the man sitting opposite her and knew she could trust him.

I saw you in some of your previous lifetimes," she began. "I saw that you have always been a healer. In one of your lifetimes you couldn't save the wife you loved from dying in childbirth. You were away hunting when she went into labour. Your potions couldn't save her. You lost your power and your soul has carried forward that feeling of loss into many lifetimes, including this one."

The professor gave an involuntary gasp at this. Saoirse continued.

"In subsequent lifetimes you tried to help as many women as you could by supplying them with herbs and potions. Your soul is still working with loss. You have learned a lot throughout many lifetimes but the lesson is still not complete. This same lesson has come up again in this life time. Am I right?"

When she finished speaking, her heart was beating wildly because for the first time she had taken responsibility for the use of her gift of inner seeing. The professor stared at Saoirse. Outside the window, she could hear Sinead calling to the dogs. The sound of her muffled footsteps in the snow seemed to heighten the silence in the room. Saoirse turned her head to the window and once again was struck by the beauty of the winter landscape. Nothing moved, the leafless trees stood sentinel in the fields, and even the birds were silent. It was Christmas Eve morning. After what seemed a long while, but must have been only a couple of minutes, the professor began to speak.

"I married young. Younger than you are now. My wife Catherine came from a well-known wealthy Dublin family. She was an only child and was used to having the privileges which money can bestow. To be fair to her though, she had a very sweet kind temperament which was what initially attracted me to her. We met around the time of the 1916 Rising and she was like a bright burning flame amid the chaos of that time. Although she was a very intelligent woman and had received the finest of educations, she had absolutely no idea what was going on in the political arena right under her nose. We married within three months of our first meeting and I was totally and utterly captivated by her. She always wore bright beautiful clothes which were sent over from the fashion houses of London and Paris. I had immersed myself in my studies and my baptism into her world of house parties and horse racing was intoxicating. While the city of Dublin lay in ruins after the Rising and war rumbled on in Europe, I willingly accompanied my young beautiful bride to every society event. I noticed the way other men looked at her as we entered a room and I felt a possessive pride in knowing that she was mine."

The professor stopped at this point and held his face in his hands. Saoirse involuntarily leaned towards him to offer comfort but recoiled when he removed his hands and she saw that his face was lit by an inner joy.

"My God!" he said, "she was so beautiful. The first thing anyone noticed about her was the blueness of her eyes and her wide smile. Her figure was statuesque and curvy and her elegance was accentuated by the expensive clothes she wore. She was never flashy but she certainly got noticed wherever she went. We set up home in one of the finest houses in Merrion Square. I continued with my research into Monastic Traditions in Ancient Ireland. My work quickly got me noticed and I was offered a professorship at Trinity College. Meanwhile, Catherine supervised the refurbishment of our home and continued to be the darling of Dublin society. I was a happy and contented man."

Suddenly his mood changed. He shot out of his chair and began thumping his fist against the wall.

"How could I have been such an idiot? How come she tricked me for so long?" As he continued to thump his fist against the wall, Saoirse became anxious that he would seriously damage his hand.

"Professor, please. You're scaring me."

He slumped back down heavily into his chair, and continued in a low bland voice.

"I came home from the university earlier than usual one afternoon and found Catherine slumped on the sofa in a state of high anxiety and distress. It was immediately obvious that something was terribly wrong. Her speech was slurred, and she wasn't making sense. I phoned for an ambulance and tried to make her comfortable in the meantime. Her skin was pale and sweaty, and despite the heat of the July afternoon she was shivering. I noticed that there were dark circles under her eyes and the skin on her face appeared thin and stretched. I sat with her through that long night in the hospital until I was told she was out of immediate danger. The kindly young doctor on duty informed me that my wife was suffering from an opium overdose and was most certainly an addict.

'Professor O'Neill, your wife is out of danger now but she will need a great deal of help to wean her off the drug.' I put my hand up to stop him going further because my heart was pounding in my chest. 'What on earth are you talking about. You must be mistaken.'

'There is no mistake I'm afraid. Your wife has imbibed an almost lethal amount of opium. There is evidence to suggest that she has been using opium for quite some time. She will sleep now and when she wakes, she may not recall with any real clarity what has just happened to her.'"

"I left the hospital in a frigid daze, unable to think clearly. My usual rational mind could not understand what exactly had just been said to me by the doctor. I absolutely did not want to accept what he had told me about my beautiful wife. I wandered aimlessly round the silent wet streets of Dublin trying to make sense of what had happened. I let myself into the house some hours later. I sat for a while without turning on the lights, going over and over what the doctor had told me. 'He can't be right' I told myself. 'Surely I would have noticed something was wrong. She's my wife for God's sake. We live in the same house.' But slowly the truth began to seep into my veins like a chill on a long winter's night. I recalled those occasions when her mood would swing very rapidly from gaiety to dark depression. She always reassured me that it was simply her time of the month and not to take any notice. I brought to mind also the many occasions I had returned from work to find she was still in her night clothes. One part of myself was still trying to find excuses for these occurrences, while the other part was being crushed by the weight of the mounting evidence."

"In a moment of intense fury with myself for not suspecting anything was out of kilter in our lives together, I threw the whisky glass I was nursing across the room. The sound of breaking glass brought me to my senses. I went into my wife's bedroom and I knew immediately the doctor was telling me the truth. The room was still reeking of that sweet floral smell which Catherine had always told me was her favourite perfume. In that instant, standing there in the middle of her luxurious boudoir, I knew she had been taking opium for a very long time. She had always, from the time we first met had that smell on her clothes and in her hair. But it wasn't perfume, it was the drug. Standing in the bedroom inhaling that killer smell, I hated the endless lies and episodes of deceit she had played me for. But I still loved her. How could I not? She was young, beautiful and the darling of high society. Surely my love could save her."

"While she was convalescing, I made arrangements to remove her from Dublin society and her sources of temptation. I resigned from my job at the university with immediate effect, citing illness as the reason. I contacted Sinead, the housekeeper at *Carraig Fada*, my family home in Donegal, which had passed to me on the death of my parents. I loved everything about the house and its surrounding landscape and I managed to spend holidays there several times a year. It always worked its calm peaceful magic on me. I was hoping it would do the same for Catherine. Sinead assured me the house would be well aired and in good order on our arrival."

"Catherine was calm and compliant on the journey up to Donegal. She had refused to give an opinion one way or the other when I outlined the plans for leaving the city. She simply fell into step with whatever I suggested. It was pitiful to see her spirit so broken and several times I questioned my decision to remove her from the city and everything she had known. She sat huddled in her train seat opposite me on the long journey, constantly wiping her nose and only spoke when questioned directly. She looked like a lonely vulnerable child and I longed to take her in my arms. Since coming out of the hospital she had pulled away from me physically and flinched if I even laid my hand on her arm. The hospital had explained to me that withdrawal from loved ones and intense feelings of shame and regret were common and normal after an overdose. I hoped that by bringing her to *Carraig Fada*, we would be able to make a fresh start in our marriage."

"The house was in perfect order when we arrived. Sinead had cooked a rather gorgeous dinner for us and had laid out places in the dining room. Catherine only picked at her food, though she hadn't eaten since breakfast. I was ravenous and felt rather ashamed of my hearty appetite. When Sinead brought dessert through, Catherine waved it away. I was about to cajole her into trying some when I remembered the advice the doctor gave me when I came to pick her up from the hospital. 'Your wife is going to have a difficult time for the next week or two. We have no way of predicting how severe her withdrawal symptoms will be and how long they might continue. Don't try to force her to eat. Her body will be making huge adjustments and she will take food when her body can handle it again.'"

Time After Time Before Time

"And so we passed those first few weeks together in *Carraig Fada*. The days were difficult enough with Catherine regularly swinging from episodes of calm stupor to periods of extreme agitation. The nights however, were almost unbearable for her, and were taking their toll on the whole household. She would sleep for very short periods, wake up in a sweat and begin vomiting. For several hours after each episode of throwing up, she would pace up and down. She moved around from room to room, banging doors and refusing to return to bed. She would finally go back to bed when exhaustion set in, only to sleep for one or two hours. Her body took the full brunt of her suffering."

"After three days of witnessing her extreme distress, I suggested to her that we go to the local hospital. She refused saying that if she could fight the cravings she would be cured. The first week rolled into the second. I cleaned up after her, and walked the floors with her, but mostly I prayed to a God I didn't really believe in, to help her. Towards the middle of the second week she had passed the crisis. She stopped begging me to take her back to Dublin and her suppliers of the drug. She slept for longer periods and began to eat again, albeit tiny amounts. She was still very agitated most of the time and unable to sit still for more than a few minutes at a time. But there were definite changes for the better. She began to take an interest in her appearance. Her beautiful city clothes no longer hugged her figure because of her weight loss and her hair had lost its sheen. But she was making an effort. She came down to breakfast now most mornings and accompanied me on a short daily walk."

"As the summer passed into autumn, she grew more robust and began to take an interest in the house and garden. We talked about her drug addiction once and once only. She assured me that it was now behind her and I was not to mention it again. Life at *Carraig Fada* shifted into a new pattern with Catherine's recovery and the return of her health and vigour. I continued working on my own research and spent most of the day shut up in my study. Catherine took it upon herself to completely change the décor of the house. I rather liked the house as it was, but I was so pleased that she had found something to occupy her time that I kept my misgivings to myself. All the way through that first autumn she organised and oversaw all the changes which transformed the house into the beautiful home it is today. She had an amazing capacity to put beautiful colours and objects together without the final effect looking contrived. As soon as the house was finished to her satisfaction, she embarked on a series of dinner parties. I knew most of the older families in the district and they were very pleased to be invited to our home to meet my wife. She very quickly became the darling of our rural social life. Everyone adored her and she seemed to be happy and content. However, I was not. I craved solitude and silence, and time away from people. Catherine was frightened of silence and needed the company of others. Perhaps this was her way of keeping her demons at bay. I began to grow very weary of the constant round of supper parties in my own home and our twice weekly trips into town simply because Catherine was bored."

"Things finally came to a head some months later. I asked her to cut back on our social engagements. She became furious and I'm ashamed to say that we engaged in a shouting match which revealed the true state of our marriage. She left for Dublin the following morning on the early train. I never saw her alive again. She died six months later from a massive overdose."

Time After Time Before Time

    The professor's face convulsed with unexpressed grief as he struggled with the effort to stay in control. Saoirse remained perfectly still. The professor, too, sat perfectly still with great silent tears running down his cheeks and into his collar. After some time, she passed him her handkerchief. He wiped his face and blew his nose loudly.

    "Thank you for listening. It all happened a long time ago."

Time After Time Before Time

Chapter Twenty-One

After some large slices of warm soda bread washed down with several cups of strong tea, Saoirse and the professor set out later that morning to walk the Colmcille turas [27]. The journey along the pilgrim route would take about three hours in total, along which they would pass fifteen sacred stopping places, known locally as stations. The professor took his dowsing rods and binoculars. Saoirse carried nothing except her grandfather's cross which continued to be a gateway into the ancient Celtic world for her. They left the house and turned sharply left, over a stile into the nearby field keeping their heads low against the swirling snow. In places the snowdrifts were building up rapidly and the going was tough. The professor led the way and Saoirse was surprised how fit and agile he seemed for a man in his late forties. Over their cups of tea in the kitchen, before they left the house, they had quickly dropped the pupil-mentor relationship in view of the professor's disclosure about his wife that morning. He asked Saoirse to call him Seth and a comfortable sense of companionship was established between them.

Looking at his back now as she trudged after him in the snow, Saoirse allowed herself to acknowledge how attractive she found him. He was tall and lean and his shock of thick white hair gave him a rather wild and rugged look. She felt a peculiar sense of kinship with him and an intuitive realisation that she could trust him with her life. Not once

---

[27] A pilgrimage route

did Seth look behind him to check on her. She had a sudden knowing, like a previously seeded thought coming to fruition, that together they had survived great hardships in previous lifetimes. Whether or not it was the effect of the swirling snow which had increased in intensity, the figure of Seth up ahead of her suddenly morphed into that of a much older man. Saoirse realised with a full lurch of her belly, that she was flooded with feelings of filial love. She just knew he had been her honoured kinsman in another lifetime.

Her thoughts were interrupted by the voice of Seth calling her. She hurried forward as he pointed out the first of the stations. They entered the field and walked towards the megalithic burial cairn. Wordlessly they circled the cairn three times. Saoirse felt that at last she was walking in the footsteps of Colmcille, the man and saint who had occupied her thoughts for so many years. They continued on their way, stopping for the ritual practice at each station. When they reached the sixth station which was known as 'Colmcille's chair', Seth proposed that they turn for home as the weather had deteriorated considerably. Saoirse agreed but asked that they sit for a while longer. Saoirse took her grandfather's cross from her pocket and placed it beside her on the sacred spot. She closed her eyes, oblivious to the biting cold, as she asked out loud for clarity of vision and purpose to be given her if the time was right. Within seconds, she could hear a humming in her head which quickly got louder and louder. She could faintly hear Seth's voice saying, "You are safe. I will be your guardian."

The humming in her head reached a fever pitch. At the moment when she thought her head would split apart, she registered a soft click and a voice in her head said, "Watch and listen. Neither time nor space has diminished the impact of what you are about to be shown."

Time After Time Before Time

She was looking at an island, where brown robed monks were walking in single file around the shoreline. Their voices rose in perfect harmony as they praised the name of the Lord. In the space of a heartbeat, she was no longer looking at the line of holy men, but she herself was a young monk among them bringing up the rear of the procession. The twenty-two men walking before her were her beloved brethren, each of them known and loved by her. She was the youngest of the monks and was known as brother Aodh. As the youngest member of the community, Aodh was responsible for ringing the bell to summon the monks to prayer throughout the day. He loved this duty, and the sweet tone of the bell filled him with love and gossamer memories of beauty. Even on those rare occasions when illness confined him to his bed, he rose to ring the bell. It was only when the abbot Molaise gave instructions that he was not to get up until he was well recovered, did he surrender his bell ringing to another. He had tried explaining to his confessor that he kept having dreams of another bell which had been hidden for safekeeping. His confessor, brother John, was a pragmatist and not much given to seeing omens and signs in dreams. He advised Brother Aodh to forget about his dreams and concentrate on worshiping the Good Lord.

Life in the island monastery was simple and peaceful. The brothers were often cold and hungry but their outdoor chores had toughened them up. Each man had his daily duties and the rhythm of prayer and work was rarely if ever disturbed. A simple beehive cell was inhabited by each man, where he slept and spent time alone. The church which stood in the centre of the circle of huts was small with just enough room for the brothers to stand shoulder to shoulder. There was a wooden seat to one side where the abbot and two of the more elderly monks could sit. Meals were eaten as a community, each brother taking it in turns to be the cook. Everyone looked forward to the day when Brother Aodh was in charge of cooking because his meals tasted so good. He had a natural way of knowing which herb to use to make the food more flavoursome, and knew all the spots where the wild herbs grew. He could often be seen at first light, hurrying with his basket to collect the choicest of herbs with the dew still fresh on their leaves. Also, he was naturally gifted in using a wide range of plants for medicinal purposes.

Aodh had imbibed a great deal of knowledge in the use of herbs both for medical and ritual purposes from the abbot. Molaise and Aodh enjoyed a close friendship not unlike that of a natural father and son. Brother Aodh had spent many hours walking the length and breadth of the island gathering the precious plants. Molaise was meticulous in making sure that Aodh could accurately identify every plant and know exactly how to use it for the best results. Brother Molaise was meticulous in his instructions to Aodh in the use of specific quantities of dried plants to be used and warned him never to become complacent. Before every session of preparation, the elderly abbot and the young brother would kneel

"We give grateful thanks to you, the spirits of the plant kingdom. We ask for guidance in our preparations today and that the infusions we make be filled with life energy and the strength which heals."

They worked quietly and harmoniously together and there was a sense of timelessness about their work. It was as if they were drawing on previous knowledge from another lifetime, so effortless did their work together become. Although he knew about the hallucinatory effects of certain herbs and plants, Aodh had made a solemn promise that he would only use his skills to heal.

Each brother had his daily duties and the rhythm of daily prayer and work was rarely, if ever, disturbed. Until the day when a boat came from the mainland with news of a terrible battle which had recently taken place in which thousands of men had been killed. The messenger told how a monk known as Colmcille, a prince of the clan O'Neill had instigated the battle because a judgement by the High King had gone against him.

Pressed for further information the messenger explained that whilst staying for a while with Finnian, Colmcille asked if he might be allowed to make a copy of one of the manuscripts. Colmcille set to work, and because of his long monastic training, the copy he made was exceedingly beautiful. When asked by Finnian to hand over the copy Colmcille refused. The two men asked the high king Diarmait to settle the dispute. He judged in favour of Finnian. In a moment of intense anger at this judgement, Colmcille forgot his monastic vows and called on his kinsmen to enter into battle to avenge his honour. He was of ancient royal blood and his call to arms was answered without hesitation by the loyal chieftains of Donegal. The subsequent battle of *Cúl Dreimhne* was a scene of savage slaughter where thousands of men perished, the battlefield strewn with the dead and dying.

Colmcille knew that he had committed the most heinous of crimes. He alone was responsible for the senseless slaughter. His wounded pride and arrogance had blinded him to his own inability to back down. He had taken vows as a young man to serve God by rejecting what would have been his legitimate claim to the high kingship of

Ireland. He had renounced the ways of the world and had dedicated his life to study and prayer. And now on this most dreadful of all days, he had caused the death of so many of his kinsmen. How could he bear to continue living when so many had perished? He walked slowly into the battlefield and slumped down among the dead and dying. He howled into the evening sky begging God over and over to forgive him. When his brother monks tried to lead him away, he refused to move. He tore away his robe and smeared his naked body with the blood of the innocent. He walked round and round the field, now and again throwing himself upon the body of a beloved kinsman. He pulled at his hair and clawed at his flesh. His screams of despair and grief were frightening. He was a broken pitiful sight. His screams and animal-like howling could be heard all through the hours of darkness. With the coming of daylight, he allowed himself to be led away to his cell.

His brothers cleaned him and gave him something to eat. For five days and nights, he remained in his cell. He prayed aloud all through the days and long into the nights. He neither ate nor slept and only accepted small amounts of water.

On the morning of the fifth day, he emerged from his cell and asked one of the boatmen to prepare a coracle for him. His wild eyes, unkempt appearance and shrunken frame spoke of the ordeal he had undergone. He spoke to none as he walked slowly down to the shore. He dismissed the boatman and prepared to row himself over to the island. One of the brothers had followed at some paces behind and he now approached and offered to take Colmcille across. Again, the offer was refused, this time more gently with the words, "Thank you brother, but I am not worthy of such kindness."

He stepped unsteadily into the boat and prepared to take up the oars.

It was immediately clear that Colmcille didn't have the energy to handle the boat. His brother monk waded in and took up the oars. Colmcille lay back and closed his eyes. When they landed on the island, Colmcille tried to rise from his seat but failed. Two of the island monks had come down to meet the boat and between them they managed to get him out of the boat and up to the visitor's hut. They laid him gently down and went to inform Abbot Molaise, who was praying in the chapel. When the abbot finished his prayers, he came to see the sleeping visitor and immediately recognised him as the great Colmcille, kinsman to many of his own brethren. That evening Molaise spoke to the whole community as they gathered for their evening meal.

"We have in our midst this evening, a man who has dedicated his whole life from early boyhood to the service and glory of God. He has travelled the length and breadth of this land inspiring all he met with his kindness and loving ways. He has momentarily stepped into darkness and we are tasked with the job of helping him; firstly to regain his bodily health and afterwards to open up the way of peace for him again."

Each monk bowed his head in obedience.

Colmcille slept for a full twenty-four hours. His first thoughts on waking were laced with despondency and despair. He tried to rise from the bed but fell back down again as a wave of dizziness and nausea engulfed him. He closed his eyes and waited for the nausea to pass. When he opened his eyes again, he was greeted by a young monk who silently handed him a clean robe. The younger man waited

Time After Time Before Time

with bowed head while Colmcille changed his clothing. Although somewhat rested, he was still weak and needed to rest on the arm of the younger man as they slowly made their way towards the abbot's dwelling. When the abbot's voice bade them enter, Colmcille turned away from the door, so deep was his sense of shame. Abbot Molaise rose to greet him with outstretched arms. Aodh remained outside. Colmcille flung himself on the stone floor in full prostration as his body convulsed with powerful sobs. No one moved and not a word was spoken until the sobs subsided. Colmcille slowly got to his feet and allowed himself to be enfolded in the abbot's embrace. Many hours passed and the door of the abbot's hut remained closed.

As the sun began to set low over the lake, abbot Molaise emerged and motioned to Aodh to go inside and assist Colmcille. The two monks slowly retraced their steps back to the hut assigned to Colmcille, the older man leaning heavily on the arm of the younger. Colmcille slept and dreamed and whenever he opened his eyes, Brother Aodh was always beside him to offer him a drink or a morsel of food. On the third day the patient was strong enough to begin to take part in the life of the community. Brother Aodh accompanied him everywhere and slowly a great and tender love grew between them.

As his body strengthened, Colmcille began to work alongside the others in the fields. The warm sun and fresh air restored his body and the hard, physical work became like a balm to his troubled soul. He prayed continuously for forgiveness and as a sign of humility he asked to be given the lowliest jobs in the community. No job was too much for him. He particularly asked to do extra duty looking after the very old and sick brothers. He bathed their worn bodies twice daily with a tenderness that belonged to the hands of a

Time After Time Before Time

mother with her new-born baby. He always insisted on being served his food last and he regularly gave half his allotted portion to others. He prayed in the chapel long after the other monks had retired for the night but he never seemed to show signs of tiredness during the daytime. His voice rang out loud and clear during the hours of the Divine Office, but when he spoke with his brothers, he always held back from offering his opinion unless pressed to do so. He was working on his personal transformation like a jeweller carving out the facets of a diamond.

There was one area of his life in the community where Colmcille did take the lead and that was in the scriptorium. He held daily teaching sessions, where he passed on his skills with the quill to the younger monks. Brother Aodh was a diligent student and his heart soared as he slowly over time became more and more adept in the use of the quill. Each time he began work on a new letter in a psalter, something deep stirred inside him that caused him confusion. As he began his work fleeting memories of another manuscript of exquisite beauty would appear before his eyes. He wondered where these memories came from but over time, he simply learned to not dwell on them as his brother confessor advised him. While teaching in the scriptorium, Colmcille was not the humble monk who worked in the fields. He demanded absolute perfection in the quality of work produced because as he would frequently say to the bowed tonsured heads bent over their work, "Only the best is good enough for our Lord."

After seven years, Colmcille still felt that he hadn't made enough reparation for the great sin committed by him. He asked Abbot Molaise to give him a penance that would cleanse his soul. Molaise was a wise and deeply loving man

Time After Time Before Time

who knew that Colmcille loved Ireland almost as much as his God. With Colmcille kneeling before him, Molaise made his pronouncement.

"You will go from here and sail away until you can no longer see the land of your birth. That will be your final punishment. Take with you those brothers who freely wish to accompany you. Use your great gifts for the honour and glory of God and you will rest your eyes upon His face when you die." Colmcille crossed his hands over his heart and bowed his head in acquiescence.

Preparations for Colmcille's departure got under way without delay. The biggest coracle was loaded with the provisions needed for the journey. Animals and sacks of grain which the monastic community could ill afford to go without, were loaded and made fast. On the third day all was ready for departure. The whole community stood in prayerful silence as each departing monk received a final blessing from the Abbot before stepping into the boat. When all was ready to cast off, Colmcille knelt and kissed the ground, his final act of love for his homeland. Just before he stepped into the boat, there was a piercing cry and Brother Aodh threw himself upon his knees before Colmcille and pleaded to be given a place in the boat. It had already been agreed that Aodh would stay behind because his skill with medicinal herbs was of huge importance to the community. And besides, he was by far the best scribe left to carry on Colmcille's work in the scriptorium. However, neither Abbot Molaise or Colmcille had reckoned on the extreme love Brother Aodh bore Colmcille. Brother Aodh clutched at Colmcille's robe and cried over and over.

"Please take me with you. Don't leave me behind!" Colmcille looked over towards the Abbot and a silent nod of consent was granted. Colmcille raised Aodh up, embraced him and said, "You shall come with us. And may God bless us all and keep us safe."

As the boat pulled away, a flock of buzzards appeared in the sky overhead, calling and calling until the little craft was out of sight.

Sitting on the stone known as Colmcille's seat, with the snowstorm swirling around her, Saoirse watched the boat make ready for departure. As it pulled away from the shore, she began to shout out "Take me with you, take me with you!" over and over as huge sobs racked her body.

Time After Time Before Time

Chapter Twenty-Two

"It's all right Saoirse, it's all right. I'm here beside you, you are quite safe."

As Seth's voice registered in her brain, Saoirse's inner eye was still trained on the little coracle. She felt the sadness that was flooding Colmcille's heart as her own chest began to convulse with sorrow.

"Please take me with you," she pleaded." Don't leave me behind!"

Strong hands gripped her shoulders as Seth said in a loud voice, "Saoirse, open your eyes." When she didn't immediately obey, he shook her again and again.

"Open your eyes. it's over."

When she opened her eyes, Saoirse was surprised to see snow swirling around her as she began to focus her attention. Her body was very cold but her cheeks were hot with tears. Seth wrapped his arms around her and gently lifted her into a standing position. When she had quietened, he said,

"We need to make tracks for home immediately before the weather deteriorates any further. The night is not far off. We can talk later."

Slowly they made their way back to *Carraig Fada*. It was hard going because the snow had drifted and blocked their passage in several places and Saoirse seemed to have little energy and kept wanting to stop to rest. Seth pushed her on regardless until finally the house lights came into view. They were greeted by the housekeeper who assessed the situation immediately. She put her arm around Saoirse and led her towards the stairs.

"I will run you a nice warm bath and have tea waiting for you when you are finished."

Seth walked slowly towards the drawing room, poured himself a whisky and sat down in one of the large armchairs in front of the fire. Sometime later Sinead brought in the tea tray and said that Saoirse was on her way down. When Saoirse entered the room shortly afterwards, long forgotten feelings of appreciation of feminine beauty took him by surprise. She came towards him, freshly bathed, her long hair loose around her shoulders and her gaze strong and steady. They stood facing one another without speaking, each knowing that there was no turning back now for either of them. He took a step towards her and crushed her against his chest. He buried his face in her hair and inhaled its smell as he repeated her name over and over. Finally, he released her, held her at arm's length and said

"I have found you. I have found you again."

They sat for several hours unburdening the secrets of their souls to each other. Seth explained to her that he had a strong intuitive feeling that they had known and loved one another a very long time ago. He went on to say that since the moment she arrived at his house he had known that he had tutored her in a previous lifetime about medicinal herbs and their uses. Furthermore, he added, "I taught you the ceremonial use of herbs and how to safeguard yourself and others." On hearing this, Saoirse simply nodded her head. "You don't seem surprised," he exclaimed.

"Of course not. I always knew I would find you again some day. I believe you were my beloved grandfather in the life we shared together. You taught me everything. We were lost to one another for a long time within that lifetime but our love was so strong that it drew me back to you from the world of the Sidhe. When you were walking in front of me in the snow this morning, I suddenly saw you as you had been in that other lifetime and I knew I would never let you go from me again. Today, when I used my inner sight and found myself back in the time of St. Colmcille. You kept me safe, just like you did in other lifetimes. Our love for one another is the thread that has drawn us together now. However, this life we are living now is the only life we have. We must not look back to the past and what has gone before. Yes, we have soul memories, some of them very strong, but we are tasked with living this lifetime now. And we are truly blessed to have found one another again."

    Seth looked at her, his eyes drunk with love and longing, a longing which he saw mirrored in her. They talked until the fire was dead and the sound of the church bells reminded them that it was Christmas Eve and nearly time for midnight mass. They wrapped up warm and walked the half mile to the tiny church dedicated to St. Colmcille. On the way they met neighbours and friends all heading for the church. Everyone seemed to know Seth and it didn't go unnoticed that Seth seemed to be very protective of the beautiful young woman who accompanied him. When mass was over, everyone congregated outside to wish one another happy Christmas. Almost everyone wished to be introduced to Seth's companion. From the look on his face as he introduced her, it was obvious to one and all, that Seth had fallen in love with the beautiful Saoirse O'Haloran.

    For the whole of the Christmas holiday Saoirse and Seth remained undisturbed at *Carraig Fada*. They laughed and loved and revelled in each other's bodies. They each experienced a sense of a peaceful regaining of a part of themselves which had been missing for a long time. Lying in

Seth's arms Saoirse explained it by saying that finally she could put to rest the sorrow and grief of her grandfather's famine experiences which had dogged her for so many years. Her soul no longer needed to carry that burden because she now fully understood that every lifetime is connected to every other lifetime that a soul journeys through. Our souls have the map but we have to live the journey we're on in each and every lifetime. Seth for his part said, that for him, knowing that each lifetime gives the opportunity to learn and grow in awareness and consciousness, makes sense of all his experiences.

"We are part of the living intelligent reality that underpins all aspects of life," he said.

"We are as much a part of the universe as the stars and sun and moon are. In each of our life spans we have different lessons to learn. Knowing what those lessons might be is the tricky part. It really helps me come to grips with events in my life if I can accept that everything that happens has a purpose."

Chapter Twenty-Three

 Five years had passed since Saoirse and Seth married in the local church. While maintaining his intense interest in Irish ancient monastic traditions and continuing to publish academic papers, Seth had recently trained as a medical herbalist and now had a thriving practice which he ran with Saoirse's help. Together they had a vast store of knowledge of the ancient ways of using herbal preparations. This knowledge was no doubt in part drawn from their memories of using herbs in other lifetimes.

 He specialised in helping women who were having difficulty in conceiving. He gave each woman as much time as she needed to tell her story. He heard from many women about miscarriages where no medical reason was detected. He listened to these same women explaining how hurt they felt when their friends and family suggested they could always adopt a child. It seemed to Seth that many of his clients desperately needed to be validated in their longing to conceive. He drew up a life and wellness plan for each woman and demanded strict adherence to it before he would officially take her on as a client. His methods began to have results. Not only did many of his clients become healthier and more energised, but they also became pregnant, and carried their babies to full term. The working partnership between Saoirse and Seth was a vibrant and happy one.

 Saoirse's main role was to educate the women in good nutrition and holistic self-care. She ran her weekly classes in the spacious kitchen at *Carraig Fada* and most, if not all of the women warmed to her immediately. Saoirse earned their trust because she was completely open and frank with them and she also had the knack of making each woman feel cherished and empowered.

These young first-time pregnant women also very much enjoyed watching Saoirse interacting with her own young daughter, Mary. The young child had an uncanny ability to be very happy with her own company. Wise beyond her years, she charmed everyone she met with her confident and calm demeanour. She loved to hear stories about fairies and magical places and would often interrupt her bedtime story to come up with her own alternative endings. As she came to grips with reading and writing she began to write and illustrate her own stories. Everyone who saw them was stunned by the complexity of the plots and the surreal quality of the illustrations.

She explained to Saoirse and Seth that she simply had to close her eyes and she could see the magic world. Saoirse quickly realised that her daughter had inherited some of her own memories of the world of the Sidhe. It was plainly obvious to her parents that Mary also had the gift of 'far seeing' to some degree. The world that the child could see in her mind's eye was the same magical world where Saoirse had spent her childhood in a previous lifetime. Because Mary's special gifts were assimilated and seen as normal within her family, she grew up a happy well-adjusted child who displayed a keen interest in everything around her. She particularly loved to watch her parents make up the herbal preparations and concoctions.

By the age of ten, Mary had acquired an encyclopaedic knowledge of the native wild plants and herbs in the surrounding countryside. During school holidays and at weekends she delighted in roaming the surrounding hills and valleys with her parents searching out medicinal plants.

Time After Time Before Time

She also expressed an interest in her parents' academic work and would frequently accompany her mother on her daily walks across the land where St. Colmcille himself had walked as a young man.

Saoirse continued her research into his life and times, and had published a great many papers which had been very well received. To further her research and to deepen her own personal connection with her beloved St. Colmcille, Saoirse had journeyed from Donegal to the sacred Isle of Iona every summer. Seth usually stayed behind to look after the infant Mary, but as the child grew, it became an annual event for the whole family to head off to Iona for several months each summer. Time after time Saoirse would find herself overcome with emotion as she caught her first sight of the sacred island. The island called to her soul. The peace of Iona called her home. Father and daughter usually spent most of each day on the white sandy beaches, looking for sea treasure, swimming, having fun, and generally enjoying each other's company. Saoirse rarely joined them before late afternoon as she spent most of each day walking the island on her own.

She especially loved to make the long hike westwards across the island, up and over and down to the Bay of the Coracle. The yellow irises growing in wild abundance on this part of the island never ceased to give her pleasure. Each time she stood on the top of the rise, where she sensed the presence of the guardian gateway, she paused for a moment at that liminal, numinous threshold before making her descent to the thunderous bay below. She had a set ritual which she engaged-in to settle her mind and prepare her for silent communication with the world of Spirit. She would spend time scouring the beach for sightings of the beautiful green Iona marble. Satisfied with

Time After Time Before Time

perhaps one or two pieces safely tucked away in her pocket, she would sit with her back to the land and enter a state of silent contemplation. With the sounds of the mighty heaving waves all around her, she was able to enter a deep inner space of perfect tranquillity.

On her first visit to the Bay of the Coracle many years before, she had experienced a deep altered state of consciousness, the intensity of which almost threatened to sever her grip on reality. On that occasion, she was overcome by a force so great, and so immediate that she had no time to set her personal safety measures in place. One minute she was Saoirse sitting on the beach watching the waves breaking, the next moment she was once again Brother Aodh sitting at the back of the long coracle as Colmcille and his monks tried to navigate the waves and land their craft safely. She gripped the sides of the boat as another huge wave threatened to swamp them. The next wave turned the boat broad side and Aodh took the opportunity to leap ashore and pull with all his might.

He was quickly joined by several of his brothers and the boat was pulled up the beach to safety. Each man then threw himself down in utter exhaustion. Brother Aodh watched as Colmcille kissed the ground beneath him before he too rested for a while. The monks were cold, wet and hungry and extremely fatigued from their sea voyage from Ireland. Some of the brothers were no longer young men, but they had willingly followed Colmcille and trusted their lives into his care. Leaving his twelve brother monks to rest, Colmcille motioned to Brother Aodh to accompany him.

They left the beach and walked up through the grassy knoll to the top. Here they stopped and turned around to face the ocean. Colmcille and Aodh stood side by side without speaking for several minutes as they scanned the horizon.

Time After Time Before Time

They could make out the huddled shapes of the brothers below on the beach who were still lying prone among the pebbles. Colmcille placed his hand on the shoulder of the younger man by his side and smiled.

"Our journey is over. We will settle here and build our community in love and service to the Lord."

As soon as he heard these words, Brother Aodh, sprinted like a young goat back down to the beach, shouting at the top of his voice

"We travel no further. We travel no further!"

The monks stood up and hugged one another, as each man took up the refrain, "We travel no further. We travel no further!"

Colmcille smiled at their joy as he gestured to the tiny band of men to kneel in prayer and thanksgiving. The sun was low in the western sky by then, so it was decided that they would bed down for the night where they were, and explore the island the following morning. Before they settled down to sleep, Colmcille led them in singing the divine office. As their voices rose and fell, a new pulse for humanity was seeded on this tiny island in the West, a note which would reverberate down through the centuries. This tiny group of men, under the leadership of Colmcille slept under the stars on that first auspicious night, with the sounds of the sea as their lullaby.

During that long starless night, Colmcille kept a vigil by the side of his brothers. He sat huddled in his blanket, bone weary and wracked with guilt yet again. He sobbed silently into his hands as his bitter grief for his past actions once more threatened to engulf him. The wind was blowing onto the land in tremendous gusts whipping up the sea into a fierce white foamy cauldron. He threw off his blanket and staggered towards the water's edge trying to keep his balance against the crushing wind. He stretched out his arms towards the heavens, seemingly oblivious to the danger of the tumultuous sea. Brother Aodh, who also couldn't sleep, had silently followed Colmcille to the water's edge. He stood behind the older man waiting to catch him should he fall. When Colmcille finally lowered his arms and turned back to the shore, Aodh stepped forward and tenderly guided his beloved Abbot back to the sleeping spot. He wrapped Colmcille in his blanket and cradled him in his arms to help keep him warm. Through the remainder of that first long night on the sacred isle, Brother Aodh kept vigil at Colmcille's side and rocked him to sleep as a mother would a sick and ailing child.

    The brothers rose with the first light, fatigued from bone chilling cold and hunger. As was their habit, they immediately dropped to their knees to await the call to prayer. Aodh reached into his satchel and withdrew the little bell he had brought with him from Ireland. He rung it three times, announcing for the first time on the Isle of Iona, the call to prayer. Colmcille, who seemed to be strangely refreshed and buoyant despite his turbulent night, led them in chanting the Divine office. When their prayers were completed, each man remained motionless with bowed head.

    Skylarks whirled high above them announcing the promise of a fine day. Despite their extreme hunger, nobody complained about the meagre breakfast of cold meal and water, because each man was happy to have arrived safely. When each man had shouldered his share of the goods and chattels they had brought with them from Ireland, they turned away from the beach and began to walk in search of the best place on the island to make their settlement. Brother Aodh, as usual, brought up the rear, keeping a tight hold on the rope he had secured around the neck of the two young goats in his charge. A couple of monks each cradled a chicken in their arms, all the while stroking them to stop them flapping around. The strongest of the men carried the sacks of grain which would be their future source of food.

Colmcille walked at the head of the line, his staff in his right hand. He carried a large satchel across his chest, which contained a manuscript he had been working on before he left Ireland. His bag also contained his quills and hand tools and some small pebbles to remind him of his native land. The men walked in single file in silence, a companionable stillness which was familiar and comforting no doubt to each man. They looked a strange and bedraggled crew as they walked, heads bent low against the sharp cold wind blowing towards them from the East. As he walked, Colmcille inhaled the clean sweet air feeling his energy levels rise with each step. Although he was passed his prime, he was still well muscled and strong. His broad frame had served him well over the years of austere monastic life. With hope and expectation filling his heart with each step, he thanked his God for all that had been given to him in his life. For the first time since that dreadful battle slaughter which had infiltrated his dreams by night and withered his joy by day, he felt that now he might be worthy of forgiveness.

When the little band of men got to the top of the rise leading from the bay, each man at an invisible signal laid down his load and turned to face the ocean. Colmcille led them in prayers of gratitude for their safe sea passage. Each monk in turn added his own personal blessing. From this point onwards each man knew that there would be no more mention of their homeland as they turned their backs to the ocean and to the land of their birth which lay beyond it. They carried on walking across the island; each man's senses primed for the best spot to build their church and monastery. By the time they reached the eastern side of the island, the wind had settled, the sun had broken through and was warm on their faces. Colmcille looked across the calm waters of the Sound of Iona to the pink rocks on the opposite shore of Mull and knew they had found the sweet spot to build their church and new home. He looked with a fatherly affection at his group of followers and felt the sustaining power of their faith and loyalty. None of them, apart from Brother Aodh, was any longer a young man, but their allegiance to Colmcille as their earthly leader on the journey to eternity kept all complaints at a minimum.

At a signal from their abbot, each man unshouldered his bundle and knelt. Brother Aodh fetched the little hand bell from his satchel and rang it three times to announce the time for prayers. The men knelt in a circle of prayer. Their soft voices merged with the sound of the sea as the buzzards called overhead. When prayers were finished the brothers set about making a fire, preparing something to eat and sorting out sleeping places. The animals were tethered and seemed content to be munching on fresh grass. The soft evening air, perfumed with the salty smell of the sea, acted like a refreshing balm on the bodies and souls of everyone.

A gentle stupor settled over the little band of men as the light began to fade. Some of the brothers were gathered in groups of two or three and the rising and falling of their voices blended with the rise and fall of the waves beyond their camp. Others wrapped their cloaks tightly around their bodies as they searched for the best spot to lie down. Evening gave way to night and those who were still awake marvelled at the beauty of the night sky above them. The heavenly kingdom felt very close that night. As Colmcille gazed up at the trillions of stars he prayed for the strength to

Time After Time Before Time

help bring the gospel of love to this island of such exquisite beauty.

Brother Aodh, settled next to Colmcille as was his habit, was not able to settle. Every time he let go into sleep, he was startled awake by what he thought was a bell calling to him. Time after time he told himself there was no bell calling and that he must have been imagining it. He searched in his satchel for his own hand bell, and felt reassured by its comforting presence. The feel and familiarity of the bell made him feel secure. Finally, he drifted into a sleep where he dreamed that he was a young shepherd boy in a time gone by.

When he awoke in the morning, he was surprised to see the brothers already eating their breakfast. He leapt to his feet, feeling ashamed that he had overslept and had missed morning prayers. But stronger than his feeling of shame was his utter desolation that for the first time ever, he hadn't called his brothers to prayers by ringing his bell.

"Do not be troubled," Colmcille said to him as he motioned for Aodh to sit and eat. After he had eaten, Aodh asked if he might speak to the brethren of the dream he had last night, a dream so powerful that he wanted never to wake from it. Colmcille recognised the fire of illumination now burning in the eyes of the youngest monk. He gave the signal for everyone to gather round and listen to what Aodh had to say.

Aodh stood before his brothers, closed his eyes and began to speak of his dream.

"I was a young shepherd on an island. I was shown a box which contained a priceless treasure. I had no idea what it was but I sensed that it had been made with great care and love. As I gazed upon it, a bell began to ring over and over. I asked if I could see what was inside the box." Aodh stopped speaking, opened his eyes and looked at his brothers with shining eyes.

"The box contained a manuscript whose beauty made the stars look dim in comparison."

Colmcille spoke for every man present. "You have been blessed in your dreaming. It is a sign for all of us that we have found our true home here on this island. We will endeavour to use our minds, hearts and souls from here on out to make our lives a living jewel for all to see."

Chapter Twenty-Four

    As the years passed, the published research of both Saoirse and Seth attracted a lot of attention which could easily have intruded into their personal and family life together. They went to great pains to protect their young daughter Mary from their own unsolicited fame. Saoirse had become the authorative voice on the life and times of St. Colmcille. Her lectures drew huge crowds and were scheduled two years in advance. Try as she might to deliver her lectures in the normal time-worn manner of an academic, she invariably slipped into her own very personal life memories of her time spent with the famous saint. Of course, this only helped to increase her fame, as everyone who attended one of her lectures felt that they had witnessed something extraordinary. It was not unusual to hear people saying to one another as they streamed out of the lecture theatre after one of her talks, "Gosh, that was so amazing! She made St. Colmcille feel so real, almost as if he was a member of her own family. How does she do it?"

    Equally intense and demanding of her time and energy, was the small mystery school which she ran from *Carraig Fada*. Over the years she had collected around her a small group of dedicated young men and women who displayed a depth of sensitivity to matters of the spirit. She trained them with an austerity and discipline which only those souls who were totally committed to the spiritual life could endure. Although some of her students lived a fair distance away, she expected them to arrive on time for the six o'clock meditation every morning. Each day was devoted to reading the works of the great mystics, punctuated by hour-long meditation sittings. After lunch each day, she insisted on a vigorous two hour walk along the headland, no matter what the weather was doing. She allowed for no exceptions, and any student who showed the slightest reluctance to obey her rules was asked to leave.

    Each year she continued to spend some time on the sacred Isle of Iona. She developed a reputation for walking the land at all hours of the day and night. Her experiences with the unseen worlds were so profound that at times she looked and behaved like a deranged person. Mostly she forgot to wash except to splash water on her weathered face each morning. She sometimes forgot to eat for a whole twenty-four hours, and she slept badly most nights. But she was always profoundly happy. Her whole being, her very essence was immersed in the ancient monastic life on the island when she herself was Brother Aodh. In her mind's eye, she saw herself leave her bed each morning before any of the other brothers had awakened. She walked on bare feet across the cold cobwebbed grass, to ring the bell to rouse her brothers for Divine Office. This was always a wonderful start to the day, especially on those early summer mornings when nothing stirred and even the sea was still sleeping. Slowly but steadily, her brother monks under the guidance of Colmcille had carved out a simple monastic settlement that went from strength to strength. The daily and yearly rhythms of work and praising the Lord hardly ever varied.

    Aodh continued to be the chief bell ringer and over time became a very skilled scribe. His deep love for Colmcille never faltered and he always tried to sit next to him at mealtimes. During fasting times Colmcille liked to go off by himself to a secluded cell away from the settlement to pray. Only Brother Aodh was ever allowed to accompany him. Aodh would sit waiting and watching at a respectful distance while his abbot sat in silent contemplation hour upon hour. Aodh came to love these times, simply sitting listening to the skylarks and sometimes the corncrakes in the early part of the summer. Turning his young face up to the warmth of the sun, Aodh knew that he was mightily blessed. His love for Colmcille and his love for God were equal in intensity. Once when Colmcille and himself were winding their way back to the monastery after a whole day at the hermit's cell, Aodh wanted to know how it was possible to sit without moving for so many hours.

"Father," he said, "how can I become like you?"

Colmcille looked at him with tender loving eyes and replied, "Brother Aodh, tell me, how can I become like you? You bring great joy to our community because of your purity of heart. I have much blackness resting in my own heart which I ask the Lord to lighten every time I pray. Do not strive to become like me. You are your own true self and your youth and vigour brings joy to these old bones of mine," responded the older man.

As Saoirse remembered those times, her face would crumble with the pain of longing and remembering. Time was cruel. She could never live those times again except in her mind's eye. When she journeyed between the worlds, the toll on her physical and mental health was enormous. Some of the older islanders who remembered her as a young woman looked out for her. Oftentimes, she could be found walking towards the north shore ringing a small bell which she always had about her person. The islanders made sure she came to no harm. Some took her into their home to rest until she seemed her dignified self once more. Sometimes when her longing to be with her beloved Colmcille again became acute, she would cry out in her anguish, to be

Time After Time Before Time

soothed as one would a tiny baby. She was not understood but she was greatly loved. Each year upon her return to the island, there were mutterings behind closed doors about how much she had deteriorated since her last visit. But she was always greeted with warmth and affection and welcomed back.

Each year, with the approach of the September weather and the threat of storms, she would finally prise herself away from Iona and journey home to Donegal - usually in a pretty low state of health. Over the years Seth grew increasingly worried about her mental health and wellbeing. He was visibly shocked each time she returned from Iona to see how thin and worn she had become. He knew she would never forgo her trips to Iona where she could walk in spirit with Colmcille and her brothers of old. Instead, he set in place a scheme whereby she would take one of her pupils with her to look after her on each visit. This took some persuasion but finally she agreed because she realised that low physical energy diminished her psychic powers.

When she was at home in *Carraig Fada*, her energy was like a blazing fire, ready to consume all in its path. She continued to demand the same rigorous discipline from her students as she did from herself. After the early meditation and hurried breakfast, the rest of the morning was spent in deep discussion with her students. She taught them everything she herself knew about living a life underpinned by deep spiritual values. She cautioned them about using their emergent psychic powers for self-glorification or worse still, for monetary rewards. She herself exemplified a simple purity of heart and soul, and she demanded nothing less in her students. Despite the demands she made on her students, each and every one of them loved her with a fierce loyalty, and tolerated her extreme shifts of moods. Throughout their years of training they learned to recognise when she was about to use her psychic powers to enter another realm, an ability which they could only dream of possessing. Sometimes in the middle of a sentence she would stop, look into the far distance and become almost another person entirely. In that state she would often give them information about the unseen realms. These episodes, although extremely valuable for her students, exacted a heavy toll on Saoirse. More often than not, she would feel extremely tired for several days afterwards. As the years went by, she did less and less of this work as her strength began to fail. She could, however, still hold an audience of more than two hundred people in the palm of her hand whenever she gave her yearly talk on St. Colmcille to the new intake of religious studies students at her old alma mater.

Time After Time Before Time

Chapter Twenty-Five

    Seth's love for Saoirse - and hers for him - increased as the years went by. During most winters, when Saoirse would slowly recover her strength, after yet another gruelling summer on Iona, they would spend long evenings sitting either side of the log fire recalling events from their past lives. Seth never loved her more deeply than during those same long evenings when the glow from the fire shone on her face and her eyes danced with the joy of their shared love. Sometimes, their daughter Mary would spend the evening sitting with them. Mary had grown into a beautiful robust young woman, quite the beauty according to the local young men who vied for her favours. She had the same graceful stature as her mother, but there all resemblance to Saoirse ended. Mary was above everything else a pragmatist. She had spent her childhood listening to her parents speaking of fairy kingdoms and unseen realms, and nature spirits. Mary used these stories as fantastic source materials for her children's books.

    By the time she reached her sixteenth birthday she had several books published and her drawings and illustrations sold for quite considerable sums of money. Although she loved writing and illustrating her books, her greatest passion was reserved for researching ancient monastic documents. Even before she attended university, Mary knew more about the life and times of St. Colmcille than most of her professors. She was heavily influenced in her final choice of career though, by the lifelong work of her father. Seth made all his unpublished research available to her. The two of them could often be found shut up in his study for whole days, oblivious of the need for food and company. Many a winter's night, Saoirse would tell Mary about the beautiful manuscript which she had seen when she was a young shepherd boy on a remote island in another lifetime. Although Mary herself didn't possess the same powers of far seeing as her mother, and secretly believed that most of her parents' past life stories were flights of fancy and imagination, nevertheless she had an unshakeable belief that the manuscript her mother described was real. Mary knew that her mother could not possibly have such intimate and detailed knowledge of such a manuscript if she had not actually seen it with her own eyes.

Following in her mother's footsteps she enrolled in Trinity College Dublin and, after her primary degree, began her own research into ancient monastic antiquities. She rarely revealed who her parents were as she didn't want any special privileges. She quickly made a name for herself due to her ability to work long hard hours and her insistence on meticulous tabulation of her findings. Although her work took her away from home quite frequently, she still managed to spend time at *Carraig Fada* whenever she could. Nothing gave her greater pleasure than to sit with Saoirse and Seth in their familiar sitting room, sipping a glass of good wine and exchanging stories. She would glance about the room noticing how the old grandfather clock still hadn't been repaired; how the same lush red curtains framed the sash windows; how the armchairs were ragged now about the arms; and above all, how the glowing fire made life feel very safe. *Carraig Fada* was the one place where Mary felt she could connect with the real glory and passion of her work.

Time After Time Before Time

Saoirse and Seth would listen with rapt attention as she described some minute detail of a manuscript whose authenticity she had been asked to validate. She valued their opinion and respected their knowledge and experience. Now that Saoirse no longer ran her mystery school, the life of the house was less formal. Her parents did very little entertaining and much preferred to sit down to eat in the kitchen. The kitchen held special memories for Mary, as it was there that she had sat listening as Saoirse gave advice to young expectant mums on how to really look after their health and wellbeing. Mary realised how far ahead of her time Saoirse was in running these classes, and how they had complemented the work Seth was also doing with these women.

Sitting in the oak armchair in the kitchen, while her parents prepared the meal, Mary was dismayed to see the same battered, well-used copper pans hanging in a higgledy-piggledy fashion above the Aga. The same dull red lino stretched unevenly across the floor, its humps and bumps waiting to trip up the unwary visitor. The main door into the kitchen from the hallway was still so badly-fitting that it was easier to keep it permanently open. She noted there was still no fitted food cupboards and half used packets of dried pulses and various other foodstuffs were scattered haphazardly over various counters. It was only by going away and coming back to visit that she had begun to notice how little her parents cared for keeping up with the times. Their energy was spent on their work and no doubt they would continue to live in the house as they had always done. This was how they liked it and any suggestion of installing central heating, or, horror of horrors, modernising the bathroom, was instantly dismissed as new-fangled nonsense. For all their blustery bonhomie however, their increasing frailty was becoming evident. Whenever Mary gently mentioned the possibility of moving to a smaller house, Saoirse would immediately react angrily with "I will never leave this house. Please don't mention it again."

Seth was slightly more pragmatic and attempted on several occasions to bring up the subject with Saoirse. But he knew how stubborn his wife could be and so the matter was dropped. Seth still walked with a straight back and was secretly very proud of his still-trim figure and full head of thick grey hair. At a distance he could easily be mistaken for a much younger man. He still accompanied Saoirse on her daily walks along the cliffs, to meet up with the spirit of Colmcille, as she would happily say as they set off. But Mary noticed how tired he had begun to look of late, and how difficult he found it to shake off a nagging cough.

Although she had officially moved out of *Carraig Fada*, Mary spent a great deal of time there when her work permitted. She loved the old house with its atmosphere of learning and study, and familiarity. She never turned down the opportunity to accompany her parents on their daily cliff walks. Even though she had grown up in this place, the breath-taking landscape around *Carraig Fada* never failed to exert its magic on her. To walk for miles along the cliffs with the thundering wild sea below, to pay attention to the circling buzzards overhead, to feel the warm sea breezes on the skin and above all to know that all of this beauty was part of her.

Once or twice since leaving university, Mary had accompanied her mother on her annual trip to Iona. She had seen for herself how Saoirse could plummet from a state of total ecstasy when she believed she was communicating with Colmcille, to a state of deep loneliness when her powers shut down. She came to a whole new understanding and appreciation of the discipline and commitment to the life of the spirit that her mother personified.

For her part, Saoirse was very pleased to enjoy the practical skills of her daughter. Most days on the island, Saoirse would go off by herself to either walk the land or to sit in quiet contemplation in a lonely spot. Mary always made sure that a sandwich was tucked inside her pocket, next to the little bell. And in the evenings, when fatigue and cold brought Saoirse back to the warmth of the cottage, Mary always made sure there was a good hot meal ready. These were good days for mother and daughter. On one such evening Saoirse revealed that she could hear a bell ringing deep in the earth underneath the Hill of the Angels. Mary tried to convince Saoirse that it was the movement of her own bell in her pocket which she could hear. But Saoirse was insistent.

"Why can't you believe me? I tell you I can hear a bell ringing at that spot whenever I pass and sometimes I also hear it down by the west shore. It calls me to prayer, just like when I was a brother with Colmcille."

Saoirse leaned forward to be closer to Mary and continued, "Although at that time, I myself - as Brother Aodh - was in charge of the bell. It was my sacred duty to ring the bell and call my brothers to prayer day and night. You must believe me."

"Is that why you always carry your little bell with you, to remind you of that lifetime?"

"Not exactly," replied Saoirse, "I carry it so that whenever I can bridge the worlds, whenever I find myself back in that blessed time, I can use it to call my brothers from their work in the fields. When Colmcille died, we heard the sound of a bell, loud and clear rising up from deep inside the Hill of the Angels. You have to understand Mary how happy I was in that lifetime when I was a young monk. I loved each and every one of my brothers. We were a small number when we landed here from Ireland. We worked hard for many years building our community under the guidance of our beloved abbot and seeding our note of love for all beings. You yourself know the story well of St. Colmcille and how he ignited the light of love and love of the Christ here in this sacred island. For me, it is not a story. It was my life. I was there."

"I believe you Mama" said Mary, "For how else could you possibly know all those things about that time that nobody else does?"

The two women sat in silence for some time until Saoirse continued, "Here on Iona I am closer to my brothers than anywhere else in this world. This island loosens the bonds of time for me and I am graced to be able to see beyond the veil which separates the worlds. I was there when the light, that is the love of Christ, shone out for the first time across these western isles and beyond."

Chapter Twenty-Six

During the winters at *Carraig Fada* when Saoirse was running her mystery school, Seth had engaged various young history students to help with cataloguing some of his more obscure research papers. Most of these students proved to be wholly unsuitable and not up to the task. Seth was a loving easy-going man in everyday life, but he was a hard task master where his work was concerned. It came to be a pattern where a bright eager new student would pitch up at *Carraig Fada*, full of youthful enthusiasm, only to pack up and leave after a few weeks. Seth was not willing to lower his expectations of the standard of work he required. To his way of thinking, no help was infinitely preferable to sloppy work which, in the long run, would frustratingly have to be undone at some point. He had almost given up on finding someone when life tossed up one of those small but glorious moments that knits events together.

Late one December afternoon, after a morning's work in his study, Seth went out walking along the headland to clear his head. The winter sun glimmered among the bare trees, and the hard-packed snow underfoot made the surrounding fields seem as if they had been freshly laundered. The wind, however, was blowing strongly onshore and it was needle sharp against his face. Seth battled on, head down, for about thirty minutes before heading back. On a whim he decided to pay a visit to the village pub, before returning home, something which he rarely did. The Golden Hare pub dated back to the 17th century and was a warm and welcoming place to find oneself in on a winter's day. Two men were sitting by the blazing fire, the only customers, quietly chatting. The older of the two looked up and greeted Seth by name. Cradling his hot double whisky, Seth came over and sat down opposite. He stretched out his legs and leaned back against the settle, letting the warmth from the fire and the whisky thaw his bones.

"How are you doing John?" inquired Seth.

"I'm doing OK, quite good in myself Seth, but to tell you the truth, things are not so good on the farm. We're struggling to make ends meet. It's been a wet summer and I'm sad to say I've had to let most of the lads go because there isn't the cash to pay the wages. I've had to sell off most of the animals to cover the debts. I'm grateful that Daniel here has come up from Cork to lend a hand until I decide what to do for the best."

Seth was introduced to the younger man who was visibly delighted.

"I'm so happy to meet you," said the young man offering his hand.

"And I you," said Seth. "Tell me, what work do you do in Cork?"

"Presently I am without work. I studied Irish medieval history at Cork University and your books and research were prescribed reading. I'm happy to be staying here in Donegal helping out on uncle John's farm while I begin sorting my notes for the book I'm planning to write."

"What is your subject?" asked Seth.

"I'm planning to write about land usage and social structure in medieval Ireland. The problem is, I spend so much time working on the farm, that by evening time I'm too exhausted to write."

Seth leaned back in his chair and surveyed the young man in front of him. Daniel O'Leary was a good-looking

Time After Time Before Time

young man, possibly the same age as his own daughter Mary. Set in an open intelligent face, his dark brown eyes blazed with life and vibrancy. His smile highlighted the many laughter creases around his eyes and mouth. Seth took an instant liking to Daniel.

"I've got a proposition to put to you," said Seth, "but why don't we have another drink first?" John went to order another round, and while he was gone, Seth and Daniel settled into easy conversation together.

When they were once again settled with fresh drinks, Seth explained how he needed an assistant to help him put some order into the extensive quantity of research notes he had accumulated.

"I can't pay much, but board and lodging are included. The work is painstakingly slow and requires a fine degree of patience and organizational skills. I'm a stickler for accuracy and order. If you are interested, call over to the house and I can show you what's involved."

Young Daniel's face lit up at the prospect of working with the famous man seated in front of him, but turning to his uncle he said tenderly, "Don't worry uncle John, I won't abandon you or the farm."

"Listen here young Daniel," said his uncle, "Lightwood farm has been in our family as you know for generations. Most of the land has been sold off over the years, and it is no longer viable as a working farm. When I die, the remaining land and the house will come to you as my only living relative. That is secure, so if you are interested in Seth's offer, please don't let any thought of saving the farm stand in your way."

The two men held each other's eyes, and the look of love which flashed between them was so intimate that Seth had to look away.

"Thank you for your offer," said Daniel. "Can I have a few days to think it over and to talk further with my uncle?"

"By all means, by all means," responded Seth, finishing the last of his whisky. "I'll be off home now. I'll await your call."

Daniel proved to be a willing and very competent assistant and quickly settled into his new job. Seth treated him like the son he never had, and the relationship between the two was one of harmony and mutual respect. Daniel had moved out of his uncle's farm and had settled in easily at *Carraig Fada*. He was given the spacious attic bedroom which faced the sea. Saoirse was delighted to have the company of a young person in the house again. Seth and Daniel had settled into a rhythm of work which suited each of them. They worked without a break all morning, had a quick lunch, then finished for the day at three in the afternoon. Daniel would usually go for a run along the cliffs, then closet himself in his room to write until suppertime. He was an easy house guest and Saoirse formed an instant bond with him. He never tired of listening to her stories of ancient monasticism and her tales of past lives.

He spent most weekends helping her in the garden. She was no longer able to do any of the heavy work, which Daniel undertook willingly. He found being outdoors and working up a sweat was the perfect antidote to a week of mental work with Seth. He found as the weeks and months passed, that the stimulation of the work he was doing for Seth, actually energised his own writing. He had yet to meet Mary, who was giving a series of lectures in Trinity College. He had built up a mental picture of her as someone who was seriously academic and unlikely to enjoy doing fun things. This image was instantly shattered when she burst through the front door a week before Christmas. Daniel was coming down the main staircase when below in the hall he saw a young woman throw down her bag and run shrieking into the drawing room. He could hear the excited voices of Seth and Saoirse and guessed that the young woman with the flaming red hair and pale freckled skin must be their daughter Mary. He turned and was about to retreat to his room when Seth came out to get some drinks and called up to him, "Come on down Daniel and meet our daughter."

When she moved forward to greet him, Daniel's first thought was 'God, she's beautiful!' With the air of confidence born out of knowing how one fits into the great scheme of life, Mary took his hand and looked him full square in the eyes. Saoirse, flushed with pleasure at her daughter's homecoming, busied herself drawing chairs up closer to the fire. The four of them sat talking and sipping their drinks until the light faded. Mary and Daniel slipped into an easy comradery together that first evening, which blossomed into love during the following twelve months. Life at *Carraig Fada* continued as normal with the added excitement of Mary's much more frequent homecomings.

The young couple were married in the local church the following year, and moved into Lightwood Farm, which they quickly made their own. They made very few structural changes apart from opening out the two smallish rooms downstairs. They both loved the land and never tired of walking up to the top field where the view across the valley was breath-taking. They were happy and fulfilled in each other's company as young lovers often are, and they were also fulfilled in their separate work roles. Mary continued to be much in demand for authenticating documents and lecturing. She had her mother's flair for captivating an audience but she never laid claim to extra sensory perception which was so predominant in Saoirse's life trajectory. Daniel divided his time between working with Seth, and continuing with his own research and writing. He had a passionate interest in documenting how the ancient peoples of Ireland had related to the land. How they had seen the hills and forests and rivers as living entities, which, if respected, would give of their bounty to humans. He spent a great many hours sharing his enthusiasms with Saoirse. From her he learned to view the natural world through the lens of his heart and not through the analytical mindset of the historian that he had become. Although he fully respected her views on the 'after life' and indeed the 'before life,' he retained his scepticism about what she called 'the world between worlds'.

    After they had settled into Lightwood Farm, it became something of a ritual that the young couple came over to *Carraig Fada* every Sunday for lunch. Saoirse and Seth no longer ate in the dining room, so Sunday lunch was an informal affair eaten in the kitchen with everyone lending a hand to prepare the meal.

    The Sunday that Saoirse died began just like every other Sunday. Herself and Seth walked down the hill to the church for Sunday mass. They briefly chatted outside after the service with some friends, then began their walk back home. Half way up the hill, Saoirse said she felt extraordinarily tired and needed to rest for a while before they continued. They sat down on a rock facing the sea. Saoirse leaned against Seth and closed her eyes. She began to mumble words and phrases which he knew from experience could be the prelude to Saoirse entering a heightened state of consciousness. In an instant, he stood up, took her arm and helping her to her feet said, "Let's get you home, my love. A little sleep before lunch will do you good."

Saoirse didn't make a fuss but he could see from her eyes that she could see and feel the cold fear that had already gripped his heart. She patted his arm and looking at him with absolute tenderness said, "It's OK Seth, my love, let's go home."

She went straight up to their bedroom and lay down. After a short while Seth came to check on her with a cup of tea. She insisted she was feeling fine and felt she might just nod off. She shooed him out of the room with instructions about lunch preparations. She asked that as soon as Mary and Daniel arrived, would he send them up to her. Despite an inner feeling of disquiet, Seth did as he was told. Downstairs in the kitchen, in an attempt to stop his thoughts racing he began to peel and cut vegetables. Several times, he thought he heard a car coming up the drive. Try as he might he couldn't get rid of the sense of gloom which was stalking his every move. When Mary and Daniel arrived, they knew immediately something was out of kilter. All three of them went upstairs to see Saoirse. She had undressed and was lying under the covers propped up against several pillows. She patted the bed and motioned for Mary and Seth to sit either side of her. Daniel continued to stand.

"Why the long faces?" she said, looking at all three of them in turn. "My time has come at last. I have no fear of death and neither should you."

"Don't talk nonsense Mum," said Mary, "You're not dying. You're simply tired and perhaps coming down with a virus. You'll be up and about in a few days I expect."

Saoirse looked at her beautiful daughter with a look of searing love and said softly, "Everything is as it should be darlin'."

Before Mary could reply, Saoirse asked her to fetch the wooden box which always sat in the centre of her dressing table. Opening it, she lifted out the tiny exquisite Celtic cross carved by her grandfather so long ago. She kissed it before placing it in her daughter's hands.

"This is now yours. Keep it safe and let it guide your heart."

As soon as she held the cross, Mary's agitation lessened. She leaned over to kiss her mother. Saoirse wrapped her arms around her daughter and held her close.

She knew from previous lifetimes that leaving was always hard but she had never experienced it to be this painful. Mother and daughter remained locked together for a long time, whispering sweet tender love to one another. Saoirse stretched out her right hand towards Daniel and beckoned him over.

"Cherish my girl," she said to him in a loud clear voice. "She has been tasked with something special in this lifetime, although the time has not yet arrived for her." Daniel could only nod as tears blurred his vision.

Seth had been sitting on the end of the bed all the while, never for a second taking his eyes off his wife. Saoirse, with total command in her voice, asked that she have time alone now with Seth. When the others had gone, Seth came to the head of the bed and held Saoirse against his heart. They talked of their present life together and those other lives when they had known one another. Seth, who could hardly speak because his heart was beating so wildly, asked in anguish, "What if I can't find you next time round?"

Saoirse placed her fingers against his lips and said, "Shoosh, I will always find you. Our souls have the map remember which shows us the way. I will never lose you, no matter how many lifetimes pass before we meet again." She slept then, leaning against him. Seth woke with a start as the afternoon light was fading. His shoulders and neck muscles were stiff from sitting in the same position for so long. It was Saoirse's voice which had awakened him. She was speaking in a clear voice to several people whom he could not see but were obviously visible to her. In her dying moments her consciousness had taken refuge where her soul and spirit had been most fulfilled. She was once again Brother Aodh and she was back on Iona with her band of brothers. Over and over she seemed to be addressing Colmcille and asking for his blessing. Her face shone with the joy of being once again with her brothers. She began to repeat over and over, "*Tá mé reidh anois, tá mé reidh.*" [28]

    Even with his minimal knowledge of the Gaelic language, Seth knew that she was preparing to leave her body. She was ready. He laid his head on her chest and began to cry softly, muttering all the while,

    "Please don't leave me my love, please don't go!"

    He felt a soft hand caressing the back of his head. With the softness of a baby's breath Saoirse whispered above his head "Let me go, my sweet love, let me go. I will be waiting for you."

    Seth lifted his head and kissed her on both eyes. He reached for the bell on the night table and gently rang it to summon Mary and Daniel. Throughout that long night, Mary and Seth each in turn recited the ancient Celtic prayers to ease the passing of the soul. The candles surrounding the death bed had burnt low and still the vigil continued. The energy in the room was soft and caressing, held in the deep black velvet silence. Just before dawn, as the light entered

---

[28]   I'm ready now, I'm ready.

the room, Saoirse drew her final breath. Those who had journeyed with her continued to sit in silence until the day itself began to stir.

In line with her wishes, Saoirse's body was left undisturbed for the following forty-eight hours. On the third morning, again honouring her wishes, her coffin was carried along the cliff path. Those mourners who followed behind, continuously chanted the ancient Celtic death prayers. She was buried in the local churchyard facing the West.

Seth grieved quietly and alone in those early days after her death. He intentionally wore himself out walking the land during the daylight hours in order to help him sleep at night. High up on the clifftop where only the wind and the gulls could hear him, his grief took on a different form. Each time he heard the lonesome mewling of the buzzards he was reminded of other lifetimes he had shared with Saoirse. He raged against her leaving him. He was a man being rent in two. He believed with every fibre of his being that he would meet Saoirse again in another lifetime but for now he couldn't see how he could live out his own allotted life with the pain of his aching for her.

"How could you leave without me?" he shouted over and over in the days and weeks after her death. When his pain and grief got too much for him, he took to throwing himself down and beating the earth with his fists. Sometimes this helped to bring a momentary relief from his anguish. Mostly it made no difference. As the weeks and months passed, he slowly began to place his grief in its rightful place in his heart. It wasn't so much that he stopped grieving but rather he directed it into his work. He called up Daniel one day and announced that they had work to do. He threw himself into new research and did something which he hadn't done for quite a number of years. He agreed to mentor some students. So once again the rooms in *Carraig Fada* resounded with the voices of young people eager to study with Seth. He enjoyed teaching and felt uplifted by their youthfulness and enthusiasm. Who was to know that he was simply marking time until he could re-join his beloved Saoirse? He was perfectly hearty during the daylight hours when his work left no time for touching the wounded space inside him.

Nightimes however, clawed at his heart and broke the seal on what he had hidden during the day. Alone in his room, he experienced the bleakness of the dark night of the soul. He lay in bed waiting for the oblivion of sleep to wash over him. Some nights when he couldn't rest, he went down to his study and sat in the darkness. By stilling his mind and emotions and going into a deep meditative state he hoped to be able to communicate with Saoirse. His longing for her was so intense though, that it blocked his ability to see beyond the veil and he saw only a void where he expected to see her. Just before dawn each day he would go back up to bed and fall into a dreamless sleep for a few hours. Mary was concerned about him and had suggested several times that he might like to come and live on the farm with her and Daniel. His refusal had caused a few angry scenes between father and daughter.

"I cannot possibly leave *Carraig Fada*," Seth would say each time Mary brought up the subject.

"This is where I am closest to your mother. Everything in this house holds an abiding sense of her presence for me. I can almost believe that she is still with me when I am here, in the house we shared together for so many years. Why would I give that up?"

"Because you're not taking care of yourself Dad." Mary would reply. "You are lonely. You don't see your friends anymore; you don't go anywhere except to walk for hours along the cliff path. I'm worried about you Dad. You are also becoming very thin."

    Seth would not be persuaded. He would on occasion accept an invitation to go down to the farm for dinner, but he was always glad to be back within the four walls of *Carraig Fada*. Several years passed with Seth becoming more and more of a recluse. He no longer took on any students and his loneliness and longing to be done with life engulfed him. In his moments of deep inner honesty, he knew that Saoirse would not have approved of his desire to cut his life short, and that he was breaking the ancient code of right timing in all things by wishing to die before his time. He was like a hollow reed with the wind haunting his heart. When yet another winter saw Seth laid low with one chesty cold after another, Mary finally persuaded him to move into Lightwood Farm.

Time After Time Before Time

Chapter Twenty-Seven

Out on the western seaboard, the evening light was fading over the Isle of Iona. Mary stood motionless at her hotel bedroom looking totally transfixed by the view. The setting sun turned the rocks of Mull on the opposite shore into a dazzling kaleidoscope of brilliant reds and yellows. In that luminous space between the ending of the day and the coming of the night, the changing light becomes a threshold into other unseen worlds. On such an evening it's easy to be taken back in imagination to a time when this tiny island resounded to the sound of monks' voices raised in song. She continued watching until a sudden restlessness made her decide to go for a walk. She walked slowly along the north strand thinking of her late father. Her heart was still sore, burdened with not only sorrow at his passing, but a deep sense of guilt.

She blamed herself for his suicide. She hadn't really understood how deeply he had felt the loss of his beloved Saoirse. His unnatural death tore at her own heart. She blamed herself for not picking up on the signs of his deep depression. Even now, four years since that dreadful day, she continues to have flashbacks. What sticks in her mind the most about his suicide, is not his mud-caked body, scratched limbs and torn clothes, but his face. The look on his face when he was found was that of a peaceful resting child. He looked happy. She knew without really understanding how she knew, that he, along with her mother, had inhabited worlds which she knew nothing about. Was this the reason for the look of bliss on his dead face? She believed he had been happy living on the farm with her and Daniel. She knew now she had been terribly wrong. Although she had had various conversations with her parents throughout her growing years about the 'unseen worlds' she hadn't fully grasped how real it was for them. They didn't just discuss the possibility of reincarnation, they had strong memories of experiencing living in previous lifetimes. In the final hours of her life, her mother chose to focus her consciousness on the monastic life she had lived on Iona. Had her father chosen to do the same thing? Had his life in the present time been so barren without his companion of many lifetimes, that he would choose to die? This would explain the almost superhuman effort it must have cost him to climb the hill to his death. Her own frantic attempt to climb the hill to get to him on that fateful day, caused her to go into premature labour later the same evening.

  The baby was small but delivered safely after a long labour. Mary named her daughter Sethanna in honour of her father. In the aftermath of the birth, her grief for Seth was submerged in looking after the baby.

  It wasn't until now, almost four years on, alone on Iona, that she feels the tide of memories rushing in. Memories as fragile as gossamer threads. Unable to shake off a feeling of melancholia, she continues walking along the shore nursing the hollowness inside her, until darkness forces her to retrace her steps. Back in her room at the hotel, she began to make sure her preparations for the following day were in order. She was billed to give the keynote speech at the annual conference of the 'Society for the Study of Ancient Monastic Manuscripts'.

  It was her first time on the island since the death of her parents and she was suddenly finding it difficult to cope with her emotions surrounding the way each of them had died. Saoirse's death had been so gentle and quick, and its arrival so eagerly welcomed by her mother, that Mary hardly gave herself permission to grieve at the time. Everyone mourned the passing of the famous lecturer and wise authority that was embodied in Saoirse. This was the woman the public knew, but only Mary knew the kind gentle mother who tucked her up in bed at night and encouraged her to draw and write stories. Mary also accepted that path of her career had been heavily influenced by her mother's minute recollection of the intricacies of ancient monastic documents.

    Theirs was a private world of family love and integrity which Mary kept close to her heart. Here on Iona however, memories of Saoirse were vivid and immediate and asking for Mary's attention. She remembered, like it was only last year, her mother's flushed and windblown face as she burst through the door of the family croft they rented here on the island each summer when Mary was a child. Saoirse was happy and fulfilled at that time, without a hint of the labyrinthine mind-struggles she would suffer later on. She exuded a tremendous life-force and charmed everyone with her stories of other worlds and eras past.

    It was only Seth, and later on Mary, who understood that Saoirse's stories were not stories, but sprung from her actual experiences. Mary loved her mother unconditionally but she spent a fair amount of her childhood in Donegal making excuses for Saoirse's eccentricities. But here on Iona, no such excuses had been needed. Everyone on the island knew Saoirse. She was a well-known figure who could be seen walking the island landscape whatever the weather. This changed as she grew older when she began to move in and out of realities more frequently. It pained Mary to recall how distressed her mother had been on the last Iona trip they had shared together. Her grip on present-time reality had been fragile then and easily snapped. She walked the land incessantly and stayed out all night on several occasions. However tired and hungry she might be after a long night at the Bay of the Coracle, or praying in the ruins of the hermit's cell, the light in her eyes never dimmed. She was on fire with love for the Divine. She had explained to Mary many hitherto unknown facts about ancient monastic life, the accuracy of which Mary was able to verify later in the course of her own work. Here on Iona she could feel her mother's energy around her which only served to increase Mary's sense of sadness and melancholia. Mary's longing for her mother had been a raw wound which time could not heal. Was this what it had been like for her father as well?

Seth had chosen death and reunion with Saoirse over the chance to see his only grandchild grow up. Mary had never forgiven him for that act of denial, but somehow being back on Iona had helped to soften her feelings of anger towards him.

The air was clear and bright next morning with a slight westerly breeze as the small group of Celtic enthusiasts assembled in the lounge of the hotel for the opening talk. Mary hadn't slept well. Her dreaming had been punctuated with bizarre images which left her feeling a little bit frazzled on waking. Something was working its way into the edges of her consciousness which was troubling her. Unfamiliar images came tumbling into her mind unbidden, causing her to feel more than slightly unnerved. Nevertheless, as she stood before her audience, she appeared calm and her usual professional self. Her talk had been billed as 'Monastic life in the time of Colmcille'. She began her talk by holding up two objects. In her right hand she held aloft the tiny exquisite Celtic cross carved by her great-

Time After Time Before Time

grandfather Seamus, and in her left, the bell which her mother Saoirse had always carried about on her person.

"These two objects," she began, "bring to life the story of Christianity here on Iona. The bell was the great regulator of life in the monastic tradition. It summoned the monks to prayer at set intervals throughout the day and night and the task of ringing the bell was assigned to the monk who felt intuitively called to this task. The cross was the symbol of the faith which the brethren held dear."

As she continued talking, Mary felt a strange buzzing in her ears which made her feel almost faint. She reached for the glass of water on the podium beside her and as she drank, she heard her mother's voice in her head saying, "Trust me."

Two hours later Mary finally stopped talking and was met with total silence from the audience. It was as if everyone had been put under a spell, which was finally broken when everyone spontaneously rose and gave Mary a standing ovation. She was totally amazed by this and even more so when she looked at her watch and realised that she'd been talking for over two hours. Many in the audience came up to congratulate her on a most enlightening talk and marvelled at how she had brought the world of 7th century Iona right into the room. One elderly man hung back until everyone had dispersed. He took Mary's hands in his own and looking lovingly at her said, "I knew your mother very well my dear. She was one of the spiritual greats. When you were talking earlier, you reminded me so much of Saoirse. Whenever I closed my eyes during your talk, it was her voice I heard. You have been blessed to be overshadowed by your mother."

Mary felt quite shaken by this but nothing else that she could think of could possibly explain what had happened during her talk. This confirmed for her why her mother had always drawn such huge crowds to her lectures. Saoirse was actually talking from her own personal experience of living, working and praying with Colmcille in those early days in the monastic settlement here on Iona. That's why her talks and lectures appeared so vital and why people felt they had been given an opportunity to look into a world which they could never find in books. Mary had no idea what she had said during her talk. She was deeply puzzled but when so many people came up to congratulate her for such a stimulating and informative talk, she had to accept that something out of the ordinary had happened. Perhaps the old man was right and she had been overshadowed by her mother. Over lunch, various people were curious to find out what Mary had used as the source material for her talk. Their curiosity was another confirmation for Mary that her mother must have spoken through her. She couldn't recall what she had actually said that had so impressed her audience. The talk she had prepared to deliver was one she had delivered on many previous occasions to various groups. At no other time had she received such a rapturous appreciation from an audience.

"What was different this time? Am I going mad?" she asked herself, "Or did my mother actually speak through me?"

While in her room after lunch, she again experienced a strong sense of something pressing in on the edges of her consciousness, which was making her feel very agitated. She felt like she was trying to walk through mud where each step was a huge effort. She lay down on her bed and tried to shake of the sense of something building up inside her. Her head began to throb, and the afternoon light streaming

Time After Time Before Time

through the window hurt her eyes. Her palms were sweaty and her heart began to beat abnormally fast.

"Perhaps I'm ill," she mused, knowing that this wasn't so. In an effort to shake off this feeling of mounting dread and anxiety which was threatening to overwhelm her, she flung on her coat and headed out of the hotel. Some of the conference participants who had already gathered in the lobby called after her.

"Are you not staying for the afternoon session?"

She hastily explained that she needed to get some fresh air but she would join them shortly.

She began to walk very fast. She took the road that led to the north of the island but on a sudden impulse she turned back and headed south towards the Bay of the Coracle. She continued to walk at a quick pace but as she reached the Hill of the Angels, she slowed her pace right down. As she passed, she thought she heard the sound of a small bell from deep within the mound. She stopped in her tracks and became very quiet. She knew all about this beautiful hill because her mother had told her so many stories about it as she was growing up. She knew that in the folklore tradition it was regarded as a fairy mound and that when the fairy folk are celebrating, soft musical sounds can be heard coming from the hill. While Mary gave no serious credence to this, she really wanted to believe that it had been the hill where Colmcille had stood in prayer and a host of angels had descended and stood about him. She wanted to believe because her mother had been so insistent that it had happened. She had always accepted that her mother was eccentric, passionate, and learned, but in the last few hours she had been forced to make a rapid reappraisal of Saoirse. Could it possibly be true that everything her mother had told her about Iona and her beloved Colmcille was actually true?

She left the hill and carried on across the machair. As she reached the high point, she could see the Bay of the Coracle below her, gleaming in the bright afternoon sun. She stopped to admire the view and when she tried to continue, she found she was rooted to the spot. A soft gentle voice in her ear said, "You must ask permission to cross this threshold."

Mary felt very shaken because the voice in her ear was the voice of her mother. Considering what had happened during her talk in the morning, Mary did as the voice bade her do. She stretched out her arms and asked the unknown forces to allow her to enter. Immediately she felt the burden of dread which had clung about her person for the previous twenty-four hours, lift from her. She felt a rush of joy and peace which she hadn't felt for a very long time. She ran down the slope towards the bay. When she reached the water's edge her mood shifted again. Her elation of a few minutes ago evaporated as she felt herself becoming silent and still and receptive. She knew intuitively that she needed to simply wait. She sat on the sand leaning against the rocks and focused her eyes on the waves. Five, ten maybe fifteen minutes passed. Mary sat motionless waiting for something, she knew not what. A warm breeze blew around her and Mary felt herself growing sleepy. As she surrendered into sleep, she distinctly heard the voice of her mother in her ear.

"Do not be afraid. I have something to show you. Look out to sea."

Out beyond the surf a small coracle was being thrown about by huge waves, frantically trying to make headway out to sea. It seemed an impossible task because despite the best efforts of those aboard, the little craft was being pushed back towards the shore where it finally beached itself. Two monks climbed out and prostrated themselves on the sand. A young man came running down the hill toward them shouting and hollering. When he reached the monks, he sank to his knees, repeating over and over, "You've come back. You've come back."

The two men got up and hugged the lad.

"Yes Fiachra, we've come back. The great treasure we were taking with us belongs here on this island." The older of the two leaned into the boat and took out a wooden box. He laid his hand in blessing upon it and handing it to Fiachra saying

"Brother Conall would have wanted you to take care of it. We are going to try again to take the boat out so we leave you with our blessing." Fiachra stood as if in a dream, clutching tightly the box containing the beautiful manuscript. He watched as the two men successfully negotiate the surf and finally manage to direct the little coracle out to sea. He stood watching until they were no longer in sight. He decided against opening the box to have one final look. He buried the box next to the bell in the cairn alongside the bones of his ancestors.

As Mary watched this scene unfolding, she was simultaneously receiving a running commentary on it via her mother's voice in her head.

"You see now Mary, that here on this island is an ancient manuscript, more beautiful than anything you have ever laid eyes upon. By revealing this to you and you alone, you are now tasked with its guardianship. Everything that you have done in your working life has brought you to this point. This is your destiny. It was decided long before you were born in this lifetime. Your soul is one with the soul of Fiachra. You can choose to call in an archaeological team and have the book and the bell excavated. You have been

Time After Time Before Time

shown its exact location. You will become famous, and your find will be known as the 'Jewel of Iona'. You have free will in this matter. Or you can choose to do absolutely nothing. You are the only living human being who knows the final resting place of the book and bell, or that they actually exist. You have until the first blush of dawn appears in the sky."

Mary woke with a start and remembered clearly what she had seen and heard in her dream. Except she knew with absolute certainty that it was much, much more than a dream. She had been shown the past and had been asked to make a choice for the future of this sacred island. All of her training in evaluating and authenticating sacred manuscripts clearly indicated to her that this could possibly be the most brilliant find, not just of her career but for posterity. She imagined the whole scenario in great detail and found she was breathing heavily with excitement. Gathering her coat about her she turned her back on the bay and began to walk at a steady pace up the hill. She walked straight past her hotel and continued towards the north of the island.

Half way along the road she turned off to follow the path which led to the summit of *Dun I*, the highest point on the island. She climbed quickly and sure footedly. The first rays of light brushed the western sky as she reached the summit. She stood in silent wonder as the vast expanse of sea and sky unveiled itself before her eyes. She turned and looked down upon the sleeping island below her and understood that the true jewel of Iona was this very peace. She walked over to the hidden pool where pilgrims come to seek their visions. She knelt down and looked into the water. She saw the whole island reflected in that tiny pool, glittering like a precious jewel, shining its light in all directions.

The End.

Printed in Great Britain
by Amazon